CONTEMPORARY LITERATURE

THE BASICS

'Contemporary literature' is among the most popular areas of literary study, but it can be difficult to define. This book equips readers with the tools needed to take an analytical and systematic approach to contemporary texts. The author provides answers to some of the critical questions in the field:

- What makes a literary text contemporary?
- Is it possible to have a canon of contemporary literature?
- How does a reader's location affect their understanding?
- What impact do print, electronic and audiovisual media have on contemporary literature?
- Which key concepts and themes are most prevalent?

Containing diverse illustrative examples, and discussing topics that define our current sense of the contemporary, this is an ideal starting point for anyone seeking to engage critically with contemporary literature anywhere.

Suman Gupta is Professor of Literature and Cultural History, The Open University. He is the author of numerous books on contemporary literature, literary theory, political philosophy and current affairs.

THE BASICS

ACTING
BELLA MERLIN

ANTHROPOLOGY
PETER METCALF

ARCHAEOLOGY (SECOND EDITION)
CLIVE GAMBLE

ART HISTORY
GRANT POOKE AND DIANA NEWALL

ARTIFICIAL INTELLIGENCE
KEVIN WARWICK

THE BIBLE
JOHN BARTON

BUDDHISM
CATHY CANTWELL

CRIMINAL LAW
JONATHAN HERRING

CRIMINOLOGY (SECOND EDITION)
SANDRA WALKLATE

DANCE STUDIES
JO BUTTERWORTH

ECONOMICS (SECOND EDITION)
TONY CLEAVER

EDUCATION
KAY WOOD

EVOLUTION
SHERRIE LYONS

EUROPEAN UNION (SECOND EDITION)
ALEX WARLEIGH-LACK

FILM STUDIES
AMY VILLAREJO

FINANCE (SECOND EDITION)
ERIK BANKS

HUMAN GENETICS
RICKI LEWIS

INTERNATIONAL RELATIONS
PETER SUTCH AND JUANITA ELIAS

ISLAM (SECOND EDITION)
COLIN TURNER

JUDAISM
JACOB NEUSNER

LANGUAGE (SECOND EDITION)
R.L. TRASK

LAW
GARY SLAPPER AND DAVID KELLY

LITERARY THEORY (SECOND EDITION)
HANS BERTENS

LOGIC
J.C. BEALL

MANAGEMENT
MORGEN WITZEL

MARKETING (SECOND EDITION)
KARL MOORE AND NIKETH PAREEK

PHILOSOPHY (FOURTH EDITION)
NIGEL WARBURTON

PHYSICAL GEOGRAPHY
JOSEPH HOLDEN

POETRY (SECOND EDITION)
JEFFREY WAINWRIGHT

POLITICS (FOURTH EDITION)
STEPHEN TANSEY AND NIGEL JACKSON

THE QUR'AN
MASSIMO CAMPANINI

RACE AND ETHNICITY
PETER KIVISTO AND PAUL R. CROLL

RELIGION (SECOND EDITION)
MALORY NYE

RELIGION AND SCIENCE
PHILIP CLAYTON

RESEARCH METHODS
NICHOLAS WALLIMAN

ROMAN CATHOLICISM
MICHAEL WALSH

SEMIOTICS (SECOND EDITION)
DANIEL CHANDLER

SHAKESPEARE (SECOND EDITION)
SEAN MCEVOY

SOCIOLOGY
KEN PLUMMER

SPECIAL EDUCATIONAL NEEDS
JANICE WEARMOUTH

TELEVISION STUDIES
TOBY MILLER

TERRORISM
JAMES LUTZ AND BRENDA LUTZ

THEATRE STUDIES
ROBERT LEACH

WORLD HISTORY
PETER N. STEARNS

WORLD MUSIC
RICHARD NIDEL

CONTEMPORARY LITERATURE

THE BASICS

suman gupta

Routledge
Taylor & Francis Group

LONDON AND NEW YORK

First published 2012
by Routledge
2 Park Square, Milton Park, Abingdon, Oxon OX14 4RN

Simultaneously published in the USA and Canada
by Routledge
711 Third Avenue, New York, NY 10017

Routledge is an imprint of the Taylor & Francis Group, an informa business

© 2012 Suman Gupta

The right of Suman Gupta to be identified as author of this work has been asserted
by him in accordance with sections 77 and 78 of the Copyright, Designs and Patents
Act 1988.

British Library Cataloguing in Publication Data
A catalogue record for this book is available from the British Library

Library of Congress Cataloging in Publication Data
Gupta, Suman, 1966-
Contemporary literature: the basics / Suman Gupta.
p. cm. – (The basics)
1. Literature, Modern – 21st century – History and criticism. I. Title.
PN780.5.G87 2012
809'.05 – dc23
2011023682

ISBN: 978-0-415-66871-2 (hbk)
ISBN: 978-0-415-66870-5 (pbk)
ISBN: 978-0-203-15306-2 (ebk)

Typeset in Bembo and Scala Sans
by Taylor & Francis Books

CONTENTS

Acknowledgements   viii
How to use this book   ix

1   General strategies   1
2   Specific strategies   25
3   Production   55
4   Reception   92
5   Perspectives and issues 1   126
6   Perspectives and issues 2   156

Index   185

ACKNOWLEDGEMENTS

The following have been reproduced with permission:

The poem 'Testimony' by Seamus Heaney from *101 Poems Against War*. London: Faber and Faber Ltd. © 2003 Seamus Heaney, reproduced with permission from Faber and Faber Ltd.
The poem 'No Mourning for Language' by Duo Duo and translated by Gregory Lee from the special issue *Writing China* edited by Suman Gupta of *Wasafiri* Volume 23, Issue 55, Autumn 2008. Reprinted with permission of Taylor & Francis Ltd.

HOW TO USE THIS BOOK

This book can be read from beginning to end as developing a consistent picture step by step, or different sections of chapters can be read independently as reasonably free-standing discussions of topics. Where a point made in a section is also discussed elsewhere, that is noted.

Observations that readers may wish to consider and explore further are italicised. For ease of reading, arguments and observations are often broken into sequences with their own numbered subheadings.

Several literary texts – poetry, plays, novels, e-texts, etc. – are referred to in order to exemplify and clarify arguments. It is not assumed that the reader will have prior knowledge of such texts. In every instance, a sufficient account of these is given for arguments made with regard to them to be clear. Poems discussed are reproduced.

Lists of references at the end of each chapter are kept to a minimum: only texts that are quoted or discussed are listed. Each chapter is followed by suggestions for further reading. These are listed under headings corresponding to the main issues covered in the chapter, and could be regarded as a next stage of reading. They also give a sense of the kind of material that informs this book, but are not representative of all the material that had a bearing on writing it.

GENERAL STRATEGIES

THE CONTEMPORARY LITERARY FIELD

This book is about what makes contemporary literature contemporary, and how to study such literature in a systematic and informed manner.

A very large number of new literary works are made available to readers every month, indeed every day. Consider what a variety of forms are broadly regarded as serious or popular literature now: various kinds of poetry, short and long fiction, theatre and screen plays, personal journals and blogs, biographies, e-fiction and fanfiction, essays, and so on. Moreover, contemplate the number of languages in which these literary works are produced, in the original or in translation. For a rough estimate, think of a wildly popular recent novel that has been translated for readers in most parts of the world. J.K. Rowling's *Harry Potter* novels are a useful example of this sort: it is available in 64 living languages. These are languages in which literary works are published now and read more or less regularly; these languages sustain, so to speak, a contemporary literature market. True, the numbers of literary works published in these languages are very uneven. A great many more appear in English or Chinese, for instance, than in Irish or Faroese. But the point is that, if we think of the totality of the production and circulation of recently written literary works worldwide, we are faced with a very large and unwieldy field. To begin with, let's think of this almost unimaginably vast field as 'contemporary literature': the literature of our time, or of the present.

We are rarely called upon to think of contemporary literature in such broad terms. By 'we' I mean all readers of contemporary literature, in whatever language and wherever, however young or old, expert or inexpert – including me. This book is addressed to anyone who reads literary works that seem to be of our time. However, having said that, this book is obviously for readers who wish to do rather more than simply read such literature. I expect you are reading this because you wish to understand contemporary literature in a more systematic and informed fashion than usual. Possibly, that's simply because you have an inquiring mind. Perhaps you are preparing for a school or university examination on, or are a teacher or researcher of, contemporary literature. This book will, I hope, prove useful for all of you – for us – in different ways.

We rarely think of contemporary literature in the broad way described above, for good reasons. Every one of us naturally reads such literary texts in an extremely selective manner. Our reading choices are limited significantly by factors such as where we live, what languages we are competent in, our education and upbringing, and the social circles we move in. That still leaves a much larger quantity of literature within reach than we can possibly read. We generally use various sorts of information to help us narrow down what we actually pick up. These may include advertisements, recommendations, reviews, the reputation of authors, displays in bookshops and libraries, film or television adaptations, literary prizes, packaging (what's on the covers, for instance), issues of current interest, what's trendy, etc. Then, of course, there are selections made for educational and academic purposes – I have much to say of this soon, so won't pause on it here. At any rate, we read contemporary literature in manageable quantities, and our thoughts are unlikely to be burdened by the great weight of all contemporary literature at any given time.

Further, we probably choose to read contemporary literature because we expect it to be directly relevant to our lives and our world. We hope to find in it expressions and issues with which we are familiar. We anticipate resonances with our experiences, attitudes and concerns, as these have developed within our lifetimes and surface in our everyday lives. Of course, reading literary texts from past periods (before our time, or the historically defined past) also necessarily call upon our present-day experiences and attitudes. We are, for instance, apt to make sense of Shakespearean sonnets in relation to our own memories and feelings. But contemporary literature is read with a sense of being closer to us than literature from the past. We feel that the literature that is written and appears in our time is more intimately connected with the complexity and messiness of our lives. It is in tune with how we speak and what we think about and observe. That means that we usually think of contemporary literature in the blurred way in which we think of our lives and times. We don't often feel the need to stand back and think systematically about contemporary literature any more than we feel the need to stand back and ponder our lives – we are generally busy simply living our lives. We tend unquestioningly to accept that this sort of literature is woven with our lives.

To move beyond simply reading thus and to begin *thinking about contemporary literature in a systematic manner* puts us in danger of feeling intimidated. It means confronting contemporary literature in all its unwieldiness and breadth, much as described above. Understandably, the prospect could be discouraging. To persevere involves developing strategies for ordering and describing the field of contemporary literature so that its relevance to our lives/world, and its place in literature generally, would become clear. Fortunately, scholars and teachers have come up with such strategies already. These provide the foundation for studying contemporary literature in schools and universities – in brief, for academic study. To approach contemporary literature in an informed and systematic manner, it makes sense to take recourse to these existing academic strategies.

As it happens, the existing strategies are functional but not necessarily satisfactory for studying contemporary literature. Nor do they lead to a consistent way of approaching contemporary literature, but to various and often contradictory ways. To begin with then, it is worth enumerating what these strategies are, and deciding to what extent they are useful for our purposes. There are two levels of such academic strategies to take into account:

- firstly, general strategies for the study of literature from different periods, which are therefore relevant to studying contemporary literature too; and

- secondly, specific strategies for dealing with contemporary literature itself, which involve ways of defining what is specifically contemporary in literature.

Chapters 1 and 2, respectively, are devoted to discussing strategies at these two levels. In both, we shall consider whether and why these strategies are useful and sensible. This chapter is concerned with the general academic strategies that have been, and still are, widely accepted – in particular, the following:

- close reading and contextualisation of literary texts;
- preferring the study of texts in their original languages rather than in translations;
- selecting texts that are worthy of attention, which should belong to the 'literary canon'; and
- presenting the relationship between texts and readers with minimal attention to the literary industry.

I should say straightaway that habitual recourse to these strategies has often been questioned by literary critics, especially of late, and sometimes discouraged. However, while misgivings about some of these strategies are well known, for the practical purposes of teaching and studying literature they continue to be used confidently. In fact, this is far from uncommon in the academic study of literature. Numerous long-standing literary notions that recently have been reconsidered and found wanting nevertheless continue to be used unthinkingly. For instance, until quite recently – say, the 1960s – literary critics largely agreed that the key to understanding a literary work is to understand what its author intended. To understand the poem *The Waste Land* (1922) properly, for instance, it was felt that the best way would be to work out what the poet T.S. Eliot was thinking when he wrote it, what his social circumstances were, and whom he was writing it for. Now, after several decades of debating this assumption, most literary critics put less weight on what the author intended. It is now largely accepted that equal – if not predominant or even exclusive – attention should be given to who is reading and where and why, and to other factors which the author may not have been aware of. Nevertheless, when it comes to actually discussing a specific literary text, teachers and critics frequently continue to put superlative emphasis on the author's intentions (this is discussed further in chapter 3). There is, in brief, often a gap between what literary critics and teachers think in principle and what they actually and habitually do.

With that in mind, let's consider by turn the general strategies mentioned above, and try to decide how useful they are for a systematic approach to contemporary literature. That also helps me to clarify some of the principles that are followed in this book.

CLOSE READING AND CONTEXT

At this stage, let me introduce you to my friend Dr Guru, an experienced teacher of literature. He has a firm grasp of what he regards as necessary principles for studying literature, and I have found it useful to consult him occasionally for the first two chapters here. When I first told him about the idea of this book, his immediate advice was: 'Don't begin with a heavy barrage of concepts and theories. They frighten most readers. Stick to the close reading of specific texts. The skills of close reading are what studying literature is ultimately about, the ability to analyse content and language and style and form. You must develop your arguments through reading particular literary works carefully; in fact it might be a good idea to do so by focusing on one text in a sustained way. I know this from experience.' This was said with the conviction that a literary text for the thinking reader is rather like a corpse for the forensic pathologist. The latter assumes that close attention to the corpse will tell all about its condition, and thereby confirm the usefulness of forensics generally. Just as a Dr Guru of forensic pathology may advise students to focus on the body, so Dr Guru of literature recommends the close reading of texts.

It seems to me unquestionable that studying literature by and large entails reading texts carefully. However, for a systematic approach to contemporary literature, I feel rather more is needed than simply reading particular literary texts closely.

What I have in mind can be made clearer with reference to a particular text. Take, for instance, this poem by Seamus Heaney, entitled 'Testimony':

'We were killing pigs when the Yanks arrived.   1
A Tuesday morning, sunlight and gutter-blood
Outside the slaughter house. From the main road
They would have heard the screaming,
Then heard it stop and had a view of us   5
In our gloves and aprons coming down the hill.
Two lines of them, guns on their shoulders, marching.
Armoured cars and tanks and open jeeps.
Sunburnt hands and arms. Unnamed, in step,
Hosting for Normandy.   10
                    Not that we knew then
Where they were headed, standing there like youngsters
As they tossed us gum and tubes of coloured sweets.'   13

(Heaney, 2003)

A close reading of the poem without any further information tells
us a great deal. The quotation marks around the whole present the
poem as the statement of a third person (not, for instance, the poet
himself). The title gestures towards something weightier than a
passing reminiscence, since legally a testimony claims to be the
truth as witnessed by the speaker. The scene can be dated to just
before the Normandy landings (6 June 1944) of the Second World
War, and the telling of it some time after. The poem describes the
passing of a regiment of American soldiers through perhaps a village
or provincial town (the perspective of the hill suggests open spaces)
somewhere abroad – perhaps in Britain or Ireland. The perspective
shifts between the American soldiers' view of the narrator and
his companions (lines 4–6), and the narrator's view of the Americans
(lines 7–10). There is thus a balance struck between the two parties
looking at each other – this isn't a one-sided view of the event.
The view of the two sides is also enacted in the cadence of the
verse: the Americans see the slaughter house workers as a disordered
crowd coming down the hill, and the verse is prosaic and flowing;
the narrator sees the soldiers in an ordered group, and the verse
there is regular and staccato. Where lines 1–10 describe what the
narrator witnessed, the break before line 11 marks the turn towards
a retrospective note (when he mentions Normandy, the narrator
admittedly does so with hindsight). But that break also marks a

pause that emphasises the ironic counterpoint of the poem: that the bloodletting in this scenario has to do with the everyday civilian activities of the slaughter house, while the playful tossing of sweets is what the soldiers do. There is a hint of a merging between the soldiers and civilians at that moment: 'standing there like youngsters' (line 12) could equally refer to the workers or the soldiers. We may wonder why this has the weightiness of a 'testimony', and may conclude that it is the irony of the counterpoint behind the apparently unmemorable event which gives it weight. Awareness of what comes in the future may render apparently unmemorable moments in the past memorable.

We can carry on in this vein, and come up with further thought-provoking observations by looking closely at the text. Undoubtedly, in doing this we bring something of our contemporary experience of life to understanding the poem (we bring, for instance, attitudes to soldiers and slaughter houses which may or may not have been common at the time of the Second World War). But beyond that, the *contemporary* impact of this poem, that which make us in 2011 (as I write this) think of the poem as a work of contemporary literature, remains unclear so far. It could have been composed any time after the Normandy campaign (that much the poem itself indicates) – to many amongst us, especially younger readers, this might not seem to be particularly contemporary, or especially relevant to our present-day world and lifetimes. But so far I have presented this close reading in an artificial manner, by concealing information that readers would normally be aware of when examining the text.

The reputation and writings of the poet, Seamus Heaney, would be known to many and are likely to colour our close reading. We might find ourselves discerning an underlying awareness of other conflicts in the poem, especially of the Troubles in Northern Ireland, which has often been Heaney's theme in verse. Further, knowledge of the date and manner in which 'Testimony' first appeared will undoubtedly give it a turn which a close reading in itself cannot – indeed, this information is likely to mould our close reading significantly. It first appeared in the Reviews section of *The Guardian* newspaper of 15 February 2003, alongside two other poems under the overarching title 'Three War Poems'. These were introduced briefly as follows: 'Poets have been among the most eloquent critics of war. Here, we publish a new work by Seamus Heaney and poems by Iraqi writer Saadi Youssef and Vietnam veteran Michael Casey.'

February 2003 was a period of intense anxiety and passionate debates about moves towards invading Iraq led by the US and UK administrations. On 15 February, some of the largest peace marches ever witnessed were organised in various cities around the world. It was a political environment that was powerfully polarised between supporters and opponents of the forthcoming invasion. Literary texts of the time, especially those alluding to war, were apt to be read accordingly, in terms of what position they took apropos the developing conflict. Clearly, the British newspaper *The Guardian*, which was regarded as having primarily an anti-invasion readership, recruited 'Testimony' as a statement against war. It subtly directed readers to Heaney as an 'eloquent critic of war'. Readings of 'Testimony' were also manoeuvred by placing it alongside Saadi Youssef's translated extract from the Arabic poem 'America, America', which has a more explicitly of-the-moment message, and Michael Casey's 'A Bummer', which is redolent with the experience of having been in a war. In April 2003, by which time the invasion was in full swing, the poem reappeared in a Faber anthology, edited by Matthew Hollis and Paul Keegan, entitled *101 Poems Against War*. The title left the reader little choice about how the poems in the anthology should be read. Youssef's and Casey's poems were also included.

When the poem appeared thus in 2003, I inevitably found my close reading inclined towards trying to work out what it meant in terms of ongoing political concerns. I wondered whether anything could be inferred from these lines about the USA as a military power, about the USA's foreign policy. How should the ironic counterpoint be read under the circumstances? How balanced really is the balance of perspectives (American soldiers' and narrator's) that the poem presents? Are these words really an expression of a position *against* war? Or does it present something else: for instance, could it be suggesting that war is an intensification of the violence that is already there in civil society (the blood from the slaughter house), and that war could be a promise of peace (the soldiers distributing sweets)? How do these implications gel with what we know of Heaney's other poems and writings?

Dr Guru's sort of conviction about the great importance of close reading, in other words, needs to be tempered when we are considering contemporary literature generally. What gave Heaney's 'Testimony' its immediate and contemporary edge in 2003 were a number of factors outside the text: the reputation of the poet, the timing and political situation, where it first appeared, how it was introduced, who was reading it – to name a few. And if the poem still seems contemporary (though in a less urgent way) to us in 2011 as I write this, it is because the anxieties arising from the invasion of Iraq are still very much with us, because Heaney is still writing, and most of us have lived through 2003. It seems to me very likely that *what seems contemporary for us usually, for most literary texts (even in less controversial times), has as much to do with what close reading reveals as with how, when, where and by whom the text is produced and received. Indeed, the latter is often of greater moment than the former.* Or, put in terms that are familiar to literature students, the importance of close reading is conditional here on the various contemporary *contexts* of a text. Close reading is moulded by a text's contexts to accentuate its contemporary status.

Although the scope of this book does not allow for detailed consideration of contexts or really close attention to many texts, the relation of texts within their various contemporary contexts is of the greatest importance here. The texts that I discuss, more or less closely, in subsequent chapters are considered within some context of current relevance – in terms of when the text was written, how it was made available to readers, who reads it and for what purpose, etc.

ORIGINAL LANGUAGE AND TRANSLATION

'The texts that you will read closely in your book,' continued Dr Guru, 'should obviously be in the original language. What's the use of reading a translated text closely, except to see how it relates to the original? And even where you won't be reading closely, you will naturally be discussing literature that you have read in the original and have a confident grasp of. So, you will mostly be writing about contemporary literature in your language, in English, in the language your book is written in. This very broad idea of contemporary literature which you have in mind is impractical; it is merely an idea, and cannot really be discussed – that would need proficiency in many languages. You will actually be writing about contemporary literature written originally in English, and that, too, in a sketchy fashion. At best, you can extend your range to the very few languages you are fluent in. In my experience, it is best to be honest about one's limitations.'

Dr Guru is right to point to my limited knowledge of languages, and indeed to that of any reader. We are very unlikely to find readers who are able to deal with more than a small proportion of the 64 languages mentioned above. All readers will feel only modestly equipped insofar as contemporary literature is understood as being read meaningfully in the original. By those standards, none of us can practically claim to have anything more than a very restricted sense of what is contemporary in literature.

It is worth pausing, though, on Dr Guru's strong emphasis on original languages. This emphasis is grounded on powerful presumptions among scholars, teachers and many non-professional readers that:

- literature is best studied systematically in terms of particular linguistic traditions; and
- there is a close and inextricable relationship between a particular language and a literary text written in it – so that, to understand a literary text *fully*, we need to pay attention to its distinctive use of a particular language.

The second presumption can hardly be argued with. But we can probably agree that it is possible to understand a text at least *partially* without looking too closely at the distinctive use of a particular language. And we might agree, too, that it is sometimes useful to try to understand a broad range of literature *partially* rather than to confine ourselves to a *fuller* understanding of a small range of literature. This might be a trade-off worth making. It seems to me well worth making when thinking systematically about contemporary literature, especially in view of objections that can be raised about the first presumption: that literature is best studied according to particular linguistic traditions.

There are understandable political reasons for the conviction that literary study should focus on separate language traditions. It can be explained, for instance, in terms of how a sense of national identity was historically instilled in different countries (in its modern sense mainly in the nineteenth and twentieth centuries), and how schools and universities were accordingly established or restructured. Cultivating a modern national identity involved promoting a distinct tradition of a national language.

In a generalised and simplistic way, the relevant reasoning about national consolidation − say, in an imaginary Any-Place − could be put as follows. The Any-Placean government realises that to be secure and strong, it would be useful if most citizens feel a powerful allegiance to their country, Any-Place, and have clear markers of Any-Placean identity other than happening to live there. One of these markers of identity can be convincingly set up by standardising and officially sanctioning a national language, even though citizens in Any-Place may well be using various dialects and several languages. Most probably the language of the majority, or of elite Any-Placeans, would be identified as the national language. The Any-Placean government would then naturally establish educational systems and undertake cultural propaganda campaigns accordingly. These would promote, among other things, the idea that literature in the Any-Placean national language written by Any-Placeans is particularly rich and confirms the wonderfulness of Any-Place country and culture. Any-Placean patriots will collaborate in the effort to promote the integrity of Any-Placean language and literature as distinct and worthy. The solidarity of Any-Placeans and sovereignty of Any-Place would seem to be confirmed by thinking of Any-Placean language and literature as nationally defined and distinct.

This is obviously simplistic, but through some such process national identities have been cultivated so successfully that now it seems obvious to think of separate nationalities and cultures as wedded to particular languages. To a great extent, however, such traditions are artificially made up. In this respect, if we consider the literature of any specific period, and especially of what we regard as our time, the following come to mind.

1. NO PURE LANGUAGE

It is quite difficult to think of any pure modern language, one that is untouched by other languages. Most modern languages have adopted words, idioms and phrases from other languages; languages constantly do so. Where populations using different languages co-exist, they tend to mix languages. Often a single language is used in quite different social and cultural contexts, and is modified accordingly in each. To take two different sorts of extremes as examples: English is an official language of over 50 sovereign states apart from the UK, USA and Australia; and in London, over 250 languages are used regularly. People and languages have, in brief, always moved and interacted relentlessly.

This is particularly the case now, in the early twenty-first century, when people increasingly move from place to place speedily and frequently. Even if they don't move, people (at least those who read literature) are now probably more aware of international contexts than ever, through the internet and global media coverage (radio, television, newspapers).

If we were determined to conduct a careful reading of a literary text now, paying really close attention to its use of language, we would probably be looking not at *one* language, but at a dominant language that is intersected by many languages and flows of languages. In other words, *we would be looking at a literary text that cannot be understood as simply within one language tradition, but as appearing amidst flows and mixtures of languages.*

2. A WHIRL OF TRANSLATIONS

We live in the midst of a whirl of translations. Actually, it is doubtful whether there's any author in, say, the past two millennia who has not been influenced by, or worked with, translations, or for that matter any reader who has not engaged with translated literary texts. Certainly, in the early twenty-first century, our lives are interwoven inextricably with translations at every level. Much of the news we read or listen to involves numerous acts of translation; we often speak to people in a common language that involves translations on one side or the other; translated manuals and instructions are encountered daily; we often watch subtitled films; and so on. Correspondingly, *contemporary literature reflects a world that works through many layers of translations. And literature in translation is an ever-increasing part of the literature that is sold and bought now in any language with a significant readership.*

Reading only texts in original languages to study what is contemporary in literature is pointlessly restrictive. That may be useful for a focused and in-depth academic study of a few texts or authors. Otherwise, it makes good sense to extend a broad perspective to literature, especially contemporary literature, by referring to translations and making the best of what they convey.

In academic circles (schools, universities, research institutes), reading and analysing literary translations has often been looked down upon, and students and researchers are still apt to feel a few qualms about engaging seriously with translations. But even within such circles, attitudes have been changing significantly, roughly since the 1980s. A few late-twentieth-century academic debates usefully clarify the current position. The following are some areas of literature studies where the use of translations for academic purposes has been debated and largely accepted.

1. COMPARATIVE LITERATURE

This has usually meant the study of the literatures of two or more languages, cultures or nations. In many universities offering Comparative Literature courses (the discipline developed from the late nineteenth century), strong emphasis was conventionally laid on comparing literatures in two or more original languages. By the late 1980s and in the 1990s, however, it had become clear that Comparative Literature needed to broaden its horizons. An exclusive focus on two or three languages and literary traditions appeared unable to cope with the growing popularity of more joined-up and interconnected perspectives of literatures from different parts of the world. Such restrictions also seemed out of synch with the histories of, and particularly with the contemporary realities of, literary circulations. Through translations and adaptations, or through various levels of influence, literary texts have often reached beyond obvious linguistic and political boundaries – and do so with ever greater frequency now. The insistence on studying literature in original languages has gradually diminished in most Comparative Literature programmes, and professional bodies representing the discipline (such as the International Comparative Literature Association) now acknowledge the usefulness of translations. I take up some of these arguments again in chapter 2.

2. POSTMODERNISM, POSTCOLONIALISM AND GLOBALISATION

These are academic perspectives that have had a powerful impact on literary studies as the above-mentioned debates in Comparative Literature unfolded. The joined-up and interconnected perspectives of literature which I mentioned above are particularly associated with these perspectives. I discuss postmodernism, postcolonialism and globalisation in chapters 5 and 6, and in passing in other chapters. Briefly, these perspectives draw attention to the manner in which economic and social networks and cultural exchanges associated historically with European colonialism, and now with processes of global integration, affect literature. To obtain an informed understanding of the relation of literature to these perspectives calls for knowledge of more languages than we can manage. It has consequently become commonplace for translations to be used in 'Postcolonial Literature' or 'Globalisation and Literature' courses in various academic programmes and projects.

3. LITERARY TRANSLATION

Literary translation has itself become a significant area of academic interest through the 1980s and 1990s. This has taken several noteworthy directions. The principles and practicalities of translating literary texts from one language to another have been carefully examined. The social and political contexts in which literary translations are undertaken have been studied. The ideological factors that are implicit in translating literature − in colonial or postcolonial or Cold War conditions, amidst globalisation processes − have been analysed. Conventional attitudes towards translations and translators (which, as I said, often disregarded them) have themselves been dissected. The role of translations in literary circulation and influences has been extensively charted. Naturally, amidst such researches, literary translations have acquired an unprecedented academic respectability of late and are now themselves regarded as distinctive literary works.

As noted, I return to some of the above observations in later chapters, but a more sustained and organised discussion is outside the scope of this book (see Further reading). Ideas and methods drawn from these are implicit throughout this book.

The main point to note in this section is: for a systematic study of contemporary literature in the broad sense, it is expedient to take recourse to translations. And indeed, in subsequent chapters I use translated literary texts as unhesitatingly as original English ones to illustrate and exemplify observations. While deciding to do so, however, I feel it is worth emphasising that *translations are translations and should be read as such, as distinctive literary texts*. We usually read literature in translation because we don't know the original language in which it was written. In using translations below, I do not assume any knowledge of the original language; on the contrary, I assume that such knowledge is lacking. We can nevertheless read and analyse translated texts confidently, with an awareness of the fact that what we are reading is a translation – that mediations and decisions are involved with regard to an original text, which we can grasp only partially. In chapter 4, I discuss in greater detail what it means to read a translation as a translation without knowing the original language.

SELECTION AND LITERARY CANON

'To get cracking, you need to make a selection of the literary works you want to talk about,' observed Dr Guru as I dithered about beginning this book. 'What you need is a good, strong list. Always begin with the texts, I say – they keep us literary people grounded. In my experience, once a list is at hand, you can talk about it to start you off. You can explain how and why you have reached your selection, and why it represents contemporary literature well. You can explain what you have left out, and why. But it is important to get your selection just right, so that it can be examined to give a strong idea of what is contemporary in literature. If you draw one up and show it to me, I will happily tell you what I think of it. As a teacher, I have a reasonable understanding of what sorts of texts will do the job.' I knew straightaway that if I did come up with a list, Dr Guru would try to change it, and we would end up never agreeing on any list.

Those who teach and do research in literature tend to be attached to lists of texts. *Conventionally, the study of literature, however narrowly or widely described, has been approached through a selection of exemplary authors and texts – thought of as the 'literary canon'.* University and school literature curricula are generally lists of texts. Literary histories and surveys typically elaborate on the relations between a list of authors and texts. Literary areas, such as Renaissance sonnets or realist novels, are often effectively described by citing a number of representative texts. Various principles for making such selections and drawing up lists have been in and out of fashion in academic circles.

A popular recourse has been to the idea that we should select the 'best' literary works, the classics, for systematic study. To many literary scholars, this recalls such formulations as Matthew Arnold's 'touchstones' in his essay 'The Study of Poetry' (1964 [1880]). This sort of formulation has had, in different guises, a powerful hold until late in the twentieth century. In Arnold's essay, 'touchstones' are simply a selection of the unarguably best ever examples of poetry, which can be used to measure the quality of any poem that one comes across. How to identify such touchstones is, however, not wholly clear. Arnold didn't say what makes a touchstone a touchstone, but did note that a touchstone isn't one because it is historically interesting, or because it appeals on personal grounds. He apparently felt that standing the test of time is an important factor, since the examples he cited were suitably classical and venerable. The thing to do, he suggested, is to measure the contemporary poem against such touchstones from the past. He warned especially against being influenced by the personal appeal of texts in making our selections of the best, something that is particularly likely to happen with contemporary texts (which often have an immediate appeal).

Arnold-like ideas of what is best in literature and how to make a list accordingly are seldom taken seriously now in academic circles, but still slip in every once in a while. It is difficult to see how literature can register and express the great changes that take place in the world if it is constantly measured against touchstones from the past. However, Arnold's warning about not allowing ourselves to be too taken by personal appeal is a sound one. I might like Heaney's poem 'Testimony' because I had a bracing drink before reading it; and you might hate it because a bee stung you while you were at it. Or we could both be serious about this, and like or dislike it because it evoked similar or different associations. In neither case would we have persuasive grounds for thinking that our selections are of interest beyond ourselves. On the whole, it is simply so difficult to reach any consensus on what is best, especially with regard to contemporary literary texts, that making a selection on that basis seems foolhardy.

Other ways of making selections and drawing lists have been fiercely debated more recently, in the first instance by scholars in the USA and Western European countries. In the 1980s and 1990s, 'canon wars' were fought in academic circles on whether existing exemplary selections (usually presented as some sort of selection of the best or most influential) shouldn't be changed to render such lists more representative of cultural and literary diversity. In summary, the two sides took positions such as the following.

- On the one hand, some argued that existing lists of 'exemplary works' of different literary traditions are too focused on dominant groups (white, middle-class, heterosexual, male writers hog the canon of English literature). Instead of exemplifying the best by any reasonable literary standard, these lists merely show that literary value is determined by who is politically powerful or part of a dominant majority. To be fair, the exemplary writings of minorities and neglected groups (immigrants, women, homosexuals, working-class writers) should be included.

- Others chose to defend the existing literary canon in terms of precisely that which Arnold also warned against – historical interest. According to this argument, selected works in the existing canon are more worthy of attention because they have been exemplary for so long, and have demonstrably influenced subsequent generations of writers and their writings.

Neither of these arguments encourages me to follow Dr Guru's advice and draw up a list. I am entirely in favour of political inclusiveness, but can't think of any list of contemporary literature that could include representative texts for every group that should be included. And the argument about the influence of texts in an existing canon gives little clue about how we should select from contemporary texts. Some contemporary texts may have powerful and immediate effects, but there is no saying whether that will last.

In brief, I find myself reluctant to follow Dr Guru's advice and start off with a list that clarifies what is important or representative in contemporary literature. I don't think a list could do that, and I can think of no plausible criteria for making such a list. Besides, it seems to me that, particularly for an area like contemporary literature, any such list would be more misleading than helpful. A list of this sort may suggest that texts that are included are more important than those left out, and that this selection is somehow a comprehensive representation of what is contemporary. The field of contemporary literature is very wide, and it is impossible for me, or any limited number of readers, to pretend that we know how much has or hasn't been left out. And the whole point of thinking about contemporary literature is that we are taking account of an open-ended and moving period. What is contemporary today will shortly cease to be so, and we haven't a clue what could become contemporary very shortly. *In contemplating why contemporary literature is contemporary and how it could be systematically studied, we need to keep in mind the open-ended and shifting character of the contemporary period. We need to consider our task in ways that are relevant to both literary texts out there that we think of as contemporary now, and literary texts that don't exist yet and will become the contemporary literature of tomorrow. No list of selected texts can help in this.*

When I pause on some literary text or other below to illustrate how contemporary literature could be approached systematically, it must not be taken as a representative or exemplary contemporary literary work. Each such reference below is purely opportunistic: I happen to know that text, it happens to be useful to illustrate a particular point, it promises to be publicly available somewhere in the foreseeable future. That's it. No further significance should be attached to the fact that some text is picked up in this book, or is not.

ON DISREGARDING THE LITERATURE INDUSTRY

'I know you have a particular interest in how literature is published and marketed,' said Dr Guru, 'but it really has only a distant bearing on how and why we read literature. Texts that may have been produced in small numbers and not marketed very well could well become much read, and texts that are produced in great numbers and widely distributed could well be forgotten in a short time. What we value in literature might seem to have something to do with who is publishing it and how it is advertised and received, but actually it doesn't. We know this from experience. Few people read, let's say, James Joyce's *Ulysses* (1922) because it was published by a famous publisher and marketed energetically. We know neither is true. What we look for in literature can be found in the text itself, in terms of how that reverberates with where and when it is read. All we have to do is look to the experience of history to confirm this. That is why, as I have said already, you would be well advised to start your book with close readings and then consider what that reveals in particular times and places – now and where we are for contemporary literature.'

Dr Guru takes too narrow a view of the processes of producing and circulating literary texts. In this he falls in with *well-worn academic attitudes that regard the material forms of literature (as books, magazine publications, electronic texts, and so on) as quite separate from the abstract literary text.* With time, of course, such a separation does perceivably occur – we think of the literary text as a somewhat abstract composition, which can appear in a wide variety of material forms. Thus, when we think of a Shakespeare play, we think of its abstract text, not of the specific material forms in which it has been or is available (the early folios, the Arden edition, the specific film version). *If we are thinking of a contemporary literary work, however, we are unlikely to overlook the material form in which it appears and is circulated: we have a more tangible sense of it as a book or electronic script, we are apt to consider how it has been publicised and reviewed, we may be quite interested in who has published it or made it public, we may well be aware of the different ways in which its translations and adaptations take material form.* All of these are likely to feed into our understanding of a contemporary work as such.

This contemporary awareness of the material forms of literary texts is considerably more complicated than Dr Guru suggests. It isn't simply to do with what we think of as the reputation of the publisher and ways of publicising (the poster or advertisement or book launch and book signing in shops). Let's take Dr Guru's example of *Ulysses* to clarify this, though it might seem a bit odd to dwell on *Ulysses* in a book on contemporary literature published in 2012. This is the only occasion in this book where I pause on a literary text that takes us back nearly a century. Doing so is, however, a useful reminder that all literary texts were contemporary in the first instance, and helps clarify the distinction between contemporary and historically placed at any given time.

Ulysses was first published in 1922, not by a reputed publisher but by a bookshop in Paris with no reputation for publishing books at all, Shakespeare and Company. It wasn't initially particularly well advertised, and the publisher suffered severe losses. Nevertheless, there are other factors that worked alongside these two bare details, which explain how *Ulysses* surfaced very quickly as one of the most discussed novels of the twentieth century. These factors, too, are part of its production and circulation in a material form (as a tangible book with a price tag) – they are part of what I call the 'literary industry' of the time.

A number of episodes from the novel, edited by Ezra Pound, appeared in a US-based journal, *The Little Review*, before the whole was published. The journal was prosecuted in the USA for publishing one of these episodes ('Nausicaa') on the grounds of obscenity, and so was the book as a whole. It appeared, therefore, with an intriguing reputation. Ezra Pound was an influential figure in modernist literary circles, and a most effective promoter of writing in which he was interested. As it happened, the bookshop Shakespeare and Company was a meeting point for aspiring and established literary writers. So Joyce had influential friends. Through his earlier writings, Joyce had already acquired something of a reputation among discerning readers, and those who kept tabs on contemporary literary experimentation already looked forward to the appearance of the novel.

Soon after its appearance, it was therefore widely reviewed by influential literary figures. A number of them were struck by the telephone directory-like appearance of the volume, the difficulty of getting hold of a copy, and its reputation for 'indecency'. Some took issue with its risqué content, some hated its obscurity, and some of the most influential hailed it precisely because they were concerned with shaping the contemporary in the literature of their time. Thus T.S. Eliot (1923), for instance, found (in 'Ulysses, Order and Myth') that the novel evidenced perfectly something of his own quest as a poet: to come to grips with the complexity of the contemporary world in literature by using the structures of myth. Or, in other words, the quest to express 'contemporaneity' by building upon and departing from tradition, as he had already famously observed in his essay 'Tradition and the Individual Talent' (Eliot, 1951 [1919]). As it happened, the first edition had numerous errors in printing, which Joyce corrected for subsequent editions, and it eventually became a serious scholarly pastime to come up with an error-free edition. Pirated editions of the novel created further controversy. Other such details can be adduced to grasp how *Ulysses* came to acquire the reputation it did.

These are all details that have to do with the material forms in which *Ulysses* appeared and circulated, and with the manner in which it was promoted early in its career. All these factors have a powerful bearing on how the text itself was read and re-read. And all these factors, with the complicated links between them, are aspects of the production and circulation process of the book – of the 'literary industry' of the 1920s. Once the initial steps of production and circulation and reception of *Ulysses* were done, subsequent generations of readers had its reputation, and tested strategies for reading it, to fall back on and develop further. At this later stage, it might seem that the text in itself is responsible for its reputation and possible critical nuances. But within the contemporary field of the novel, it was awareness of its production and circulation, the material forms in which it was available or censored, the ways in which it was publicised, that crucially enabled an immediate and systematic approach to it.

Just as an awareness of the literary industry, understood in that broad way, enabled Joyce's contemporaries to come to grips with *Ulysses*, so our attempts to come to grips with contemporary literature are based on our awareness of the literary industry now. *To study contemporary literature systematically, then, we need to foreground some necessary aspects of the literary industry now.* The literary industry of our time is quite different from that of the 1920s, and we need to be explicit about how the production and circulation and reception of literature takes place now – and is likely to in the foreseeable future. Consequently, it seems important to me that, in a book such as the present one, some general characteristics of the prevailing literary industry should be kept in view, and chapters 3 and 4 are particularly devoted to this.

This leads me to make a more general point arising from the above. To a great extent, thinking systematically about contemporary literature involves thinking about texts that are new to most of us.

In general, these are texts that have been produced recently enough to not have been considered in depth yet, or for which considered interpretations haven't yet evolved. Put otherwise, these are texts about which there is little firm consensus on how they should be understood – not enough firm consensus for us to either agree or disagree with. Nor is it entirely clear yet how these texts reflect their contexts, since the contexts of the text are effectively our contexts. Our contexts are what we live through, and that is usually less clearly understood than some relatively distant period and location, such as, for instance, 1920s France or the USA (when *Ulysses* appeared). Our time is still unfolding and being charted by observers and scholars, whereas the 1920s has already been charted and thought about in definite ways. We already know to a reasonable extent what were the important social events and ideas of the 1920s and what were the significant literary texts of the time; whereas we are still working out what these are for our recent times.

Under these circumstances, a systematic study of contemporary texts depends largely on our ability to make connections between the text and what could be relevant to it in our world, as we live in and perceive it. The literary industry provides an obvious and immediately available structure in terms of which we can understand some aspects of a contemporary literary text. There are other structures that are equally important. What are dominant social and political concerns of our time, what are the familiar experiences of people living now, what are the dominant tastes that are cultivated, and so on – we can bring some or all of these to the task of understanding a contemporary literary text. And that works the other way around, too: approaching contemporary literary texts in a systematic fashion will also clarify how the various aspects of our world work. It is a two-way process: *we approach contemporary literature systematically by thinking about the connections to our world; and equally, by doing this we begin to think about various facets of our world more systematically.* Subsequent chapters aim to explain briefly how we can capitalise on this two-way process.

REFERENCES

Arnold, Matthew (1964). 'The Study of Poetry' (1880). *Matthew Arnold's Essays in Criticism: First and Second Series.* London: Dent.

Eliot, T.S. (1923). 'Ulysses, Order and Myth'. In Robert H. Deming, ed. (1970). *James Joyce: The Critical Heritage*. London: Routledge & Kegan Paul.
———(1951). 'Tradition and the Individual Talent' (1919). *Selected Essays*. London: Faber and Faber.
Heaney, Seamus (2003). 'Testimony' (along with Saadi Youssef's extracted poem from 'America, America', and Michael Casey's 'A Bummer'). 'Three War Poems'. *The Guardian* (Review section), 15 February, p. 36. Reprinted in Matthew Hollis and Paul Keegan, eds (2003). *101 Poems Against War*. London: Faber and Faber.
Joyce, James (1922). *Ulysses*. Paris: Shakespeare and Co.

FURTHER READING

Relevant further reading on postmodernism, postcolonialism, globalisation, and themes relevant to comparative literature and the literary industry appear in the Further reading lists for subsequent chapters.

ON CLOSE READING AND CONTEXTUALISATION

Barry, Peter (2007). *Literature in Contexts*. Manchester: Manchester University Press. [Covers both what is implied by contextualising literature and what is entailed in reading literature in context.]
Lentriccia, Frank and Andrew Dubois, eds (2003). *Close Reading: A Reader*. Durham NC: Duke University Press. [A collection of essays on close reading as the common ground between formalists and non-formalists. Together, the essays give a strong sense of the different nuances of close reading and of the contexts in which close reading is undertaken.]

ON LITERATURE IN RELATION TO ANALYSING LANGUAGE AND TO TRANSLATIONS

Bassnett, Susan and André Lefevere, eds (1998). *Contrasting Cultures: Essays in Literary Translation*. Clevedon, UK: Multilingual Matters. [Various perspectives on translating literary texts or reading translated texts.]
Bassnett, Susan (2002). *Translation Studies*, 3rd edn. Abingdon: Routledge. [A general introduction to the area.]
Carter, Ronald and Peter Stockwell, eds (2008). *The Language and Literature Reader*. Abingdon, UK: Routledge. [Essays on analysing literature by using the tools of linguistics. A useful entry point for considering the various levels at which the inextricable relationship between literary text and language work.]

Venuti, Lawrence, ed. (2004). *The Translation Studies Reader*, 2nd edn. Abingdon, UK: Routledge. [Selection of key texts in the area, arranged by chronological phases up to '1990 and After'.]

ON THE FLOWS AND INTERPENETRATIONS OF LANGUAGE RELEVANT TO CONSIDERING CONTEMPORARY LITERATURE AND CULTURE

Alim, H. Sami, Awad Ibrahim and Alastair Pennycook, eds (2009). *Global Linguistic Flows: Hip Hop Cultures, Youth Identities, and the Politics of Language.* Abingdon, UK: Routledge. [Useful in being anchored to hip hop, which does involve texts.]

Risager, Karen (2006). *Language and Culture: Global Flows and Local Complexity.* Clevedon, UK: Multilingual Matters. [Not to do with literature, more language teaching; but pertinent in analysing contemporary language flows in relation to concepts of culture.]

ON COMPARATIVE LITERATURE

Apter, Emily (2006). *The Translation Zone: A New Comparative Literature.* Princeton, NJ: Princeton University Press. [Covers most of the debates about the use of translations in comparative literature.]

Bassnett, Susan (1993). *Comparative Literature: A Critical Introduction.* Oxford: Blackwell.

Saussy, Haun, ed. (2006). *Comparative Literature in the Age of Globalization.* Baltimore, MD: Johns Hopkins University Press. [Reckonings with the state of the discipline of Comparative Literature in the early twenty-first century.]

Tötösy de Zepetnek, Steven (1998). *Comparative Literature: Theory, Method, Application.* Amsterdam: Rodopi. [A wide-ranging account of the discipline and recent developments therein.]

ON LITERARY CANONS AND 'CANON WARS'

Bloom, Harold (1994). *The Western Canon: The Books and School of the Ages.* New York: Harcourt Brace. [The most influential defence of the integrity of the Western canon.]

Guillory, John (1993). *Cultural Capital: The Problem of Literary Canon Formation.* Chicago, IL: University of Chicago Press. [A sustained argument about the need to open the Western literary canon.]

Kolbas, E. Dean (2001). *Critical Theory and the Literary Canon.* Boulder, CO: Westview. [Part 1 gives a useful overview of the debates mentioned above.]

2

SPECIFIC STRATEGIES

DEALING WITH CONTEMPORARY LITERATURE

'The recent, the present day, our time, our world, the contemporary – what a lot of vague, slippery phrases you use,' complains Dr Guru. 'They don't really say anything or refer to anything. The problem with your book is that it is about literature along the moving boundary of time. Of course, we read this literature in an ongoing way, and write about, and teach, and study it. We are on this moving boundary. It is true that there is hardly a school or university programme about any living literary tradition that doesn't end with the contemporary. If we consider reviews and media discussions, what's highlighted in bookshops and chatrooms and literary events, what's performed or adapted for the stage or screen – if I think about these, it's obvious that what you call contemporary literature is the most visible part of all literature. But I'm not sure you can really discuss methodically something that we simply do according to our current habits.'

These views are evidently shared by many. At any rate, there are very few guidebooks or textbooks on how to study contemporary literature in a systematic and informed fashion – I mean, contemporary literature *broadly*. Perhaps this paucity is because currently favoured critical principles (Dr Guru-like principles) for studying literature need modification when it comes to contemporary literature. In chapter 1, we discussed some such strategies for studying literature generally.

There are, however, a multitude of anthologies and textbooks on contemporary literature *of particular sorts*: that is, of such-and-such place or language (German, Chinese, Russian, Tamil, and so on) and/or such-and-such genre (fiction, short stories, poetry, and so on). These feed courses in schools and universities featuring contemporary literature, and practical methodologies for studying contemporary texts are constantly used in classrooms. Numerous scholarly works also discuss particular facets of contemporary literature (in ways that I elaborate in subsequent chapters). These prevailing approaches to the academic study of contemporary literature already have a respectable history.

For an indicative sense of when academia started tackling contemporary literature systematically, we can turn to the example of English literature. Literary histories and anthologies stretching from the beginning to the 'present day' began appearing frequently in English from roughly the mid-nineteenth century (for example, publisher Robert Chambers' edited *Cyclopædia of English Literature*, 1844; or scholar Thomas Arnold's *Chaucer to Wordsworth*, 1870). Bibliographies of contemporary literature in English started being produced from the late nineteenth century (publisher William Swan Sonnenschein's *A Reader's Guide to Contemporary Literature*, 1895 – covering literature, art and sciences – is an early example). During the nineteenth century, British schools and universities gradually moved from the study of Greek and Latin classics towards English literature. It is therefore understandable that books which try to systematise contemporary English literature appeared in significant quantities in the mid- to late nineteenth century. However, a higher regard for 'great works' that have stood the test of time, and nervousness about contemporary literature, persisted well into the twentieth century. The study of current literary productions nevertheless gained ground steadily through the twentieth century, and there has been a constant proliferation of anthologies, textbooks and scholarly books on the contemporary literature of, as I stress above, particular sorts.

In the latter, we find certain academic strategies for dealing with contemporary literature *specifically*, which are the subject of this chapter.

This chapter complements chapter 1 on strategies for studying literature *generally* and their relevance for contemporary literature. Some of these strategies for dealing with contemporary literature specifically are best understood with reference to a typical textbook. Judging by the title of Steve Padley's *Key Concepts in Contemporary Literature* (2006), it promises to cover roughly the same ground as this book. The first couple of pages, however, outline a different agenda, and in the process exemplify some of the strategies we are interested in here. Padley opens by observing that: 'The term contemporary denotes an open-ended period, up to and including the present day, but there is a marked lack of consensus about when the period can definitively be said to have begun' (p. ix). So, more or less arbitrarily, he decides to affix a beginning – he starts with 1945, after the Second World War. In doing this, he takes it for granted that the literature his readers are interested in must be exclusively and originally in English, but he goes a step further by confining himself to British literature alone. By way of explaining this, Padley observes: 'Ideally, it would be desirable to trace the development of all literatures written in English since 1945, but the resulting volume would either be impossibly long or wholly inadequate in the depth of its coverage' (p. x).

In brief, the academic strategies involved here are:

- affixing a *period* as the contemporary period;
- limiting the appraisal of the contemporary period to a specific language and/or *territory*; and
- putatively providing adequate and in-depth *coverage* for the affixed period and place – which suggests that a survey of representative texts and ideas clarifies what the contemporary in literature is about.

These are actually useful and tested strategies, and they are worth examining closely. Useful as these are, they are *not* the strategies adopted here (in the previous chapter I decided against using surveys and representative lists). For us, their usefulness rests in providing points for discussion in this chapter. My reasons for not adopting these strategies must be evident to some extent already: in brief, these strategies actually led Padley to write a useful book about *post-1945 British literature* instead of *contemporary literature*.

Also, due to these strategies, Padley's book turns out to be an implausibly limited account. It is apparently innocent of globalisation processes, pays no heed to translations and intercultural flows, ignores the fact that we read as much in electronic forms as in print, overlooks our involvement in networks, disregards our adeptness with audiovisual media, and so on. There are a couple of familiar strategies that Padley doesn't exploit:

- addressing specific forms or *genres* (confining critical appraisal to contemporary poetry, contemporary popular writing, electronic fiction); and
- focusing on some *perspective or issue* that is recognisably of contemporary interest ('war on terror', environmentalism, globalisation).

The idea behind strategies such as those in the five bullet points above is to consider contemporary literature broadly by looking at a limited bit of the field. This seems to me a rather optimistic and unrealistic idea. The contemporary world, and therefore contemporary literature, is characterised more by links and connections than by artificially cut-out bits in themselves. In favour of such strategies, it is usually urged that they are practical – the alternative would be unmanageable. But the alternative is unmanageable only if we assume that the study of literature involves either mainly close readings or a comprehensive survey. Neither, I have argued in chapter 1, is necessarily the way forward, and I chart a different approach there.

As I have said, though, such strategies are useful because each draws attention to one way of describing what is contemporary in literature. If we consider each of them further, by the end we should have a clearer sense of what our understanding of the contemporary in literature broadly consists in. The four sections that follow take up these strategies by turn, and are entitled 'period and territory' (the first two strategies discussed together), 'coverage and intertextuality', 'genre and change', and 'issues and perspectives'.

PERIOD AND TERRITORY

At the beginning of Carlos Ruiz Zafón's novel *The Shadow of the Wind* (2002; translated from the Spanish by Lucia Graves, 2004) there appears the intriguing notion of a Cemetery of Forgotten Books. The fictional narrator Daniel is taken to one as a child (in 1945) by his father Sempere, a bookseller. It turns out to be a vast and labyrinthine library, which is described by Sempere as follows:

> When a library disappears, or a bookshop closes down, when a book is consigned to oblivion, those of us who know this place, its guardians, make sure that it gets here. In this place, books no longer remembered by anyone, books that are lost in time, live forever, waiting for the day when they will reach a new reader's hands. In the shop we buy and sell them, but in truth books have no owner.
>
> (p. 4)

The Cemetery of Forgotten Books is obviously a metaphor for the opposite of the bookshop or library that makes books in demand available. In Zafón's novel, it is described as a vast collection that is completely randomly stacked, naturally secreted away from the public eye in no discernible order. Insofar as Daniel gets to see it, he seems to come across primarily forgotten literary books in various languages: during his first visit, he picks up an unknown novel (bearing the same title as this novel) which becomes a prolonged obsession, and when he visits on several later occasions, he comes across novels, plays and the odd philosophical work. It is a useful metaphor for us, in that it gives us a backdrop against which several of the sections in this chapter can be approached.

Imagine setting a dedicated literary scholar (with bibliographical interests) or librarian (with literary interests) loose in the Cemetery. After a brief, despairing tantrum, she will immediately set about imposing order on the Cemetery, starting with literature – pulling all the books down and sorting the texts according to some principle. Putting the texts in order will in fact bring them back to life: it will be possible to find them again, and the very act of putting them in order involves consulting them and arousing them from oblivion. The ordering of texts is therefore central to what the academic study of literature – as of librarianship or the book trade – involves. It would be natural for our bibliographical scholar to take recourse to chronology to order the texts. It might make sense to, say, arrange all the texts by the years in which they were first published. But that's actually a cumbersome and clumsy process, in which she might easily lose track of the very great number of texts at hand. It would be easier to arrange a finite number of large piles rather than lay out the texts according to date in one line that seems to stretch forever. It is, in brief, better to divide up the texts between broad periods rather than simply in a sequence of consecutive years. There are, it occurs to her, two ways in which she could go about this.

1. MECHANICAL PERIODISATION

She could choose her periods in a strictly mechanical fashion: for instance, periods of 100 years by the Gregorian calendar, so that she will end up with neat piles of sixteenth-century, seventeenth-century, eighteenth-century, and so on literature. The last pile here would be the most recent − now, the twenty-first century literature pile, which, being far from complete yet, she might label 'contemporary literature'. Or, since she finds that there are actually far more books in the more recent periods than in the earlier, she might decide to start sorting into decades for the twentieth and twenty-first centuries, and decide that the texts of the past five decades should be regarded as contemporary because 50 is a nice round number. Or, she might go for the past five decades and three years, because we happen to be three years into the ongoing decade. If she does this, she finds that her periodisation, though mechanical, acquires retrospective meaning − she seems to find links in texts according to which century or decade they appeared in. She suspects that this might be a kind of trick of her mind, a bit like an optical illusion.

2. SOCIALLY RELEVANT PERIODISATION

Alternatively, she could decide to choose the less mechanical path of trying to *determine periods according to the content of the texts in relation to the social circumstances and events* (such as the rule of dynasties, developments in social and economic relations, epoch-defining historical events such as wars and famines). This is considerably more interesting, and seems to be less inclined to tricks of the mind. Since our bibliographical scholar is not fond of purely mechanical categories, and wants to arrange the texts in terms of potential readers' interests, she finds this path more to her taste. To demarcate meaningful periods thus means to think of what is meaningful for a large group of people, like the citizens of a country or speakers of a language. So she begins demarcating periods accordingly, and decides that the latest meaningful event thus understood would determine where the period for contemporary literature would begin.

Where the contemporary begins would naturally be different for different groups. If she were thinking in terms of countries, for instance: in many European countries the contemporary may well begin with the end of the Second World War; in postcolonial countries it may begin with independence; in East European countries it may begin with the fall of communism in 1989; in many contexts it may begin with the terrorist attacks in USA on 11 September 2001; in China it may well be placed from Liberation in 1949 or after the Cultural Revolution ended in 1976; and so on. Of course, our bibliographical scholar might also choose to set periods with regard to a country in a less political way, perhaps according to the appearance and development of influential literary or cultural ideas or movements.

In fact, the logic that our bibliographical scholar may follow to organise the Cemetery of Forgotten Books is precisely the rationale that is followed in academic circles for periodising literature in relation to territories. It is through some such rationale, mechanical or contextual, that periods are demarcated in literary histories, in school and university curricula, for research specialisations. Insofar as setting where the contemporary period begins, unless the mechanical path is chosen, it is evident that this will depend on what territory is in question – for what group of readers and writers, where and when. There is therefore no general consensus on where the contemporary period begins, as Steve Padley observes. But there is a perfectly understandable range of possibilities arising from what is practical and meaningful, mechanically pragmatic or contextually relevant for those studying the matter. Where it is set may be different for different groups of readers in different places and different times, but in a manner that is consistent with our bibliographical scholar's reckonings in the Cemetery.

A couple of further observations on the periodisation and territorial demarcations of the contemporary in literature are worth taking on board. Going back to Zafón's novel: the book that

Daniel picks up during his first visit to the Cemetery (his father tells him he is allowed to take one), and which leads to his subsequent adventures, turns out to be a fairly recent one. It is a novel published in 1935, a mere ten years earlier, though it has practically disappeared since. It appears someone has been systematically burning all the known copies. There is, in other words, an ambiguity about how contemporary the novel is. In a mechanical sense, a gap of ten years is by most measures 'contemporary' enough in literature (consider your own sense of what counts as a contemporary novel). However, to Daniel and other readers, all resident in Barcelona, it seems to belong to a different age – and with good reason.

A change of epoch-defining proportions has occurred for these characters in the interim: the Spanish Civil War has taken place and the pre-war socialist government has been replaced by a fascist government under General Franco. In Spanish history and letters, the scars and implications of the Civil War have been extensively (and are still being) pondered. So, from a contextual point of view, the novel that preoccupies Daniel after 1945 has already receded into a past pre-Civil War period, and symbolically has been absorbed in a burning ritual – which could be taken to symbolise the upheaval and consequences of the Civil War. *The tension here between the mechanical way and the contextual way of setting the contemporary period is worth noting.* They don't work neatly together. From a contextual point of view, where we set the beginning of our contemporary period depends on where we feel a previous period has come to a close.

To take a different tack, as I write this in the early twenty-first century, thinking of periods in terms of countries or other relatively limited groups of people often seems to limit our approach to contemporary literature unnecessarily. While a country-specific understanding of the present is, of course, still very pertinent in some ways, in others it is obvious that there is a constantly growing sense of the present in larger terms – in international or even global terms. That has increasingly been the case for the past few centuries, and it is particularly so now. Significant social and political events are reported and absorbed very quickly and widely around the world nowadays. A larger number of economic, administrative and communication organisations and systems operate multinationally or globally now than ever before to ensure this. This is not merely reflected in literary works, but also influences the way literature circulates. A popular novel such as Zafón's reaches readers more widely and quickly than was likely a few decades back, for reasons I go into in chapter 3. It is translated, read and assimilated within a multitude of linguistic and national contexts. In being made available widely and quickly to be read and considered in numerous contexts simultaneously, it becomes part of a broad sense of the contemporary in literature – it becomes a component of what is contemporary for readers not just in Spain, but also in the USA and UK (it is a bestseller in both) and elsewhere.

Naturally, our understanding of the contemporary period in literature *now* has to take this into account – take into account that, for many of us, Zafón's novel appears as a work of contemporary fiction in London and Paris and New York and Barcelona and Beijing within a very compressed period. *Our understanding of what is the contemporary period in literature is, in many ways, an international or perhaps even a global sense. Even though widely dispersed, from this international or global perspective we are now increasingly likely to be able to agree where the beginning of the contemporary can be meaningfully set.*

For this situation, too, there's an intriguing literary metaphor of a library that comes to mind, in Jorge Luis Borges's short piece, 'The Library of Babel' (1941; translated by Anthony Kerrigan and available in the collection *Fictions*, 1985). Here we have a playful consideration of the universe itself as a library, and the vagaries that arise in trying to impose order on this library. It isn't directly relevant to our consideration of periodisation and territory in this section, so I won't dwell on it here. But there is a suggestive metaphorical thread between Borges's library and Zafón's Cemetery of Forgotten Books. You might wish to explore this connection yourself.

COVERAGE AND INTERTEXTUALITY

Here's another novel I picked up recently: Mansoura Ez-Eldin's *Maryam's Maze* (2004; translated from the Arabic by Paul Starkey, 2007). Here Maryam, a young woman, wakes up from a disturbing dream to find herself in an unfamiliar room, though all her things are there. Naturally at a loss, she throws some clothes on and goes out into the streets of Cairo to look for her boyfriend, or her friend, someone she knows. She is unable to find them. She returns

to the room anxious and frustrated and falls asleep, and starts reminiscing – perhaps dreaming – of her childhood and adolescence in
an aristocratic family. Memories, dreams and reality merge gradually
as Maryam's story unfolds, and her confusions are never quite
resolved. What does become clear to her is that she is in the midst
of an agonised search, which she understands thus:

> Feelings that cannot be contradicted are mankind's secret, the place
> where his superiority lies. Being deprived of them was her death spot,
> her private Achilles' heel. She wouldn't behave like Grenouille, the hero
> of *Perfume*, a novel that Maryam had read and become crazy about. She
> wouldn't embark on an epic journey with the aim of 'perfuming' her
> feelings as he had done when he embarked on a journey to find a smell
> that suited him. Her aim was different. She had to nurture the one wish
> she had been able to nurture: the desire to escape, to finally leave her
> dilemma behind her, the maze whose frightening walls she had been
> left to bang herself against from time immemorial without the slightest
> mercy.
>
> (pp. 86–87)

The reference is to Patrick Süskind's novel *Perfume* (1985; translated
from the German by John E. Wood, 1986), which is set in eighteenth-century France. Its hero Grenouille has a preternaturally
developed sense of smell and becomes adept at distilling perfumes.
A powerful desire to distil the smell of a woman which he finds
particularly appealing leads him to commit a series of murders. He
kills young women and distils and mixes their aroma in the hope of
achieving that sought-after perfume.

What we have here is an intertextual reference: one relatively
recent novel referring to another, which is not too distant either.
The first thing that strikes me, as a reader who happens to be
familiar with Süskind's novel, is how clarifying the reference is:
Grenouille's quest is an apt counterpoint to Maryam's situation.
Where Grenouille's quest for the perfect perfume is single-minded
in the extreme, Maryam is swept along by circumstances beyond
her control into a sort of oblivion. Grenouille's distinctively male
quest makes him a predatory killer of women, whereas Maryam's is
the fate of a woman trying to overcome the constraints of an
oppressive, male-dominated world – one who is keenly aware of

other women in her life who have become victims of oppressive circumstances. Grenouille is endowed with a superlative sensory ability and accordingly maps the world so that it works in his favour, while Maryam is overcome by material conditions that confuse and trap her, and from which she seeks release. The other thing about this passage that interests me is how casually that reference to Süskind's novel is given. The reader is barely even informed in Ez-Eldin's novel of what Grenouille actually does, and there's nothing of where and when *Perfume* appeared. It doesn't in the least seem to matter that quite different, conventionally distanced, social milieux and languages are involved, Arabic and German; or that one is set and written in contemporary Cairo, the other set in eighteenth-century France and written in 1980s Germany. Only something a little over a decade separates them – referring to Süskind's novel is not like referring to some venerable common denominator of 'world classics' such as *Gilgamesh* or Homer's epics or *The Arabian Nights*. And yet Ez-Eldin assumed that the reference has a reasonable chance of making sense to the reader. This is not misplaced confidence. In fact, Süskind's novel was a remarkable international success, and was translated into 46 languages. Ez-Eldin could justly anticipate that many of her readers would have read Süskind's novel. Indeed, the chances of the reader's knowledge of it increased dramatically by the time the English translation of *Maryam's Maze* appeared, since *Perfume* was produced as a film shortly before (in German, directed by Tom Tykwer, 2006).

Such intertextual references are far from uncommon. In fact, they are more the norm than the exception. Literary texts are littered with such references, across the most dispersed languages and territories and periods. It so happens that the example I have chosen illustrates how such intertextual references may be used explicitly in a text; if we consider the kind of intertextual connections that we, as readers, constantly make across every sort of boundary when reading, it is evident that these are a constant part of reading. Thus, even before I had reached the reference to *Perfume* in Ez-Eldin's novel, I was already trying to make sense of it in terms of books I have read. It had occurred to me, for instance, that though *Maryam's Maze* begins with a mystery, the novel does not develop like the mystery thrillers and detective stories that I am fond of reading: Maryam is the opposite of the single-minded hero or determined detective who resolves mysteries. In other words, I had already started making intertextual connections with other texts, such as mystery thrillers and detective stories I have read.

In fact, *reading consists very largely in our constantly charting such intertextual connections to make sense of a new text, sometimes from the most distant precincts of the literature we are familiar with. Arguably, this has always been the character of reading, and such intertextual references are legion in all sorts of literary texts since classical antiquity. In the contemporary period, however, we may feel that the possibility of making such references and connections is intensifying, simply because literary texts can circulate now across languages and territories more fluently and speedily and widely than was possible heretofore.* At least certain texts (such as *Perfume*) circulate thus very successfully, in print and in electronic forms and through audiovisual adaptations. It is more likely now for writers and readers confidently to make intertextual connections between texts from widely dispersed origins that have appeared within a relatively short time. Like Ez-Eldin's intertextual reference to Süskind's novel, such references appear to us to make good sense and need little explanation – we don't find ourselves particularly baffled or taken aback by them.

Returning to the issue of trying to achieve comprehensive coverage of contemporary literature within any context, the growing and speedier scope of intertextual connections in writing and reading does present a particular problem. That is, a problem arises with conventional ways of trying to cover the contemporary in literature by delimiting our field in terms of period, territory or language – by confining ourselves, for instance, to post-1945 British literature alone (an expanse in itself). Such delimitation simply doesn't gel with the pervasiveness of intertextual connections that the writing and reading of post-1945 British literature inevitably contains. The authors of this literature have been aware of and influenced by, and have deliberately referred to, texts from other languages and cultures. Correspondingly, their readers have constantly brought their awareness of texts from other languages and cultures to bear on these. Even if we were to confine our attention to the post-1945 period, given the increasing speed with which texts and translations and audiovisual adaptations have circulated since, what we are faced with is British literature that is British only in a legalistic sense (writers with British passports and texts published by

British publishers). The legalistic sense has little relation to the realities of the production and reception of such literature. The conventional ploy of trying to understand the contemporary in literature by focusing in depth on (for instance) post-1945 British literature is, therefore, not simply stiflingly limited, but also misleading: a ploy that distorts the manner in which literature is produced and read now, and misconceives what our literary experience in the contemporary world is like.

Given the above circumstances, it would appear that *a systematic and informed approach to contemporary literature (actually literature from any period, but especially contemporary literature) should be underpinned by a broad awareness of literature from different languages and territories. Under these circumstances, the idea of undertaking any kind of comprehensive coverage of contemporary literary texts within a delimited area is best abandoned.* It is really our faith in comprehensive coverage and in-depth surveys that explains the prevailing nervousness about what we actually need here: a broad awareness of literature across languages and cultures. Nervousness about the latter has been debated at considerable length in academic circles under the guise of discussing 'world literature'. A few notes on debates about world literature cannot but be useful here, and they refer us back to 'comparative literature', which I mentioned in chapter 1.

NOTES ON WORLD LITERATURE

- The phrase 'world literature' (*weltliteratur*) was proposed first by Goethe (in a letter to poet Johann Peter Eckermann in January 1827) as an idealistic concept of the sum total of all the literature of the world. For over 150 years after that, the phrase largely continued to be regarded as an abstract concept, which can be contemplated with awe, but which cannot really be practically studied or researched. In departments of Comparative Literature where the phrase cropped up occasionally, it was regarded as a rather useless conceptual horizon, while the real toil of academic study is confined to comparing two or three literatures in their original, usually European, languages.
- It was the prospect of comparing literatures in what were regarded as distant languages and cultures, such as French

and Japanese literary texts, that brought back the notion of world literature as a possibly useful one in the 1980s. This mainly involved soul-searching about the academic credibility of using translations to compare a wide range of literatures from different languages and cultures.

- By the late 1990s, it seemed obvious that the narrow method of comparing literary texts in original languages was increasingly unequal to contemporary literary practices – as I have noted above, texts move in our time across media, languages and territories with increasing speed and reach. Consequently, formulations of world literature that are less idealistically total than Goethe's, and more useful for students, teachers and researchers, began to be considered.

- It has thus been proposed, for instance, that world literature should entail the study of how texts move across territorial, linguistic and cultural boundaries (through translations and adaptations, via the spread of dominant languages such as English) and media (print, electronic, audiovisual). It has also been suggested that to obtain a world literature perspective, the academic study of literature should not be as centred on original texts and close reading as it has been. Instead, such study should perhaps take recourse to the work of critics who have already undertaken close readings and in-depth surveys of literatures in specific languages, and try to discern broad patterns and links across them (conduct, in other words, 'distanced reading'). Such practical ways of thinking about world literature have little relation to Goethe's idea, and seem more plausible and useful. They are particularly useful for trying to come to grips with the manner in which we experience the literature of our time – indeed, I suspect that they have appeared relatively recently in response to the circumstances of our world.

The prospect of cultivating some sort of world literature awareness to study contemporary literature systematically is still apt to cause some anxiety. This is really an inherited anxiety, derived from thinking about world literature in a Goethean way, and from thinking of systematic study in terms of comprehensive coverage. For our purposes, what this involves pragmatically may be no more than the following points, which give little cause for worry.

- Taking note of evident intertextual references and allusions, if any, when reading a literary text, and also of any other kind of cultural and linguistic boundary-crossing that is apparent in the text (even, say, a protagonist travelling somewhere).
- Being cognisant of the intertextual references, allusions and patterns that we as readers inevitably bring to reading a particular text.
- Being aware of how we have come across the text we are reading (whether through recommendation, or publicity, or interest) – which is just one way of being aware of how others might get to this text. Also, making an effort to be aware of the forms and adaptations in which the text is available, in what mediums and in which languages and territories.
- Perhaps making a conscious decision to read, whenever possible and of interest, literary texts not only written originally in the language and territory we are most familiar with, but also in other languages and from other cultures (including translations and adaptations) – especially those that relate in some way to a text we have read.
- Being generally aware of social, political and cultural developments of different cultures and linguistic contexts, which may feed into whatever we read. This could be a simple matter of following world news, or tapping into other broad-based information sources (up-to-date encyclopaedias, reference books, journals, statistical sources, etc.).

Engaging with contemporary literature in a systematic and informed way now does involve a broad awareness of literature in different languages and cultures to this extent. Beyond these points, of course, we could go into more sustained consideration of existing academic theories about, and studies of, world literature, if we wish to (see Further reading).

There is no particular condition of being broadly informed in the above sense that has to *precede* our systematic and informed study of contemporary literature. The argument above is that we, contemporary readers, already bring a wide awareness of literature to our readings – we generally do this as a matter of course and inevitably. The argument is also that being systematic and informed involves being aware of what we already do, and cultivating such a broad awareness self-consciously.

Further, the necessity of this broad awareness for studying contemporary literature should not in the least be regarded as discouraging the in-depth study of literature in one language or territory, if we so desire. That broad awareness, according to the argument above, necessarily informs such a narrower or more focused kind of study insofar as it is to do with the contemporary. We can choose to focus meaningfully on the contemporary literature of one language or territory (say, post-1945 Britain), but that cannot do away with the fact that this literature has been, and will be, woven into and with the literature of many languages and cultures.

GENRE AND CHANGE

Let's go back to our imagined bibliographical scholar in Zafón's Cemetery of Forgotten Books. After sorting the books according to period and territory or language, she will have a number of large heaps. By way of trying to bring order within each heap of books, she might decide to sort them next by genre.

'Genre' is a somewhat confusing term that most scholars and readers seem quite comfortable with. Following a classical tradition that still makes reasonably good sense, most think of genre in the first instance as a way of classifying literature into three broad forms: poetry, prose and drama. Each has proliferated into numerous further categories according to form (for example, poetry into epic, sonnet, *haiku*, *jintishi*, *ruba'i*, *ghazal*), which are sometimes referred to as 'subgenres' and sometimes, confusingly, as genres too. To add further confusion, in some instances genre categorisations seem to take account of not only the form, but also the content of literary texts, and sometimes merely the content (for example, the genre of drama could break down into the genres of tragedy, comedy, farce and so on, all of which are to do with the content of plays). And by way of adding confusion to confusion, relatively recently publishers and booksellers have started referring to a certain kind of popular fiction as 'genre fiction' (such as formulaic detective stories, action thrillers, romances) as opposed to the serious 'literary' stuff – so that genre seems to become the preserve of popularity.

If our bibliographical scholar in the Cemetery of Forgotten Books wanted to get along with the business of imposing order, she could decisively cut across the confusion. She could build up a consistent system of genres, subgenres and subsubgenres, which would still make sense to readers, and arrange each heap accordingly. She would naturally take account of the fact that for each period and territory/language there are variations in what the prominent subgenres and subsubgenres are. If she were in a contemplative mood, however, she might ponder the ways in which the confusing fluidity and ambiguity of the term 'genre' is itself indicative, especially for a systematic study of contemporary literature. The following are likely to cross her mind.

1. HARDENING GENRES

If we take a historical view of the evolution of literary genres, there are several distinct and contradictory directions that can be seen. Some categories of genre seem to harden and take a very definite and formulaic shape with time. At present, these appear as market categories – categories of literature that authors, publishers and readers agree upon as following a predetermined form, content and style. What we think of now as genre fiction is essentially along those lines: these publications follow formulae that are repeated constantly in new works, with small variations. That could also be said of some genres of theatre, such as documentary drama, domestic drama, testimonial theatre, family comedy, and so on.

In fact, *at present (and this is true for as long as there has been a large market for literature), it seems that genres can be divided into two broad areas: the 'popular' and the 'serious' or 'literary'.* Popular literary genres harden into formulae and are constantly replicated (obviously because readers in significant numbers like them as they are); serious literary genres are less predictable and stable. However, such a broad division is somewhat suspect: it is created by publishers and others who want to exploit the market, and doesn't necessarily coincide with a systematic approach to literature. Thus, what is sold and bought as literary fiction is also really a market-defined genre. It is designed to attract certain kinds of readers who cultivate seriousness and literary values, and tries to impose a sort of formula on such literature too.

2. MIXING GENRES

With a historical view, too, *it appears that in a general way genres proliferate and mix up with time*. To some extent, this occurs with relatively formulaic (or popular) genres: thus gothic horror fiction can be mixed with detective fiction, or science fiction with action thrillers. These generically hybrid works are still read in terms of the hardened formulae, which they mix up, and rarely break down the latter – but these may occasionally form distinct genres themselves. Less predictable categories of literature (usually thought of as serious or literary) involve a constant testing of the boundaries of existing genres, either in terms of form or of content (sometimes both). Thus such new novels may try to cover unremarked areas in original ways relative to previous novels, and new poems may try to deliberately disturb the formal conventions of poetry already in place. This probably accounts for the proliferation of genres with time, and confusion about how the term 'genre' is used.

Naturally, the attempt of new works to test the boundaries of an older genre means that the former refer (implicitly or explicitly) to the latter; they are self-conscious about their originality in relation to the existing genre. *Testing the boundaries of existing genres in a self-conscious, referential way is a constant preoccupation in such new writing, and could be a useful way of understanding what is contemporary in literature.* This is what the strategy of examining contemporary literature *within* a delimited generic (e.g. in the novel, drama, poetry) or subgeneric (e.g. in detective fiction, lyric poetry, tragedy) area usually focuses on.

3. CHANGING SOCIAL CIRCUMSTANCES

Each of the above-mentioned *processes of proliferating, testing, mixing or hardening genre categories is due not only to decisions taken by writers, readers and publishers, but perhaps more fundamentally to changing social circumstances in different contexts.* By changing social circumstances, I mean shifts in political, economic, intellectual, educational and technological arrangements and conventions. At one obvious level, such changes can be traced through the manner in which languages change by adopting new expressions, idioms and conventions, and relegating those that seem inappropriate – which become obsolete or seem quaint. Thus we can distinguish quite easily between, say, the English used in the Victorian period in England, and that used in the 1920s or the 1950s, and the English we are accustomed to now. These linguistic shifts are inevitably registered significantly in literary texts, and are one of the ways in which genres develop over time: for example, the Renaissance sonnet is quite different from a Victorian sonnet, neither of which is likely to be emulated in a sonnet written now.

Social circumstances, which change with time, could also account for some genres becoming unfashionable (very few ballads or courtly romances are written these days, for instance), just as they account for the emergence of new or hybrid genres. So contemporary practices in and the current shape of literary genres, and our sense of what literary genres are now, say a great deal about contemporary literature generally.

It is likely to occur to our contemplative bibliographical scholar in the Cemetery of Forgotten Books that underlying all these points there is a deeper question. Is it possible that it is not just genres that shift and proliferate and are tested, she might ask herself, but also that literature as a whole changes? *Is it possible that what we think of as literature now (our contemporary literature) is different in a fundamental way from what was regarded as literature, say, 100 years back (what was contemporary literature then)?* This is a provocative question on which there is little consensus. My own feeling is that the answer should be 'yes', but there are many of us who would differ. However, let me explain why I am inclined to say, 'Yes, our understanding of literature itself, as a whole, has changed in the past 100 years.' To do that, we need to leave behind our bibliographical scholar in Zafón's Cemetery and take a quite different tack.

I have used Zafón's Cemetery above as a starting point to think about ways of imposing order on the area of literature. A similarly useful, but quite different, starting point to explore what our idea of literature consists in is provided by one of the best known of Hugo Ball's 1916 'poems without words or sound poems', the first section of which goes as follows:

gadji beri bimba glandridi laula lonni cadori
gadjama gramma berida bimbala glandri galassassa laulitalomini

gadji beri bin blassa glassala laula lonni cadorsu sassala bim
gadjama tuffm i zimzalla binban gligla wowolimai bin beri ban
o katalominai rhinozerossola hopsamen laulitalomini hoooo
gadjama rhinozerossola hopsamen
bluku terullala blaulala loooo

This is made up of invented word-like sounds, combining syllables,
which are in fact not words in any language. Ball performed such poems
in costume at the Club Voltaire in Zurich (these were performances
rather than recitations or readings), and in the same year introduced them with the first 'Dada Manifesto' of 14 July 1916, in
which he says:

I shall be reading poems that are meant to dispense with conventional language, no less, and to have done with it. [...] All the words
are other people's inventions. I want my own stuff, my own
rhythms, and vowels and consonants too, matching the rhythm and all
my own.

(Ball, 1916, p. 220)

The early twentieth-century Dada movement with which this
sound poem is associated, and which was announced through several further manifestos thereafter, entailed questioning and rejecting
received ideas in the arts and literature by creating shocking and
mocking works. Effectively, that also clarified what the prevailing
ideas about art and literature were. For the above sound poem, for
instance, the following observations come to mind.

1. IS IT A POEM?

It raises the question of whether this is a poem at all, which in turn
makes us aware of the degree to which the meanings of words *together*
with their sounds are the key to what we regard as poems. If the
meanings are removed from the sounds, as in Ball's composition, the
result still rings rhythmically to our ears and looks like poetry on
the page, but we are left unsure whether this is poetry. We may then
be struck by the arbitrariness of the poetic forms we are familiar with,
which have to do with metre, rhyme, pauses and other such qualities

of sound (their aural qualities). We are simply unaccustomed to thinking about such aural qualities as poetry without relating them to the meanings of words; and yet, as Ball's verse shows, these qualities are not inevitably linked to meanings. In brief, we are pushed to reconsider what our basic assumptions about poetry are.

2. IS IT LITERATURE?

Further, 'gadji beri bimba' pushes us to reconsider our assumptions about literature in general, not just poetry. We are usually disposed, in a common-sense way, to think of literature as having to do with written texts used for creative expression – and, as such, dependent on communication by the use of language. This doesn't mean that the written text is *all* that we regard as a literary work. For instance, theatre is conventionally thought of as literature, on the understanding that behind the performance there is a written text to refer to (a play script). Our understanding of literature usually extends, in other words, to performances insofar as they relate to written texts in some language or other. Now, in Ball's sound poem we do have a written text, but it is not in a recognisable language. Moreover, it was first performed and is therefore akin to theatre, but it is obviously not quite a play or dramatic monologue. So, while appearing to be a written and performable text and therefore a literary work, by not having a recognisable language it poses a considerable challenge to attempts to read and understand it *as* literature.

3. IS IT MUSIC OR VISUAL ART?

It may occur to us that such a collection of sounds is actually more like music, and it may be useful to understand it as music rather than literature. That side of the composition has been used subsequently to challenge our idea of what a (popular) song is: the rock group Talking Heads, with lead songwriter-singer David Byrne (1979), produced the hit song 'I Zimbra' using rearrangements of the sounds in the first five lines of 'gadji beri bimba' for lyrics. But then, Ball's sound poem could equally be regarded in terms not so much of aural qualities, as of the visual shape of the text as it appears on paper – perhaps it should be regarded as a drawing of sorts, a work of visual art. That appears to be just as plausible as any other way of thinking about it.

In fact, the more we contemplate 'gadji beri bimba', the more we tend to blur the distinctions between literature, music and drawing as art forms. In the process, our usual understanding of what literature is becomes sharper. We have a vivid sense of the importance of meaningful and recognisable language as the medium of literature, as the heart of literary expression. Otherwise, we often take language and writing rather for granted in reading literature, and don't think about them much.

Let's fast-forward now to 2010: to an e-poem put up that year by Talan Memmott entitled 'The Hugo Ball'. This cannot really be quoted or read, it has to be experienced in the electronic form in which it appears – either by going directly to www.drunkenboat. com/db8/panlitjudges/memmott/hugo_db/thehugoball.html,   or by approaching it via the Electronic Literature Directory at http:// directory.eliterature.org/node/825 (which features a useful brief introduction, and has a link to the e-poem). The screen that opens when we click on the URL of the e-poem has in the middle a framed circle (which looks like a glass sphere), through which we can see the faint outline of a face, and there is a kind of low background noise (perhaps the sound of people in a café). When we move the cursor on the circle the face becomes distinct and starts speaking a series of meaningless, word-like sounds, which are in fact the syllables of Hugo Ball's 'gadji beri bimba' mixed up to make a different sequence of word-like sounds. At the same time, the word-like sounds appear in writing on the screen as they are enunciated. The picture of the face does not speak these in a continuous fashion; it itself appears as a series of very quick but discontinuous images making the appropriate facial movements to say each syllable. When we move the cursor away from the circle it reverts to the faint background cafe-sounds and the glazed-over, still appearance of the face.

If we contemplate this electronic composition systematically in relation to Ball's 'gadji beri bimba' (which the playful title, and the mixed-up syllables we are likely to recognise, invite us to do), the following may occur to us: just as Ball's sound poem pushes us to reconsider our understanding of literature, this e-poem also pushes us to do that. The reference to Ball's sound poem serves to recall that push in the terms of Ball's time, and to relocate that push in the terms of our time. What has changed in the interim is our understanding of literature. *Ball's kind of questioning of what literature is continues to be relevant, but needs to be updated because our sense of literature has been modified in the interim – without, however, losing touch with earlier understandings of literature.* This change works in several ways.

1. REFERRING BACK

We, readers of literature now, have Ball's original sound poem to refer to – the breakdown of language and poetry in it is well known to us. It cannot be repeated now with the same disorienting effect that it had when it first appeared. To retrieve that feeling to some degree, we need to break down Ball's familiar word-like sounds yet again, and mix up Ball's meaningless words to generate other meaningless words, which this e-poem does. But we are aware that we are doing this now only by referring to Ball's composition from the past. So, our contemporary sense of literature can continue to recognise the relevance of Ball's take on poetry and literature, but is different *because* we can refer to Ball's sound poem.

2. NEW ASSUMPTIONS

For 'gadji beri bimba', assumptions of literature at the time were questioned because the sound poem appeared as a written text or as a live performance. The assumptions about literature in question were foregrounded accordingly. For us, the e-poem 'The Hugo Ball' foregrounds our assumptions of literature by displaying on a single screen simultaneously a tightly knitted written text, spoken performance, audio recording, manipulated visual image and digital programme. For us, now, assumptions about literature involve all those elements in close connection with each other, interwoven.

3. CHANGING HABITS

For 'gadji beri bimba', the prevailing habitual ways of engaging with literature were relevant: by reading from print, or being part of an audience for a performance. For 'The Hugo Ball', the habitual ways of engaging with literature still include those, but also extend further to reading on personal computer screens, and watching and listening to audiovisual media – television, movies and radio, and so on. All these ways of reading and listening and watching are habitual to us. We move the cursor on the computer screen and experience the sounds, images, written words on the screen in a practised and instinctive fashion when 'The Hugo Ball' opens. Moreover, we are aware of being able to intervene in 'The Hugo Ball' beyond simply reading and listening and watching, by simply moving the cursor (we have added 'interactivity' with this e-text). We are aware of ourselves as readers of literature in a different way.

I discuss the implications of these changes further in chapters 3 and 4. At any rate, *just as genres of literature change with changing social and political and cultural circumstances (technological developments are but an aspect of these), so too does the understanding of literature as a whole.* The differences outlined above between the understanding of literature in 'gadji beri bimba' and in 'The Hugo Ball' track the changes between the 1910s and 2010s (or, for our purposes, the contemporary).

ISSUES AND PERSPECTIVES

In a cycle of short plays published as *Shoot/ Get Treasure/ Repeat* (2009; first performed in April 2008), British playwright Mark Ravenhill includes one entitled 'Fear and Misery'. In this we have a couple, Olivia and Harry, reminiscing over supper about the moment when their child was conceived. Harry is eager to confirm that Olivia was 'calm' at the time, at peace with herself and the world, but she is unable to do so:

> Sometimes I'm ... Sometimes ... you're inside me. We're ... making love. We really are ... making love. But it feels like, it seems like – there's a sort of ... rape. Sorry. Rape. Sorry. Rape. Sorry.
>
> (p. 40)

Naturally upset, Harry presses her to explain herself, and it becomes clear that they are attached to each other and Olivia is determined to nurture their relationship and the baby, but nevertheless she is unable to forget that in the midst of the pleasure of making love she is often assailed momentarily by a feeling of being raped. It also becomes evident that this is not due to anything Harry does, but because of her insecurities and anxieties about the world at large and her immediate environment. Seeing how upset Harry is, Olivia admits that 'our child was born in love and tranquillity' and expresses her anxiety as a plea: 'We will work together. Keep away from the addicts. The madwomen. The bombers. The soldier with his head blown off. We will keep them away – yes?' (p. 44). As they discuss this further, they discover that the anxiety is shared. Eventually Harry finds himself shouting:

THE WORLD IS ATTACKING US, THE TERROR IS EATING US UP AND YOU ... WE NEED GATES. WE NEED TO, TO, TO ... DRAW UP THE DRAWBRIDGE AND CLOSE THE GATES AND SECURITY, SECURITY, SECURITY, SECURITY. I CAN'T FIGHT THIS WAR.

(p. 48)

The short play evokes a fear that is unspecified and yet very real, which invades the most intimate moments amidst the most personal of relationships. It is expressed variously in terms of racial fear, the anxiety generated by images of war on the news, worry about possible acts of terrorism, feelings of insecurity about local gangs and immigrants, fear of violation and rape – but it is at bottom simply the fear that simmers without clear definition in the society and world Harry and Olivia live in.

This fear and sense of insecurity is the subject of all the short plays in Ravenhill's cycle: in domestic and everyday spaces, at home and abroad, in war zones, among couples, friends, strangers, soldiers. Sometimes the fear beats intangibly in the minds of characters (as above), and sometimes it is tangibly out there. The title of the short play, 'Fear and Misery', gives a clue to what Ravenhill is doing here: it refers to Bertolt Brecht's *Fear and Misery of the Third Reich* (1957; translated from the German by John Willett, 1983). This features 24 scenes from everyday life – in homes, offices, streets, among friends, acquaintances, strangers – under Nazi Germany, from 1933, when Hitler came to power, to 1938, the beginning of the Second World War. And it also captures the pervasive fear and anxiety that gripped everyday life under the regime.

However, unlike Brecht's play, where the specific place and year is given for each scene, and where the title announces the political context, Ravenhill's cycle does not specify places and periods – it is up to the reader to locate the action. And, indeed, Ravenhill doesn't need to be more specific in this regard than he is. He can safely assume that most of his contemporary readers would fill those up in very similar ways. To most contemporary readers, the fear that Harry and Olivia are gripped by, the anxieties and violence that affect other characters in other short plays, have to do with a shared experience. This is, in brief, the experience of a persistent spiral of conflict and violence both within countries and internationally, which is associated with the 11 September 2001 terrorist attacks in the USA and consequent 'war on terror': the bombing of Afghanistan and invasion of Iraq, growing threat of terrorist attacks, religious and inter-ethnic discord, and political polarisation. Ravenhill deliberately doesn't actually mention any of these, rendering the atmosphere of fear and anxiety and violence all the more stark and universal. Few contemporary readers would fail to recognise it and make the specific associations themselves.

The so-called 'war on terror' and the surrounding conflicts and anxieties are unmistakably a significant issue of our time, widely contemplated from different perspectives and changing existing perspectives. These need no annotation or explanation at present; as readers and writers, we simply share an awareness of these by dint of living now in our social world. An enormous number of literary works surround and link up with Ravenhill's play from different parts of the world. Those, in turn, are all connected to films and documentaries, news reports, mass media discussions, debates in internet chatrooms and classrooms and informally among friends and colleagues, and so on. Some of us have experienced the violence of the military and of extremist organisations; all of us have been aware of these in an everyday way, either in close proximity or from a distance. We, contemporary readers, therefore immediately recognise and respond to the depiction of a contemporary social environment in Ravenhill's plays, even if the author gives no overt hint of the real-world events this environment is associated with. Our ability as readers to do this, and Ravenhill's playing with the assumption that we would, draws upon our shared experience in our social world. In this way, *the appearance and recognition of such contemporary issues*

*and perspectives relevant to them, which resonate with our lived experiences
and daily lives, determine what we regard as contemporary in literature.*

Academic attempts to undertake systematic study of contemporary
literature in teaching and research often focus on such contemporary
issues and perspectives. The example of Ravenhill's 'Fear and Misery' is
but one way in which a contemporary issue appears in a literary
text/performance. There are numerous such examples that can be
identified as contemporary in literature, as recognisably of our time.
The following are some of the familiar categories of such issues and
perspectives.

1. NOTEWORTHY EVENTS

Noteworthy recent or ongoing events and their repercussions, within a well-
defined territory or internationally. These are generally events that
have received considerable attention in the news and current affairs
media, such as the 11 September 2001 attacks and 'war on terror' (and
connected events). Other examples could include the collapse of East
European communist regimes in 1989 and the aftermath; the various
recent economic depressions and duplicity of capitalist corporations;
major natural disasters such as the 2010 earthquake in Haiti or the
2011 earthquake and tsunami in Japan; popular anti-government
demonstrations in North Africa and the Middle East in 2011.

2. CONCEPTUAL PERSPECTIVES

General conceptual perspectives of our time. These are often identified
with scholarly or media formulations such as 'globalisation' or 'post-
modernity' (discussed in chapters 5 and 6). Specifically, these could
include literary reckonings with such patterns as growing consolidation
of social networking and communication technologies; exacerbation
of, or rapprochement in, broad cultural conflicts (between East and
West/North and South); the current patterns of generation or
gender or ethnic or class relations.

3. EVERYDAY LIFE

Our experience of everyday life, wherever we may happen to be (discussed further in chapter 5). As opposed to the big events and

developments of our time, our sense of what is contemporary usually rests solidly on small, day-to-day matters. That could be the kind of daily transactions we are involved in, such as buying food, clothes and other things; being aware of brands and advertisements; our experience of dealing with institutions such as offices and schools; our leisure activities, such as being tourists, enjoying music or films, reading newspapers and magazines, chatting with friends; our domestic arrangements; and so on. Finding resonances in literary texts with our everyday life, in small details, is often the key to recognising them as contemporary.

4. LANGUAGE AND IDIOM

The language and idiom of present times. The manner in which we speak and think and write now is implicated in all the above, but it is worth considering this as a separate point. In reading literary texts, we are likely to be aware of language in a distinctive way. We are likely, in other words, to be sensitive to formal and informal usage, idiomatic and set phrases, the employment of different linguistic registers. I have noted above that, in terms of such nuances, every language is in a constant state of change according to changing social circumstances. Naturally, our (often unthinking) recognition of a literary text as contemporary depends crucially on how attuned we feel to its language.

The manner in which these kinds of themes figure in the literature of our time is discussed further in subsequent chapters, particularly chapters 5 and 6.

REFERENCES

Arnold, Thomas (1870). *Chaucer to Wordsworth: A Short History of English Literature from the Earliest Times to the Present Day.* London: Thomas Murby.
Ball, Hugo (1916). 'gadji beri bimba'. Quoted in Dietmar, Elger (2004). *Dadaism.* Cologne: Taschen, 12.
——(1916). 'Dada Manifesto' (14 July). In Elderfield, John, ed. (1974). *Flight Out of Time: A Dada Diary by Hugo Ball.* Trans. Ann Raimes. Berkeley, CA: University of California Press, 219–21.
Borges, Jorge Luis (1985). 'The Library of Babel' (1941). *Fictions.* Trans. Anthony Kerrigan. London: Calder.

Brecht, Bertolt (1983). *Fear and Misery of the Third Reich* (1957). Trans. John Willett. In *Collected Plays, Volume 4*. London: Methuen.

Byrne, David (1979). 'I Zimbra'. www.talking-heads.nl/index.php/talking-heads-lyrics/16-fear-of-music (and widely available on the internet elsewhere).

Chambers, Robert, ed. (1844). *Cyclopædia of English Literature: A History, Critical and Bibliographical, of British Authors, from the Earliest to Present Times.* Edinburgh: W.R. Chambers.

Ez-Eldin, Mansoura (2007). *Maryam's Maze* (2004). Trans. Paul Starkey. Cairo: American University in Cairo Press.

Memmott, Talan (2010). 'The Hugo Ball'. www.drunkenboat.com/db8/panlitjudges/memmott/hugo_db/thehugoball.html, or in the Electronic Literature Directory at http://directory.eliterature.org/node/825

Padley, Steve (2006). *Key Concepts in Contemporary Literature*. Basingstoke, UK: Palgrave.

Ravenhill, Mark (2009). 'Fear and Misery'. *Shoot/Get Treasure/Repeat*. London: Methuen.

Sonnenschein, William Swan (1895). *A Reader's Guide to Contemporary Literature*. London: Swan Sonnenschein & Co.

Süskind, Patrick (1986). *Perfume* (1985). Trans. John E. Wood. London: Penguin.

Zafón, Carlos Ruiz (2004). *The Shadow of the Wind* (2002). Trans. Lucia Graves. London: Weidenfeld & Nicolson.

FURTHER READING

ON PERIODISATION

Besserman, Lawrence, ed. (1996). *The Challenge of Periodization: Old Paradigms and New Perspectives*. New York: Garland. [The introductory essay by the editor usefully covers debates about periodisation with a historical perspective.]

Brown, Marshall, ed. (2001). 'Periodization' (special issue). *Modern Language Quarterly* 62: 4. [The editor's introduction summarises some recent debates.]

ON INTERTEXTUALITY

Allen, George (2000). *Intertextuality*. London: Routledge. [Mainly on the development of theories of intertextuality.]

Orr, Mary (2003). *Intertextuality: Debates and Contexts*. Cambridge: Polity. [Also takes account of the contexts in which intertextuality is formulated, and the different kinds of literary expressions and practices that are intertextual.]

ON WORLD LITERATURE

Damrosch, David (2003). *What Is World Literature?* Princeton, NJ: Princeton University Press. [This and the next consider the various ways in which literature crosses linguistic, political and cultural boundaries.]
——(2009). *How to Read World Literature.* Chichester, UK: Wiley-Blackwell.
Prendergast, Christopher, ed. (2004). *Debating World Literature.* London: Verso. [Gathers a selection of influential contributions to the conceptualising of this area.]

ON GENRE

Bawarshi, Anis S. and Mary Jo Reiff (2010). *Genre: An Introduction to History, Theory, Research, and Pedagogy.* West Lafayette, IN: Parlor Press. [Takes a broad view of the concept of genre, including literary perspectives alongside linguistic, sociological, educational. Also considers the contexts – new media, academic, etc. – where it appears.]
Frow, John (2006). *Genre.* Abingdon, UK: Routledge. [General introduction to the concept with a primarily literary perspective.]

ON CHANGES IN LITERATURE AND CONSEQUENT CHANGING CONCEPTIONS OF LITERATURE

Pettersson, Anders, ed. (2006). *Literary History: Towards a Global Perspective, Vol. 1: Notions of Literature Across Times and Cultures.* Berlin: Walter de Gruyter. [The editor's introduction discusses recent changes in concepts of literature and culture in a general way.]
Stephens, John and Ruth Waterhouse (1990). *Literature, Language and Change: From Chaucer to the Present.* London: Routledge. [Discusses, with a long historical perspective, changes in the language of literature, with reference to English literature. Useful to contemplate the notion of change in the scope and content of literature.]

3

PRODUCTION

LITERARY INDUSTRY

Chapters 1 and 2 discuss some of the academic strategies for approaching contemporary literature systematically. These are strategies that prompt the teaching and learning, research and scholarship of such literature – usually in an institutional setting such as a school or university. Nowadays, academic institutions and academics play a considerable role in how we think about literature and what we read, even if we sometimes don't realise it. Especially when we consider the literature of a well-defined period or territory – not as open-ended as the contemporary period – our attitudes and received notions are usually mediated by what literary teachers and scholars have done. However, when it comes to reading and thinking about the literature of the present, of our time, academic mediation is comparatively less influential. Other institutions and professions have a more immediate role in this regard. It is naturally necessary for us to take those into account for our systematic understanding. And, though conventionally neglected, those are increasingly given greater attention within academic circles. I have in mind here the kinds of issues that were raised briefly in chapter 1 as related to the 'literary industry'.

If the word 'industry' conjures images of factories and corporations and workers and managers, that doesn't quite apply here. Here, *by* '*industry*' *I mean something a bit more abstract: a system that enables the production of literature in material forms (print, electronic, etc.) and encourages readers to consume (buy or invest in) literature so that the system can be sustained and expanded.* The literary industry obviously includes such processes as publishing novels or staging theatre, but alongside these are a number of other processes and factors which may not be as obvious.

The various aspects of this system can be broken down into two main sides: production and reception (or consumption). *Production has to do with making literary texts and performances available to those who are interested; reception has to do with the ways in which these are obtained or accessed, read or watched, etc.* This division is, in fact, a somewhat problematic one. Literary production and reception are very closely interlinked, as we shall see. However, in this chapter I focus primarily on the productive side; in chapter 4 I examine the receptive side of the contemporary literature industry.

There are various kinds of producers involved in this industry, of whom the most significant has to be the literary author – the novelist, playwright, poet, etc. The first section below discusses:

- the role that authors of contemporary literature play in the literary industry.

The other key producers are considerably less visible than authors. Therefore, instead of discussing their particular roles, it is easier to think of them as variously contributing to the production process of the particular material forms of literature that are now available. The subsequent sections of this chapter are consequently on:

- literature in printed texts;
- literature as live or recorded performances; and
- literature in e-texts.

AUTHORS

There are three more or less distinct ways in which we usually think about authors.

1. THE AUTHOR AS IMPLIED IN THE TEXT

This is the idea that, as readers, we can discern what the author intended and what sort of person the author is by reading the text carefully. As mentioned in passing in chapter 1, what the author intended used to be regarded as the key to understanding a literary text properly. I also noted that the reader's input and other factors are now considered as, if not more, important. Nevertheless, the feeling that a literary text is the expression of a particular personality usually seems too obvious to be gainsaid. Occasionally, authors and scholars have made strenuous efforts to counter that perception. Thus, in the early twentieth century, the modernist poet T.S. Eliot and novelist James Joyce felt that their writings should deliberately do away with expressing the personality of an author. And when the literary critic Roland Barthes (1977 [1967]) dramatically announced the 'death of the author' and emphasised attention to writing itself, he effectively let loose a catchphrase which has been repeated *ad nauseam*. Nevertheless, such pronouncements have been up against our habitual language itself. We simply speak of literary texts as being by such-and-such author, or as such-and-such author's work – which takes us to the following two points.

2. THE AUTHOR AS A PUBLIC FIGURE

Authors usually publicly claim to have written their texts, and make public appearances, and explain how they came to do so and why; authors are publicised with their works, and we often choose what we read in terms of what we are told about the author; authors gain reputations from their works, and are sometimes celebrated or denigrated or even punished for the texts they have written. In other words, we are accustomed to thinking of authors as public figures who are briefly introduced on the back covers of books, feature in advertisements, give interviews, talk about their works, receive prizes or get thrown in prison, pronounce on current events, and so on. These are all ways in which the author's presence as a public figure is continuously confirmed for us. The connection between the author and the literary text consequently seems so close and unavoidable that we constantly try to reconcile the person we had inferred from the text with the public figure. And we often try to understand the literary text with reference to what the author has said elsewhere. Indeed, our sense of what is contemporary in literature derives significantly from the living presence – or presence within living memory – of the author.

3. THE AUTHOR AS A LEGALLY RECOGNISED PERSON

We seldom think of literary texts as legal documents when reading them, but they are covered now as the intellectual property of authors and their inheritors (usually). This establishes authorship as a legally defined activity, and authors as legal persons. This also puts authors and their inheritors in a position constantly to have a say on the extent to which their work can be reproduced and performed – which, tacitly but continuously, regulates and modifies our access to them and ability to discuss them. Since this has a relatively subdued (though not unimportant) part in the task of studying contemporary literature systematically, we do not need to dwell on it at length here. As a matter of immediate interest, such intellectual property laws are time-bound. By the international agreement known as the Berne Convention, authors and inheritors can exercise property rights for literary texts within the lifetime of the author and for 50 years thereafter. In some countries, this extends further: in the European Union and the USA, for example, it is for 70 years after the death of the author. Thus, in a way, a strict *legal* definition of what period can be regarded as contemporary for literature seems to be offered in terms of the author's life.

At the core of these somewhat distinct ways of thinking about authors is a perfectly commonsense understanding of what the process of writing involves. We know, of course, that the author wrote the text over a period of time, and that in this period her experiences and knowledge and the circumstances of her everyday life were brought to bear on writing. Therefore the process of writing the text is closely interwoven with who the author was and what she did while writing it. It seems natural to assume that, by retrieving as many details as possible about the author at the time, we can get close to the very impetus that brought the text about. This understanding explains why the importance of the author's intention is usually taken for granted, and why the author's intellectual property is accepted, and why we are inclined to feel that the author has special insights into her text. That's the reason for the immense popularity of well-known literary authors' biographies, diaries and letters – themselves a distinctive genre ('life-writing') in literature. We expect to understand her literary texts better (perhaps even to emulate her achievement, if we have literary aspirations).

Obvious as all this seems, however, these expectations are all actually somewhat idealistic. In fact, while the close interweaving of the author's life and the process of writing undoubtedly happened, there is no way of retrieving what that actually involved. The literary text we usually read is a finished product and itself gives no particular hint about that process. Whatever the author claims is only retrospective, and we all know how unreliable everyday memories can be. Such details as we can check are usually themselves recorded or written documents, which are open to the same vagaries of reading and interpretation as any literary text. So, *any attempt to know for sure how the author's life and writing were really interwoven is chimerical and after the fact. But the illusion exists that it can be done or is self-evident, and much common-sense thinking about, and practical arrangements for, literary matters are currently based on it.*

When we think of contemporary literature, we usually assume a process of writing that is close to our time, to the present. The living author's text, or the text that appeared within our lifetime, usually seems to be a vague but quite practical guarantee of this closeness – it *feels* contemporary. This circumstance seems to put the process of writing in relation to a world that is, in some sense, our everyday world too. We assume a kind of kinship with the author and her writing by dint of having shared our world, which is somewhat more tangible to us than having to dig up the records of a long-dead author's life and writing.

Keeping the slipperiness and limits of these expectations in mind is crucial for a systematic approach to contemporary literature. As it happens, these expectations are constantly played with and pondered in literary texts, including in the texts of our time. A couple of somewhat disparate examples may help us clarify the situation in familiar terms.

Javier Cercas's novel *Soldiers of Salamis* (2001; translated from the Spanish by Anne McLean, 2003) appears to be an unusually sustained account by the author of the process of writing what is effectively this novel itself. In it the narrator bears the author's name and repeatedly reminds us that he has set out to tell not a fictional tale, but a true one. Cercas builds his true tale around an incident that happened to a historical figure, the nationalist ideologue (Falangist) Rafael Sánchez Mazas (1894–1966) towards the end of the Spanish Civil War. The incident in question and the biographical details about Mazas are not especially relevant here; what is of interest is what Cercas does with them. The novel is set out in three parts. The first describes how the author–narrator Cercas, whose fiction-writing career has ground to a halt, finds himself growing interested in this incident, conceives the idea of writing a true novel, and researches it. The brief second part consists of the text he writes as a result. The third part describes his dissatisfaction with that text, and the further research he undertakes to fill in a missing bit of the jigsaw puzzle that the incident turns out to be. The novel as a whole is, therefore, a detailed record of why and how he writes it, and the interim result of at least one of the stages of writing.

In a broad way, we may say that the novel is about the manner in which historical events and individual memories and records play off against each other, and the choices that are made communally about what to forget and what to remember. These reflections are underlined by the travails of writing and research themselves: by the ambiguities that the end result – this novel – presents to us. It is impossible to say whether it should be regarded as a historical account, a biographical narrative, or a work of fiction, or to what degree it is a combination of all of those. By blurring the boundary between reality and fiction, between narrator and what we know of the author – by creating the illusion that this is a record of the reality of writing itself – it questions both our certainties about the world and particularly about authorship.

Typically, we might feel curious whether Cercas, the public author, has himself given any hints about the degree of truth and fiction in this novel *after* writing it, retrospectively. The novel was adapted as a Spanish film, *Soldados de Salamina*, in 2003 by the director David Trueba. At the time of its release, a collection of conversations between the author and the director was published, in one of which Cercas interestingly observed: 'my aspiration was to lie anecdotally in the particulars, in order to tell an essential truth'.

My second example is from a quite different sort of novel and in a contrary direction from the above: it is from the second of J.K. Rowling's Harry Potter fantasy novels (the last appeared in 2007), *Harry Potter and the Chamber of Secrets* (1998). Here, too, an author appears as a major character, in the guise of a famous wizard–author Gilderoy Lockhart. Where Cercas's novel tries to create an illusion of being a record of the reality of the process of writing as well as of what is narrated, Rowling's is fantasy narrative, and Gilderoy is a fantastical characterisation of an author who is the hero of his own magical adventure stories.

However, this all-too-fictional author also tests our preconceptions about authors. In Rowling's novel, the publicly celebrated *author* Gilderoy Lockhart, revered as such and as the hero of his own books, turns out to have no relation to the *writer* Gilderoy Lockhart. Gilderoy is unmasked at the end as neither the author nor the hero people regard him as, because his stories are stolen and the deeds his books describe were the deeds of others. When it comes to the final confrontation with the truly heroic Harry Potter, he is forced to face up to his misdeeds and tries to shift the blame from himself. Gilderoy observes that his books wouldn't have sold well if readers didn't think he was the hero of the adventures he recounts, especially as he is more presentable to his image-conscious admirers than the actual heroes (p. 220). It is clear that Gilderoy did *write* his successful books, yet that in itself is not enough to make him a successful public *author*. The characterisation of Gilderoy in fact reveals slippages at several levels in relation to the three distinct ways of thinking about authors and the process of writing outlined above.

- There is no necessary connection between the author who is implied in the text (in this case, more thrust forward than implied as the hero of magical adventures) and the person who writes the text.
- There is no necessary connection between the public figure of the author of certain texts (the celebrity) and the person who writes those texts (who, in a way, hides himself). The author as public figure is due to how he is presented and what expectations

readers have of him, neither of which is necessarily representative
of what's really involved in the process of writing.

• And there is no necessary connection between the author who
  is implied in the text (Gilderoy the heroic protagonist in his
  books) and the author as a public figure (Gilderoy who speaks
  publicly about himself, signs books, and is widely adored).

These different levels of slippage could well apply to Cercas's novel too:
Cercas as narrator/protagonist may not be the same as Cercas the
person who wrote this text, and neither need be the same as Cercas
the public author who speaks about his text later. However, Cercas
makes an exaggerated effort to make all these glue together. In an
opposite direction, Rowling makes an exaggerated – indeed overtly
fantastical – effort to make Gilderoy the writer, Gilderoy the protagonist in his books, and Gilderoy the public author fall apart. By
these two quite different kinds of exaggerated effort, Cercas and
Rowling help us to reconsider some of our commonly held
assumptions about authorship.

The fact that, in most respects, Cercas's and Rowling's texts are
of completely different sorts suggests that they are dealing, within
their different styles and formats, with widely held ideas about
authorship.

Incidentally, it may have occurred to us while reading the above
that Cercas and Rowling are different kinds of public author:
one an author of 'literary fiction', the other a celebrity author of
popular fantasy fiction. And, indeed, the narrator/protagonist
Cercas in the novel (an author with a modest reputation) is not to
be compared with the character Gilderoy (a celebrity author in the
wizard world, as Rowling is in ours). There are, in brief, various
gradations in the public figure of the author. However, these gradations are more important for understanding the reception than
the production side of literature.

PRINTED TEXTS

When we think of literature, we usually think of printed texts, texts
that are available in books, journals, magazines, pamphlets. The
history of literary production and scholarship has been conducted in
print to an overwhelming extent. There are, of course, other

material forms in which literature appears — in later sections we consider performance and, of particular relevance now, electronic texts. It is arguable that oral texts (such as folk tales of various sorts, ballads, fables) should also be thought of as literature; however, it is undeniable that these have received wide attention primarily on being printed. I do not touch on unprinted or unrecorded oral texts here.

Between the text written by the author and its printed version, there is the process of publication and distribution. Scholarly studies of literature have conventionally given this process cursory attention, or often regard it as a dry, specialist business (for bibliographers and book historians to deal with) that doesn't really impinge significantly on reading. However, it seems unquestionable that this process has a constant and pervasive influence on our engagement with contemporary literature. Our literary tastes and analytical interests are significantly, if tacitly, mediated by this process. Awareness of some of the current features of this process clarifies a great deal about contemporary reading habits and expectations of literature.

In the following, what I have to say applies mainly to literary production as a firm- or corporation-based venture, which could be quite different from literary publishing through government programmes or for charitable purposes (in the public interest). Insofar as contemporary literature goes, in most contexts the former now far outstrips the latter. Besides, increasingly, public-interest publishing (such as state-controlled publishing in China) is made to comply with corporate models. The idea here is therefore to reflect on the norm, rather than attempt to discuss different systems. Broadly speaking, our understanding of contemporary literature is mediated by the prevailing process of publication and distribution in three ways.

1. DOOR-KEEPING

The agencies and publishing firms involved in the production process determine what should or shouldn't be valued in literature by regulating access to readers.

Typically, the publication process entails selection from the work of a large number of aspiring authors. The reputation of publishing agencies and firms usually depends on how well their selected authors go down with readers, which is another way of saying that it depends on how ruthlessly they reject unappealing texts. The success of a published text, however, cannot be established until after it becomes available to readers – so a publishing firm's decision to accept or reject a particular text is based on a number of more or less intractable factors. These could include the experience of that firm's assessors of publishing other texts successfully, personal likes and dislikes, 'gut instinct', perceptions of what readers are currently interested in, ideological commitments, the opinions of peers, discernment of factual inaccuracies or unfortunate phrasing, and so on. It might also depend, of course, on whether a particular assessor has just received an unexpected bonus, or is dealing with a drink problem. In other words, the selection that takes place is simply made by informed contemporary readers amidst their everyday lives, like us (and perhaps less systematic than we are trying to be here) – but with an important difference.

Publishers' readings generally come with a financial stake. Their livelihoods depend on selecting carefully, and their reading is with a view to taking a gamble on whether to put money into printing and selling a text. These are readers who, and firms which, have a clearly defined purpose to their reading and selecting. Understandably, insofar as they read in a systematic and informed way, they are much like us. And insofar as they read as gamblers about to toss dice – to put money into printing a text – they are under pressure to make indicative connections between their reading and the contemporary world more urgently than most of us. We could think of this particular position as, so to speak, being on the edge of what is contemporary in literature – being on the margin, where what is contemporary is taken into account, pondered, evaluated and acted upon.

For authors, the usual way of circumventing the constraints of this selection process for publication has been to undertake some kind of self-publication. Although it is possible to recall a number of significant literary works that were initially self-published, as far as the printed text goes, the above process is more the norm. Altogether, the agencies and firms involved act as doorkeepers for what is easily available and discussed widely in literature, which in turn decides what our understanding of literature is largely based on.

2. TASTE-MAKING

Any experienced gambler would try to stack the odds in favour of winning their bet; publishers similarly try to make sure that the texts they publish would be profitable. Selecting appropriate texts is part of that, but that is based on a sense of what readers *already* want. From the publishers' point of view, it would be better if they could *mould* readers to want what they publish. So, *this process involves not just catering to existing tastes and demands, but also trying to create new tastes and demands.* Numerous bids to mould taste can be discerned in current publishing practices.

These could include dividing potential readers into sections (segmenting the market) and making sure that book designs (every aspect of how a text is presented in print, from covers to paper) are geared to appeal to specific sections. Advance publicity is a crucial part of what publishers and distributors are concerned with: making sure their texts are visible in various ways, through catalogues, advertisements, creating author profiles, organising events and festivals, and so on … here we are straying into the receptive side, though.

In some cases, existing tastes and demands can be moulded in a conservative manner. For instance, once a particular romance novel is successful, others of that sort are produced and targeted at the readers who bought the first one. As a consequence, our reading habits may become rather set and narrow (fan readerships are a form of narrowing). But for this, there does have to be at least a first text that was new and unexpected; so, alongside conservative directions, publishers also constantly try to set new directions. If this logic is followed through, it may happen that publishers evolve limits of conservative safety within which variations of newness to keep things bubbling are allowed.

Further, publishers and distributors make agreements with each other about how to price their texts and how to operate for mutual benefit. Equally, these could be left to open competition between publishers. Firms involved in the publishing and distributing process may find that centralising their operations is useful – the more the various parts of the process (selecting, designing, printing, publicising, distributing, selling) are coordinated centrally, the more profitably they are likely to work. Contrarily, they may also find that distributing parts of the publishing process among more or less autonomous firms is more profitable. Each such consideration has direct consequences for what contemporary literary texts we are able to get hold of, and how; and for what we choose to read, and why.

3. DISSEMINATING

This is really an aspect of the previous points, but with a somewhat different emphasis. *If publishers want to increase profits from investing in a new literary text, ideally they should make it available to as many readers as possible.* Even if a literary text is usually of interest only to limited audiences (for example, poetry is usually of interest to relatively small numbers of readers), we might think that it would make sense to make it available to such readers in as many territories as possible. However, there are impediments to such a very sensible idea: it is quite costly to do, and often more costly than it is worth. There are transportation and distribution costs; different regulations apply in different countries about importing and exporting printed matter; translation costs (where relevant) are significant; in different countries, readers' ability to spend may differ; and so on. Many firms (smaller independent publishers) therefore prefer to maintain their operations within clearly defined territories and often cater to loyal groups of readers with particular tastes (niche markets).

Naturally, the most commercially ambitious publishers do expand their reach across territories in various ways: by simply expanding and setting up branches in different countries, by making agreements with local publishers, by setting up collaborative organisations, etc. It is now well known that processes of centralising and expanding have led to the emergence of some very influential multinational publishing corporations (especially since the 1980s). These tend to take over smaller firms within particular countries to become stronger therein, as well as to establish international operations to extend their reach. They also seek to strengthen their influence by working closely with mass media corporations. Their emergence has led to two kinds of somewhat contrary effects on contemporary literature.

On one hand, such mega-corporations enable very wide international dissemination of the texts that they invest in, and they tend to select such texts from a wider range of contexts than smaller publishing firms usually manage. Such corporations thus have a hand in defining what we think of as contemporary literature, and, indeed, in our attempts to cultivate an awareness of international or world literature (discussed in chapter 2). On the other hand, they tend to narrow down the range of texts that receive such wide attention –

mainly to bestsellers and the work of celebrity authors. Since they thus reduce the paths to publication and distribution of other kinds of literature (perhaps more demanding or original texts), it is arguable that contemporary literature as a whole is becoming narrower and less varied. Our reading habits and understanding of what is contemporary may well, thus, be influenced by publishers and distributors without our quite realising it.

I observed above that the production process of the printed literary text is often neglected in systematic accounts of contemporary literature, or in studying literature generally. Teachers seldom mention such factors as those outlined above in their lectures, and they rarely appear in school or university textbooks. The great majority of critics writing about contemporary literature also overlook them, unless they happen to be book historians or bibliographers. The conventional notion that literary texts are abstract, and separate from the printed objects they appear in, has much to do with such neglect. There are also well-ensconced moral attitudes at work, which suggest that the elevated pleasure and intellectual stimulation to be had from literature should be untainted by such down-to-earth matters as corporate management and finance. On consideration, however, it might seem to us that such neglect in academic studies of literature is misleading. After all:

- a teacher usually teaches such contemporary texts as his students can easily find and afford;
- students and critics are usually interested in the contemporary literature that has already made a mark with readers; and
- financial and management issues have as much bearing on how academic work (including teaching and research) is done as on publishing.

The production process for literature in print is, in other words, intimately connected to all systematic and informed approaches to contemporary literature. And this is not just in terms of thinking about contemporary literature generally, but also with regard to thinking about specific contemporary literary texts.

To clarify how the production process for printed literature may bear upon a specific work nowadays, let's imagine a novel *X* written by

An.Author (this is easier than tracking the actual experiences of particular novels, which can be very varied). To obtain a sense of its
passage after An.Author writes a first draft (or even a few chapters)
and before we come to hold the book X in our hands as readers,
consider some of the people this novel meets along the way.

1. THE LITERARY AGENT

An.Author is likely (it is now commonly done) to start by sending
his draft, or a few chapters, to a firm of literary agents. Like the
publisher, the literary agent is looking to make a profit from literary
texts – perhaps by charging the author for giving advice, but mostly
by persuading publishers to publish texts on behalf of authors and
then getting a cut from the proceeds. Before working on behalf of
An.Author, the agent will read novel X and give advice on how to
make it more acceptable to publishers (make it marketable). The
advice given may well entail asking An.Author to change his draft
of X substantially, or perhaps even write a quite different novel, Y.
If An.Author and the agent reach an agreement, the agent then
looks for a publisher. If the book is published through the agent's
efforts, the agent naturally develops a protective attitude towards An.
Author, and does everything he can to make An.Author famous
and his writings more profitable.

2. THE COMMISSIONING EDITOR

An.Author may also send X directly to a commissioning editor (an
unsolicited submission), who represents a publishing firm. Whether
X comes directly from An.Author or from a literary agent, the
commissioning editor plays a key role in deciding whether X
should be published. She doesn't decide by herself usually, and has
to work with other colleagues and systems in place, but certainly if
she isn't interested in X, her firm won't go for it. Like the literary
agent, the commissioning editor may ask for changes, sometimes
very substantial changes, or even encourage a quite different
novel, Y. The selection process described above under
'Door-keeping', with the interests of the firm in mind, is very largely at the behest of the commissioning editor and her colleagues in
the firm.

3. THE MARKETING/PUBLICITY EDITOR

The commissioning editor will consult the marketing editor before making a decision about whether to propose publication of novel X. The marketing editor will make a judgement about how well the novel is likely to fare with potential readers, and what strategy for marketing the novel should be adopted. The latter would include a plan for where it should be distributed, what sorts of readers should be targeted, what sort of pricing might be appropriate, what sort of publicity material should go along with the published text, etc.

Incidentally, these editors and their colleagues, in some instances, don't really need to receive proposals and submissions to keep themselves busy. They can, naturally, simply invite appropriate authors to write the books they wish to publish. More inventively, they can produce texts by celebrities who haven't actually written a word (by using ghost writers), or even by non-existent or dead authors. If we are sometimes bemused to find that bestselling authors such as Robert Ludlum (who died in 2001) and V.C. Andrews (who died in 1986) continued to write popular fiction posthumously, it is because they are ghost-written (the real author's name might appear in small print). Such conjuring tricks are far from uncommonly pulled off by publishers, and the flesh-and-blood An.Author may well have more competition than he expects.

4. THE ADVISORY READERS

The commissioning editor may ask for advice on the quality and prospects of novel X from other novelists and experienced or expert readers, to get support for her view, or if in doubt. Advisory readers, if favourably inclined towards X, may well recommend substantial revision, to the extent of suggesting that An.Author write a quite different novel, Y.

5. THE DESIGNER

Once a final version of novel X – or perhaps novel Y by now – is in hand, the designer gets down to preparing the cover (and other publicity material, like catalogues and notices) in consultation with the above and An.Author. This is a not a task anyone takes lightly: the first impression that a reader has of this new novel X is powerfully decided by the material on the covers, and other aspects of design. And thereafter, the reader is also likely to read in terms of the presumptions suggested by these, even if only to be disappointed in them.

6. THE DISTRIBUTOR

When shiny, printed copies of novel X are ready, the lot is sent to the distributor and his colleagues. The distributor makes sure that these copies get to the bookshops and internet vendors (retailers) and libraries where we, readers, can finally get hold of them. The distributor has a good understanding with the publishing firm's editors and various retailers, and makes sure that they can convey the thinking behind publishing X. Distributors might put together their own catalogues for the purpose, and feature X in particular ways there.

7. THE RETAILERS

How retailers present novel X to their customers (us) is another factor in forming first impressions and reading accordingly. A bookseller in a bookshop may put a copy of X in the window display, or on a bestseller shelf, or the bottom shelf in the basement stock – such decisions make a difference to us if we are browsing. Internet vendors may put up lots of information about novel X on their website, invite readers to leave comments, rate it according to sales, whet readers' appetites by displaying a few pages, produce their own recommendations list, and so on.

These are just some of the people who contribute something to the process that brings An.Author's efforts to us in printed form. And the process doesn't end there. Others may turn up to act upon the text even after it has appeared in print: for subsequent editions, for translated versions, for extracting in anthologies, for television or film or other kinds of adaptation, and so on. As systematic and informed readers of contemporary literature, we cannot be indifferent to any of the above. Our notion of the authorship of a recent text may become hazier if we know about the extent to which the above persons have shaped it. Our confidence in our independence as readers making choices of, and judgements about, new literary works may need qualification in terms of their efforts. We might need to pause and consider how the design and publicity of the text have influenced our reading. Especially with regard to literary texts of the present, about which opinions are yet relatively fluid or unformed, the more or less unheeded and seemingly marginal matter of how the printed text comes to be produced – which is actually carefully engineered – is of some importance. For older and more familiar texts (not contemporary), of which numerous different editions exist, and for which received critical perspectives and contextual relevance are clearer, these might seem to matter less. But there, too, any serious interest in the reception history of those texts from the past should encourage taking account of such production processes in the past.

LIVE AND RECORDED PERFORMANCES

We are accustomed to thinking of drama as literature due to a tradition that goes back to the classical periods of several languages and cultures. For instance, literary criticism about European traditions usually refers back to Aristotle's *Poetics* (fourth century BC), which was devoted largely to drama and verse, much as literature and art criticism in India often recalls Bharata's *Natya Shastra* (the beginning of the first millennium AD), which was on the aesthetics of drama, dance and music. Literature as written, and later printed, text naturally emerged from oral and performed narratives. But the recent development (primarily over the past century) of diverse kinds of performance and audiovisual technology has complicated the relation of performance to literature. While we are comfortable, as a matter of habit, with thinking of play scripts and theatre as firmly *in* literature, we appear less certain whether we should correspondingly include screenplays and feature films or television drama in literature too. We seem inclined to think of the latter in a different way: while the role of playwright as author of play scripts, and therefore progenitor of theatrical performances, is accepted, when it comes to feature films we give a lot more attention to the director and seldom note who the screenplay writer was.

In considering academic perspectives of these matters, it seems that the study of theatre and film production – live and recorded performances generally – is largely kept separate from that of literature. The former involves, we understand, technical knowhow and analytical methods specific to audiovisual and performance media, which is a distinctive area. Consequently, in schools and universities, different courses and programmes are devoted to these. In literature curricula and literary criticism, we very seldom come across screenplays, although play scripts and theatre appear consistently. At the same time, from a somewhat different direction, it is evident that feature films and television productions are having an increasingly powerful effect on reading habits and notions of literature. This is particularly because of the popularity of film-based adaptations from various sorts of literary texts. These circulate easily and are watched more widely than live performances like theatre, and indeed have a reach that printed texts do not. University and school teachers often attest that students increasingly think about literary texts in terms of not just print, but also film adaptations, and numerous courses examining the relations between them have been devised. It is impossible to be indifferent to the intricate interconnections that have developed between recorded and live performances and written/printed texts; at the same time, the degree to which such recorded, and indeed live, performances are legitimately literature still seems uncertain.

When it comes to our particular focus in this book – contemporary literature – such confusions appear unnecessarily inhibiting. There is little doubt that our time is characterised by the unprecedented proliferation and reach of recorded performances. The technology for both creating/recording such performances and making them widely available is both cheaper and more widely used than ever. And the grip of television and radio programmes and feature films produced on an industrial scale is usually more a part of everyday life than printed literary texts. For many of us, much of what we know of literature in general, not to speak of recent and new literature, is sieved through audiovisual means. So contemporary literature and literary studies especially cannot afford to neglect live and recorded performances; these have to be regarded as part of the remit of literary study along with written texts.

For a systematic approach to contemporary literature, a further question that arises is: to what extent should contemporary performances of literary texts of the past be regarded as an aspect of contemporary literature? Should recent screen or stage adaptations of Shakespeare's plays, or Kalidasa's Sanskrit plays, or the four classical novels of China, be regarded as subjects for study in contemporary literature?

It seems to me that such questions, and any doubts about the place of performances in literature, are best answered by assuming a clear and consistent policy. We might as well adopt a reasonable one here.

So here it is, a policy for our times: *live and recorded performances are within the remit of literature and literary studies insofar as they relate in some way to written/printed texts. It is the nature of this relationship that is within the remit of studying literature systematically, rather than the nuances of performances in themselves or of performances without reference to written texts.* This relationship could be of various sorts:

- where a written text is for the purpose of generating a live/recorded performance (such as play scripts and screenplays);
- where a live/recorded performance adapts or otherwise draws upon an existing literary text (such as novels being adapted for television series);
- where a literary text is produced from a live/recorded performance (sometimes a popular feature film can lead to fanfiction or published popular fiction);
- where readers of literary texts find their views influenced by certain live/recorded performances (say, a reader's reading of a play is coloured by watching a performance of it beforehand);

and so on. Our interest as readers and students of literature extends to live and recorded performances *only* insofar as these are related to written or printed texts, in any of the ways mentioned above, or in other ways.

Further, *since it is the relationship between text and performance that is important, and there is no time-limit on such relationships, so long as either the text or the performance in question is regarded as contemporary it is relevant to us as contemporary literature.* So, a recent adaptation of a Shakespeare play in film, or a play by Kalidasa recently performed on stage, should be studied as contemporary literature. Such live and recorded performances are of literary interest to us because they are contemporary and are *related* in some way to a written literary text which may or may not be contemporary.

Like printed texts, live/recorded performances that are regarded as literature – particularly contemporary literature – can be analysed in terms of production and reception. The following are some observations that could inform a systematic approach to the production of live/recorded performances as contemporary literature (reception is taken up in chapter 4).

1. SELECTION

The production of live (such as theatre or televised drama) or recorded (say, feature film) performances usually involves selection processes that are similar to those of text publishing. As with publishing, there are agents, producers, directors, publicity managers, designers, etc., often attached to firms (theatre companies, media production companies, film studios, etc.) who either select from a pool of submitted proposals and work on them, or come up with their own. Naturally, these involve in the first instance a written text (a proposal at the least, perhaps a complete script), which is read much as a commissioning editor might read a written text for publication – with a sense of what will appeal now, and with a stake in the gamble involved in producing it. Their calculations will, however, be rather different in that the medium and the prospective audiences are quite different. The implications of costs and returns are significantly different, among other things. Arguably, public-interest media productions (such as government-sponsored films in keeping with policy, live performances for charitable or educational purposes) play a more significant role for performance than in print publishing – so that should also be kept in view. I don't go into the details of these processes, partly because I have done so for publication and these processes are analogous, and partly because our interest is in literature and therefore anchored to literary texts, not performance in itself.

2. CONVENTIONS

The conventions and expectations that attach to particular kinds of performance are quite different from those for written literary texts. For theatre, understandably, the history of different productions, the ways in which a stage can be used, the styles of acting, the audiovisual effects that are possible, and so on, establish a set of conventions and expectations. Similarly, in feature films, the screen of the cinema, the resources of the camera, the nuances of acting, the history of different film genres, also have the same weight. Let's call these, broadly, 'performance frames'. When a literary text is adapted for live or recorded performance, a translation between media takes place – from the conventions and expectations of written literary text to those of performance. *Performance frames are used to produce adaptations of a text from page to stage or screen.*

3. CONTEMPORARY RELEVANCE

When a literary text that is not contemporary – such as a classical play or a nineteenth-century novel – is produced on stage or screen now, we have, I have argued above, a work of contemporary literary relevance. This contemporary relevance is not necessarily only for audiences/readers to discern; *it is very likely to be inserted in some way within the production itself* (however historically authentic it may appear). The contemporary relevance may be apparent in terms of inflecting the performance to remind us of issues that concern us, or by making what is implicit in the text more explicit, or overtly by using present-day backdrops and costumes, and so on. Such insertions to highlight contemporary relevance are distinct from the effect of 'performance frames'.

4. READING AND PERFORMANCE TEXTS

It is useful to distinguish between literary texts that are for general reading, and those that are geared towards the production of a particular performance. Play scripts are accordingly often available in different versions: a version that is open to general reading, and which different directors may interpret differently; and a version with annotations and instructions that dispose the play for a specific performance (production play scripts). Screenplays are generally understood to be written for a specific film production. *Production play scripts and screenplays are useful in occupying an interim place between a literary text out there and a specific live or recorded performance. They can be used to track what the relationship between literary text and performance consists in.*

I am conscious of having stated the above points in a rather abstract fashion. Their implications become considerably clearer if we have an example to contemplate. Let's turn to one.

Eileen Chang (Zhang Ailing)'s short story 'Lust, Caution' (first published 1979, though probably first drafted in the 1950s; translated from the Chinese by Julia Lovell, 2007) is set in the early 1940s in Japanese-occupied China. In this, as part of the resistance to the brutal occupation, a group of students decide to organise the assassination of a powerful Japanese collaborator, Mr Yee, by setting him a 'honey trap' – using a young woman to lure him out of his secure environment. One of their number, Wang Chia-Chi, successfully infiltrates his home by befriending his wife, and after a considerable period manages to become his mistress. A suitable moment is engineered for the assassination, but just before this is due to take place, she has a moment of doubt – she considers the possibility that she might be in love with him – and warns him. Consequently Mr Yee escapes, and in the final scenes is found back at home with his wife and her friends, thinking about Wang Chia-Chi and her love for him (more confident that it was true love than Wang's thoughts showed her to be). He has, meanwhile, had her and her accomplices executed.

This very bare outline naturally doesn't convey the many layers of the story. It is economically written, in a spare but vivid fashion that often focuses on small details to convey the menace in the air and pettiness of many of the characters. The crucial moments in the story's unfolding and denouement depend on readers being allowed into the minds of the two main protagonists: knowing, for instance, what Wang thought when she warned Mr Yee, and what Mr Yee thought afterwards. Though quite a lot happens in the course of the story, much of that activity doesn't really figure straightforwardly. The story foregrounds the quiet, low-key moments and thoughts: characters playing mahjong, sitting in cafés, visiting a jewel shop, thinking, and looking at each other. The rest is outlined quickly and minimally, or merely suggested.

When well-known film director Ang Lee made a two-and-a-half-hour film (2007) based on the short story, he evidently had to work on making explicit in film what was implicit in the text – to make the text amenable to the performance frames of film. In particular, the film compensates for not being able to show the thoughts described in the story by using audiovisual devices. The usual strategies appeared in the screenplay put together by Wang Hui Ling and James Schamus, and in the film that followed. Plausible sequences fleshing out events minimally outlined or implied in the story were written up; as much as possible was made of the expressions, close-ups, gestures, costumes of characters, of the carefully recreated late 1930s and early 1940s settings, and of the background score. Since the film was first released in the USA, and was produced for a worldwide audience, a huge publicity campaign preceded it. Eileen Chang's story was relatively unknown outside China; it was translated and published several times in a short period with her other stories, and with the screenplay. The appearance of the story and screenplay in English underlined an interesting (tried-and-tested) strategy of consolidating audiences across print and performance media. These texts also invited readers/viewers to consider how successfully the short story had been translated across time (1940s setting/ 1950s to 1979 writing, to 2007 performance) and, indeed, across space (from China to a global audience).

The text-to-film translation worked at several levels. Most immediately, it worked in the expensive production values of the film: for instance, what were seedy interiors in the story became opulent in the film; where the story focused narrowly on intimate (claustrophobic at times) spaces and occurrences, the film came up with several grand-scale vistas and events in the style of historical romance movies. But nothing made more of an impression in the publicity effort and reception of the film than its explicit sex scenes. Arguably, the film's attempt to render the story relevant for contemporary audiences, and to transform what was barely articulated in writing into audiovisually striking images, occurs in these sex scenes. These exemplify both a particular performance frame and a contemporary insertion. Let's pause on the interesting topic of the sex scenes in the film *Lust, Caution* – at least, on those between Mr Yee and Wang Chia-Chi. More precisely, let's pause on scenes of sex and violence, because these are inextricably connected in the film.

In Eileen Chang's story, the sexual encounters between Yee and Wang are summarised in one sentence: 'The two occasions she had been with Yee, she had been so tense, so taken up in saying her lines that there had been no opportunity to ask herself how she actually felt' (p. 28). These encounters evidently have little to do with her contemplation of the possibility of love for Yee, which makes her warn him. Her thoughts on the matter immediately before touching fleetingly on their two sexual encounters go thus: 'Surely she hadn't fallen in love with Yee? Despite her fierce skepticism toward the idea, she found herself unable to refute the notion entirely; since she had never been in love, she had no idea what it might feel like' (p. 28). She is aware that this possibility crosses her mind partly because of her repugnance for the other person she has had sex with, and partly because of the closeness of the moment in the jewel shop. And she warns Yee because she sees a sad look in him, which makes her think that he might love her.

In Wang and Schamus's screenplay, these fleeting reflections are turned into three significant sex scenes. The first of these, obviously without dialogue, is described as follows: 'He flips her around facedown, unbuckles his pants, and enters her from behind. // What follows is more or less a rape.' The other two follow in quick succession, less carefully described, except that in one of them Wang Chia-Chi pauses in mid-coitus to look at Yee's gun on the chair and starts crying. The screenplay associates sex and violence: it is a 'more or less a rape' that somehow tames Wang and establishes a sort of loyalty; and in different dialogues both Yee and Wang fantasise about having sex while someone's blood and brains spatter on them. The screenplay, incidentally, also invents a kind of collective gang killing, a graphic episode of Wang's resistance colleagues stabbing and ultimately breaking the neck of a blackmailer while Wang watches in horrified fascination. And the execution of Wang and her colleagues at the end is also vividly depicted. Other episodes of intimacy between the two were also inserted, including one set in a geisha house where Wang sings for Yee.

Ang Lee made the most of these in the film. The scenes of violence were as viscerally realised on film as the screenplay suggested, and the sex scenes were more explicit and protracted than the screenplay suggested. In the 'more or less a rape', Yee doesn't just unbuckle his belt but also uses it to whip Wang Chia-Chi, and in the other scenes various well-lighted and carefully choreographed sexual positions and consummations are fully depicted. During the publicity phase for the film, Ang Lee observed that the film didn't so much adapt Chang's story as return to her 'theatre of cruelty and love'. Assistant director Roseanna Ng recalled the care with which the sex scenes were shot, because the 'complex and convoluted nature of the relationship [...] relied solely on those scenes'. In a way, the development from Eileen Chang's story to Ang Lee's film could be regarded as an elaboration of sex and violence, though there was little in the former to suggest that sex or physical violence was as central to understanding Wang and Yee's relationship as it was made out to be, or that the emotions of love played as effective a role. Evidently, in translating the story on to screen, and in updating its effect on contemporary audiences, Ang Lee felt it expedient to highlight the sex and violence.

This account exemplifies how the relation between literary text (short story and screenplay) and recorded performance (feature film) work in contemporary modes of production. Several of the points made above in an abstract manner are relevant to this. It is arguable that explicit sex and violence are particularly effective in live and recorded performances, and almost invariably have a pro-vocative effect on an audience. Ang Lee's reference to a 'theatre of cruelty' recalls a literary tradition that can be traced back to classical antiquity. In film, action involving sex and violence, in combination, has a potent public appeal even in indifferently made films, and is now staple in a great deal of popular and serious film-making. Using a familiar frame of audiovisual appeal to make explicit in the film what was possibly (doubtfully) implicit in the story – compensating thereby for the insights into the char-acters' thoughts – is one of the strategies through which the relation between the literary text and the performance work. Even the screenplay, written to enable the film, is an interim written text that cannot convey what the sex scenes achieve in audiovisual form.

From a related but different perspective, the public acceptability of the performance of sex and violence has evidently consistently increased in many contexts. We are generally aware that the extent to which explicit sex and graphic violence can be *performed* for public consumption now is considerably greater, and gives rise to less controversy, than in both the 1940s (when the story is set) and the 1950s–70s (when Eileen Chang was writing this). Arguably, we are more habituated now to seeing such performances in public, and we generally take it in our stride. Quite possibly, rendering the story by heightening the sex and violent action could itself be regarded as updating it – as rendering it audiovisually amenable to contemporary sensibilities. Doing so certainly has some advantages for publicity purposes, which were played out when the film was released. If it did cause controversy, that only contributed to publicising the film more widely.

The passage from Eileen Chang's literary text 'Lust, Caution' to Ang Lee's film *Lust, Caution* thus exemplifies several of the points I made early in this section. It is, however, a particular rather than typical example, and shouldn't be thought of otherwise.

E-TEXTS

In Maniyambath Mukundan's novel *Dance* (2000; somewhat indifferently translated from the Malayalam by D. Krishna Ayyar and K.G. Ramakishnan, 2007) we have the story of a dancer, apparently called Agni. His experiences are recounted, from learning a traditional dance form in a Keralan village (in India) to his recruitment into a Paris-based dance troupe, eventual rise to fame, relationships and loves, and later visit to his childhood home after contracting AIDS. Of interest here is the narrative device that frames this story. It is presented as a series of emails from an unknown person with the username Agni to the narrator, T.P. Sreedharan, soon after he opens his first email account. Sreedharan becomes hooked on the story and awaits subsequent emailed episodes impatiently, and thinks about them often. He searches for, but is unable to find, information about any dancer that fits, though the story is well informed, convincingly narrated, and appears to be based on experience. As Agni's story reaches its end, Sreedharan asks for a photograph of his unknown correspondent, and receives the following response:

> Do you remember what I wrote once? I am only an email address without a house, street, or country. I have no signature. What is the use of seeing the photo of such a person? But alright – you who have patiently read my story, have asked merely for a photo. So before I erase my email ID, agni@aol.com, before I disappear into cyberspace beyond your reach, I send you this,

A picture emerged on the monitor. An emoticon, with a funny mouth like a cave – now shrinking, now swelling. And from the speakers issued forth a loud laughter.

(p. 123)

These are the last lines of the novel.

The use of this email-based epistolary narrative device is suggestive in several ways. It conveys the basic features of the electronic environment, wherein texts are produced and received, from a low-tech perspective, which becomes acclimatised to that environment as the novel unfolds. The mobility of writing and reading is registered: Shreedharan is aware that the emails originate from different locations around the world, and he himself accesses them while travelling. Agni's story unfolds in a serialised and potentially interactive form (mainly in the final exchanges between author and reader), which is characteristic of many kinds of e-text. That Agni's story is apparently told to a stranger, at length and with literary flair, entirely outside any evident commercial or public-interest framework, is noteworthy. It is apparently driven simply by a desire for creative expression, confined to written articulation, which is arguably an impulse that drives the great proliferation of e-texts on the internet. The pervasive uncertainties about authorship, the ambiguities of assumed identities, doubts about the contexts of production and reception, are all signalled here and are all distinctive to the electronic environment. The mocking emoticon at the end seems to reflect the conventional reader's anxieties about this environment, wherein received assumptions about writing and reading are challenged in various ways.

In fact, by the time this story appeared, the electronic environment in question had already been well developed for at least a decade, accommodating an ever-increasing circulation of literary e-texts. And it had involved a great deal more than the kind of one-to-one correspondence that *Dance* uses. The developments in question had a great deal to do with innovations in the technologies for accessing and networking on the internet: with, for instance, the development of blogging and web chatrooms in the mid-1990s, and the growing popularity of social networking websites such as *MySpace* and *Facebook* post-2000 (after *Dance* was written). The implications of these for literature, and for the systematic study of literature, are enormous, and are yet to be fully exploited and explored. These implications extend to the manner in which contemporary e-text literature is both produced and received. As earlier, here I confine myself to production; I return to the reception of e-texts in chapter 4.

A few quick definitions may be useful to take this discussion forward, though most of us are generally aware of these already. *By 'e-text' I mean something that is accessible as an image on a screen, rather than on the printed page; for our purposes, especially on a personal computer (PC) linked to the internet* – which, increasingly, most of those of us with literary interests use. Keep in mind that we think of a literary text now as not merely written, but also related to performance – that is, incorporating images or sounds; accordingly, our understanding of the e-text must include all these. Insofar as producing literary texts in e-text form goes, there are four underlying processes:

- *digitisation* – turning different kinds of texts into a uniform and workable code, which can be transported easily and decoded as e-text when needed;
- *programming* – constructing a system (for many of us this comes down to the software we employ) that determines how the decoding occurs and how the e-text is manifested and used;
- *hyperlinking* – creating easily used and immediate links between different e-texts working in different programs; and
- *networking* – where all the above processes are garnered to facilitate communications and exchanges across different computer systems and programs that work with e-texts.

Our interest in these definitions is generally perfunctory; by and large, we are accustomed to handling e-texts on our PCs and through the internet without necessarily knowing how they work. The situation is similar to our constantly using electronic appliances without knowing much about power grids and electronic circuits. *By 'electronic environment' I mean an environment – both technological and social – wherein we habitually use the facilities put at our disposal through the above processes.*

In terms of production, the relatively recent development of widely accessible literary e-texts is relevant for both *how we understand the content of literature* (literary texts and forms themselves) and *what the overall process of e-text production involves* (in comparison with the process of print production outlined above). The following observations about each by turn should set the ground for further systematic study of this area.

Let's start with the content of literature.

1. DIRECTIONS OF TEXTS

The printed texts that we generally associate with literature appear as books in the form of a codex – a number of pages bound within covers, where the text is read in a natural direction – from left to right or right to left, top to bottom, following a numbered sequence of pages from front to back or back to front. The book as a rolled-up scroll, as an alternative to the codex, also involves a firm direction, but we seldom think of contemporary literary texts in terms of scrolls. To cross-refer and look back involves some effort, which is at odds with the physical form of the codex and its natural direction. The e-text can, however, be programmed and hyper-linked to make departures from that seemingly natural direction much easier. A book in e-text can be followed back and forth, and connected to other texts (to create hypertexts), in various directions by following simple instructions in the margins or ensconced habits of e-reading, according to the programmer's design. We may say that *the e-text eases non-linear reading.*

The linearity of the text has been a fundamental presumption in structuring literary texts. Given that the codex form seemed inevitable, a powerful conviction about the usefulness of clear beginnings and endings and sequences in literary texts has often been enjoined. Much twentieth-century experimentation in literature has been about questioning and undermining strong subscriptions to linear reading and formal sequences. The most radical of these considered dismantling the integrity of the codex itself: for instance, B.S. Johnson's novel *The Unfortunates* (1969) appeared as unbound pages in a box, which could be shuffled and arranged as the reader wished. At the time this seemed a laborious process, but in the era of e-text this seems quite natural, and very close to what we do habitually when surfing the internet. So, when Geoff Ryman wrote his interactive novel for the internet, *253* (1996; www.ryman-novel.

com), which does something similar to Johnson's *The Unfortunates*, it seemed an obvious thing to do in its e-text form. (Incidentally, you can try out the difference between reading Ryman's novel on the website and in printed book form, since it appeared as a book in 1998.)

The various ways in which the assumed direction of the printed text can be played with in e-text format has inspired a great deal of literary creativity (easily sampled through the Electronic Literature Directory, http://directory.eliterature.org). Apart from playing with direction, these e-texts (as hypertexts) enable a more fluid and immediately meaningful use of intertextuality (discussed in chapter 2) than printed texts.

2. HYPERMEDIA E-TEXTS

Digitisation makes it possible to build *programs that bring together, and even overlap, written, visual and audio aspects of texts (to create hypermedia e-texts)*. The printed text, of course, allows still images and texts to be juxtaposed, but moving images and sounds can only be tagged on as an attached, non-print component (and only relatively recently, with the mass marketing of cassettes, CDs and DVDs). By and large, literary texts tend to stick with print. Hypermedia e-texts allow for wide-scale engagement with a kind of literary creativity that was rare not long ago. The e-poem 'The Hugo Ball' by Talan Memmott, discussed in chapter 2, is a good example of literary hypermedia e-text. The possibilities here are only beginning to be exploited to literary ends now, and perhaps in what will become contemporary literature, such e-texts will soon appear less exotic than they do at present.

3. INTERACTIVENESS AND GENRE

Networking programs consolidate the advantages of digitisation and hyperlinking by *increasing the reach of authors and readers on the internet, and encouraging interaction between authors and readers and within literary communities*. This opens up various possibilities that are significant for contemporary literature, and will probably become more so soon.

It allows, for instance, authors to write texts bit by bit in consultation with readers, so that readers can comment and perhaps influence the author as he writes. Several distinctive genres have emerged as a result, such as Ryman's kind of interactive novel, and, far more prolifically, blogs. An enormous number of authors maintain publicly accessible personal blogs about their day-to-day lives and experiences on the internet, which can be regarded as a literary genre in the same way as published diaries are. But whereas the process of writing diaries was generally a closed personal matter, and their publication involved retrospective editing, blogs usually unfold through a process of writing in which readers are involved. Further, I have mentioned social networking facilities such as *Facebook*; such websites host a prolific number of literary communities of various sorts (various kinds of reader and fan-communities, creative writing communities, etc.). These contain a constant flow of literary e-texts that are formed interactively, by communal consultation or for specific communities (like fanfiction).

Importantly, under these circumstances, various well-established conventions of systematic literary study need to be reconsidered. The notion of a fixed author for literary texts is naturally one of them, which suggests that we need to think further about points made early in this chapter. The convention in the electronic environment for participants to assume identities – and uncertainty about whether what any participant claims is true – also undermines the potency of the idea of the author. Correspondingly, the idea of a context for a literary text (the place and time where it is written) also becomes less certain, since e-texts continuously cross all sorts of territories and boundaries without necessarily affixing a definite origin.

I have described the contents of literary e-texts with reference to written or printed texts above. It makes similar sense to present observations on the production of e-texts in relation to the publication of print texts.

1. SELF-PUBLICATION

Becoming habituated with the electronic environment means that we can easily (without spending much money or effort) make our own literary writings available on the internet, and optimistically hope to reach a wide – potentially global – readership. Many have taken advantage of this, and there are now countless literary texts of every sort to be reached through the internet. In fact, there is such an extraordinary surfeit of texts that the odds against any one surfacing to wide attention are astronomically high, but we can always be hopeful. And, as it happens, a significant number of contemporary literary texts have already surfaced in this fashion.

What we have, in other words, is *a burgeoning of self-publication in e-text form, which by-passes the gate-keeping that institutional print publishers have exercised.* Such self-publication in print form used to be regarded with great scepticism precisely because of that; as a magazine article recently put it, 'saying you were a self-published author used to be like saying you were a self-taught brain surgeon' (Grossman and Sachs, 2009, p. 54). That still applies to self-published e-texts, but with some let-outs – mainly, e-texts can do things that print texts can't, so such e-texts can't be regarded as pertinent to the conventional publisher's domain. Easily used hyperlinking and networking facilities also mean that communities of literary readers and writers can set up their own mechanisms for selecting and gate-keeping and publicising that do not adhere to the commercial or institutional considerations which have largely determined these.

2. PUBLISHERS' TACTICS

Naturally, publishers, whose bread and butter depends on disseminating texts, have been interested in the development of the electronic environment and the growth of self-publishing. They have consequently developed several tactics that are germane to how contemporary literature is accessed and understood now. The following are some of these.

First, some have chosen to pay attention to the kinds of literary works that are surfacing through self-publication in e-text form, on the understanding that these have a proven market value. So, numerous e-texts have been published thereafter by established publishers, including several blogs by soldiers and Iraqi citizens during the 2003 invasion of Iraq; novels such as Ryman's *253* (mentioned above); and quite a few Chinese *Harry Potter* fanfiction novels.

Second, most major publishing corporations have carved out controlled territories within the internet (in cyberspace) and transferred their gate-keeping and taste-making credentials to those virtual territories while trying to capitalise on the reach that e-texts enable. Typically, this involves setting up a branded and subscription-based e-text library website, or making agreements with internet vendors who have these set up.

Third, some corporations have sought to develop publishing technologies which they can control for e-text readers, such as portable e-book readers and downloadable programs for displaying compliant e-texts, which are then sold.

Fourth, in some cases there have been successful attempts to commercially control the process of readers and writers forming communities wherein writing and reading happens in an ongoing and interactive way. Notably, for instance, popular Chinese fiction community sites such as www.qidian.com, www.qdmm.com, www.jjwxc.net, or fiction areas within well-known news and blogging sites such as book.sina.com.cn and book.sohu.com, have categorised readerships (along gender or age lines) and compartmentalised self-published texts (horror, fantasy romance, slash, *ZhongMaWen* or 'stud' writing, beautiful writing). These enable the website providers to set up access pathways and charge readers to make profits. They often contract authors whose writing is proving popular as it is gradually posted and readers become hooked.

3. PUBLICITY AND INFORMATION

The facilities of *e-texts and the internet are exploited by all sorts of interested parties for dispersing information about, and categorising, literary texts.* Such publicity strategies have a powerful influence on how we approach and understand contemporary literature. Authors and publishers and booksellers use the facilities to profile texts; we can often, for instance, 'preview' parts of a new book (like browsing in a bookshop) through *Amazon* or *Google Books.* The search engines are set up to favour certain kinds of search and certain texts. Internet-based communities provide information in ways that often predispose readers about specific literary works and authors. Thus prospective readers now frequently check out authors and texts before buying books by looking at blogging sites or consulting the popular communal e-encyclopaedia *Wikipedia.*

4. SYSTEMATIC STUDY RESOURCES

Finally, since we are concerned here with the systematic study of contemporary literature, we cannot but be interested in the impact of the internet on such study itself. Much of what is involved in study exploits the advantages that digitisation, programming, hyperlinking and networking provide. Gigantic digital archives and libraries of literary texts from different periods and contexts have been, or are being, put together. These are easier to search and access; comparing texts (say, the same text in different editions, or a text and a related one) becomes simpler; negotiating annotations and ancillary information across different media is facilitated; and so on. Like networks of general readers, networks exist of scholars and teachers and students and librarians, and such networks can be bridged.

There is, of course, a great deal more to be said about each of the points made above. Here, only a sketchy outline is possible. We return to these areas from a reception point of view in chapter 4.

A LITTLE QUESTION

Dr Guru, whom I haven't stopped consulting, but who has been uncharacteristically subdued for a while, raised a little question on reading the above: 'But aren't you extending the scope of literature and the study of literature impossibly here? The manner in which you have brought in live and recorded performances and hyper-media e-texts has significant implications for the study of the literature of any period. Why shouldn't we consider such conventionally separate areas as music and painting and sculpture as within the study of literature too?'

My argument above has been that live and recorded performances are within the study of contemporary literature insofar as they relate to written texts. It is on the same principle that hypermedia e-texts are picked up: these are relevant to us insofar as writing is a component within them. All this naturally applies equally to music and paintings and sculpture and so on. Insofar as any of these are connected to written literary texts, they are within the purview of literature and the study of literature. I doubt any scholar or teacher will quibble with that, because that has been the case for as long as literature has been considered systematically. And that is certainly consistent with what we, as readers of literature, experience now.

REFERENCES

Barthes, Roland (1977). 'The Death of the Author' (1967). *Image, Music, Text*. Selected and trans. Stephen Heath. London: Fontana.

Cercas, Javier (2003). *Soldiers of Salamis* (2001). Trans. Anne McLean. London: Bloomsbury.

Cercas, Javier, in conversation with David Trueba (2003). *Diálogos de Salamina*. Barcelona: Tusquets. Extract in English at: http://wordswithoutborders.org/article/from-conversations-about-soldiers-of-salamis

Chang, Eileen (Zhang Ailing) (2007). 'Lust, Caution' (1979). *Lust, Caution: and Other Stories*. Trans. Julia Lovell. London: Penguin. [Quotations from the story are from this edition.]

Chang, Eileen and other contributors (2007). *Lust, Caution: The Story, the Screenplay, and the Making of the Film*. New York: Pantheon. [Quotations from the screenplay by Wang Hui Ling and James Schamus, and comments by assistant director Roseanna Ng and director Ang Lee, are from this.]

Grossman, Lev and Andrea Sachs (2009). 'Books Unbound'. *Time International* (Atlantic edition) 173(5), 2 February, 53–55.

Johnson, B.S. (1969). *The Unfortunates*. London: Secker and Warburg.

Lee, Ang, dir. (2007) *Lust, Caution* (DVD). Orlando, FL: Universal Studios.

Mukundan, Maniyambath (2007). *Dance* (2000). Trans. D. Krishna Ayyar and K.G. Ramakishnan. New Delhi: Katha.

Rowling, J.K. (1998). *Harry Potter and the Chamber of Secrets*. London: Bloomsbury.

Ryman, Geoff (1996). *253*. London: Flamingo. www.ryman-novel.com

FURTHER READING

ON THE PUBLISHING INDUSTRY

Feather, John (2003). *Communicating Knowledge: Publishing in the 21st Century*. Munich: K.G. Saur. [Not particularly on literature, but a wide-ranging survey of the current state and practices of the international publishing industry. The effects on literature are noted in passing.]

Greco, Albert N. (2005). *The Book Publishing Industry*. Mahwah, NJ: Lawrence Erlbaum. [Nor is this especially on literature, but a useful account of the publishing process and agents involved.]

ON THE LITERATURE INDUSTRY, MAINLY BOOK HISTORY

Eliot, Simon and Jonathan Rose, eds (2009). *A Companion to the History of the Book*. Chichester, UK: Wiley-Blackwell. [Has useful accounts on the history, theory and practices of book production and reception, with sections on book history beyond the West and considering media other than books.]

Finkelstein, David and Alistair McCleery, eds (2005). *An Introduction to Book History*. New York: Routledge. [A useful survey of the area, companion to the following.]

——(2006). *The Book History Reader*, 2nd edn. London: Routledge. [Influential texts on the history of the production and reception of books, and theorising book history from different perspectives.]

Masten, Jeffrey, Peter Stallybrass and Nancy J. Vickes, eds (1997). *Language Machines: Technologies of Literary and Cultural Production*. London: Routledge. [With sections entitled 'pens', 'presses', 'screens' and 'voice'.]

ON AUTHORS

Bennett, Andrew (2005). *The Author*. London: Routledge. [Overview of concepts of authorship associated with different literary and cultural periods.]

Burke, Sean, ed. (1995). *Authorship: From Plato to the Postmodern*. Edinburgh, UK: Edinburgh University Press. [Collection of significant writings on authorship from different periods.]

ON LIVE AND RECORDED PERFORMANCES IN RELATION TO LITERARY TEXTS

Aston, Elaine and George Savona (1991). *Theatre as Sign-System: A Semiotics of Text and Performance*. London: Routledge. [On interpreting texts for theatre performance.]

Corrigon, Timothy, ed. (2011). *Film and Literature: An Introduction and Reader*. Abingdon, UK: Routledge. [Most aspects of the relationship between text and screen performance are covered.]

Stam, Robert and Alessandra Raengo, eds (2004). *A Companion to Literature and Film*. Oxford: Blackwell.

Worthen, W.B. (2010). *Drama: Between Poetry and Performance*. Chichester, UK: Wiley–Blackwell. [On how writing is realised in performance, with case studies.]

ON E-TEXTS

Browner, Stephanie, Stephen Pulsford and Richard Sears (2000). *Literature and the Internet: A Guide for Students, Teachers and Scholars*. New York: Garland.

[Guide on the internet as literary medium, resource and teaching tool, and theoretical implications for literature.]

Hayles, N. Katherine (2007). *Electronic Literature: What Is It?* At the Electronic Literature Organization website, www.eliterature.org/pad/elp.html [Considers the context for and genres of electronic literature, its relation to print, and how such literature should be archived and managed.]

——(2008). *Electronic Literature: New Horizons for the Literary.* Notre Dame, IN: University of Notre Dame Press. [A comprehensive survey of the field, covering different genres and considering the implications for literary theory.]

Schäfer, Jörgen and Peter Gendolla, eds (2010). *Beyond the Screen: Transformations of Literary Structures, Interfaces and Genres.* Bielefeld, Germany: transcript. [Essays dealing with how electronic texts and cultural products are changing perspectives of literariness, genre, space and time, and archiving.]

Schreibman, Susan, Ray Siemens and John Unsworth, eds (2004). *A Companion to Digital Humanities.* Oxford: Blackwell. [Gives a broad overview of the 'electronic environment'.]

4

RECEPTION

WHAT WE DO

Studying what is contemporary in literature depends very largely on understanding what we, readers of literary texts, do. It is readers who read texts in the midst of their ongoing lives and times (their present), recognise texts as contemporary or otherwise, and make sense of them accordingly.

As I have observed in chapter 1, we naturally bring our present-day perspectives to reading any literary text, whether recent or from the distant past. It is therefore likely that we perceive some degree of contemporary relevance in all the literature we read. However, it is equally the case that we do make judgements of contemporary relevance with an awareness of what is recent and what isn't. For instance, when we read a play by Shakespeare, we understand it in terms of present-day concerns, but at the same time we do not lose sight of the fact that it appeared in the historical context of the sixteenth/seventeenth century. Such a juxtaposition of our sense of the present and awareness of the past usually clarifies our understanding of both present and past. When we read contemporary literature, we do not necessarily call upon a clear sense of history; we usually plunge into the contemporary text without much reflection because it appears to speak to current concerns in an immediate fashion.

This chapter explores how our sense of contemporary relevance influences our literary choices and engagements with texts (our reception of literature). For a systematic study of contemporary literature, attention to reception is as necessary as to production. Production and reception obviously complement each other; accordingly, this chapter on reception complements chapter 3 on production, and there are overlaps between them. To some extent, this chapter follows the structure of chapter 3 and starts off with three sections – on reading written/printed texts, viewing live and recorded performances, and engaging with e-texts. These are followed by two further sections – on reviews and criticism, and on reading translations.

READING TEXTS

The process of reading a literary text (or any text, really) is something we, experienced readers, undertake without much thought – we just do it, generally quickly and effortlessly. If we pause to reflect, however, it is evidently a fairly complicated process in which various sorts of guesses and expectations work. The process of reading has been much discussed by scholars, and some of their accounts are worth recounting briefly. It seems very likely that what we regard as contemporary has something to do with this process.

Four much-discussed accounts of reading come to mind, which are most easily presented with some text in view. Any bit of text would do, and the following is quoted simply because it is closest to hand for this reader. These are the opening sentences of a novel entitled *Q & A* (2005) by Vikas Swarup. I have more to say on the novel later; for the moment, the following brief quotation is sufficient:

> I have been arrested. For winning a quiz show.
>
> They came for me late last night, when even the stray dogs had gone off to sleep. They broke open my door, handcuffed me and marched me off to the waiting jeep with a flashing red light.
>
> There was no hue and cry. Not one resident stirred from his hut. Only the old owl on the tamarind tree hooted at my arrest.
>
> (p. 11)

For our purposes, and with this passage before us, two questions arise: what happens as we go through such a passage, and how could that lead us to gauge its contemporary qualities (or lack thereof)? I address the former question first, in relation to the four main accounts of the reading process; the latter question is taken up afterwards.

According to the four accounts of the reading process, working through the quoted passage involves the following considerations.

1. IMPLIED READER

By this account, *what the reader does depends on what the text directs or nudges the reader to do*. In the above passage, for instance, the reader is manoeuvred into the story in several ways. The opening two sentences could actually have been presented as one, but are deliberately broken down into effect (arrest) and cause (winning a quiz show) as separate sentences. The reader's expectations are thereby quickly played upon. The first sentence might lead the reader to expect some sensational reason for the arrest; the second sentence is almost an anti-climax since the reason seems so counter to expectations. Behind that quick readjustment of expectations, the reader brings her own associations with both what getting arrested usually means (being suspected of a crime) and what winning a quiz show means (something to be applauded rather than punished). The quick shift in the reader's expectations calls for an explanation, and the intrigued reader is tempted to find it by reading further.

A similar shift in expectations is also suggested by the next two paragraphs. In these, the location of this intriguing situation is still unknown, and the reader will naturally look for hints to make sense of these events. The second paragraph evokes a fairly public late-night arrest, and the third observes that there is no public interest in this event – again, somewhat contrary to usual expectations. The blasé attitude of neighbours to an arrest might suggest a city environment; while the hut, stray dogs, tamarind tree and owl have a country air about them. Depending on where they are, to some readers the tamarind tree would immediately evoke an exotic location (they might need to look it up in the dictionary), while to others it might evoke a familiar neighbourhood (perhaps tamarind was an ingredient in their last meal). The chatty, colloquial style, not too fussy about syntax, might sound friendly to some readers and over-familiar to others, according to their background.

The text seems to play subtly with the reader's associations and preconceptions, direct the reader's attention and draw her in, and generally anticipate how the reader might make sense of the sequence of words as she reads them. It appears, in other words, that *the text unfolds with an idea of what the reader might think.* This implicit idea of the reader in the text is a fairly flexible one, because it can accommodate and manipulate a wide variety of associations and experiences that readers may bring to their reading. This implicit idea of a reader, which the text seems to work with, is roughly what the literary theorist Wolfgang Iser dubbed the 'implied reader' of the text (see Further reading: Crone *et al.*, 2010).

That the language, form and structure of a literary text (say, a novel) can anticipate a reader in particular ways leads to two broad kinds of manipulation of the reader. Either the reader's expectations are met half-way and generally confirmed, which can be satisfying if the reader wishes to have them confirmed. Or these expectations are thwarted, which can also be satisfying if the reader likes a challenge. It is some such process that explains the appeal of formulaic 'genre fiction' and of what is thought of now as 'literary fiction' (I touched upon this in chapter 2).

2. INTERPRETIVE COMMUNITY

By this account, *the process of reading is dependent upon factors that are not contained in, but precede, the literary text.* In reading the quoted passage from *Q & A*, for instance, we already know that this is a novel because we have, at some point, agreed to call certain kinds of texts a 'novel'. We have, perhaps simply in learning a language, agreed on what certain words mean and how they should be understood. Moreover, in schools and universities, we collectively agree (by being taught or by talking to others) that generally a novel should have a plot, depict characters in a specific location, and so on. So, even before reading the beginning of *Q & A*, we are already disposed to ask some questions about it: what is the key to the plot? who are the main characters? where is it set? and so on. It is only because we have these questions in mind already that we are able to make sense of the text. As we get down to reading the quoted passage, we are already looking for certain novel-like patterns, and the passage is read accordingly: in the first two sentences, we happily find a conundrum that could be a key to the plot because we are looking for it; we are intrigued by the silence of the neighbours during the arrest because we expect a novel to intrigue us; we are interested in the owl in the tamarind tree, the hut and stray dogs because we are looking for clues about the location; we wonder about the narrator because we are accustomed to identifying a narrative position and voice; and so on.

In brief, *reading consists not so much in responding to how the implied reader is anticipated within the text, but in deploying strategies for reading that are acquired before reading the text.* Insofar as any of us knows a language and has experience of reading, we have agreed upon some such predetermined strategies. Some of us might be professional literary critics, and might have agreed upon a few more such strategies than are used generally by readers. In bringing these to bear on any literary text, we are therefore doing something that is collectively determined in advance – in the literary critic Stanley Fish's terms, we are behaving as part of an 'interpretive community'.

3. REAL READERS

Both the above accounts seem plausible, but they are contradictory and emphasise different factors. It isn't clear to what extent one or the other applies to the experience of readers. *The logical thing to do is to look for some kind of evidence to settle the differences between the above accounts – to find some empirical basis for either or both. And the obvious way forward is to appeal to real readers*: to, for instance, set up an experiment with real readers, ask them to read a text and tell us (in response to questions) what they think they did, and then analyse the answers. This sort of thing has often been tried. Researchers have gone about setting up such experiments and gathering 'response statements' and analysing them, and though the results are interesting, they don't necessarily give clear answers either.

Consider me as a real reader, for instance, of the *Q & A* novel. By the time I finished the novel, it was impossible for me to recall the details of how I had read one bit or the other, and I wasn't able to retrieve any consistent pattern to my progress through the text. The arguments made above are about processes that are so close to the text, and so habitual and quick, that I found it impossible to be conscious of and clear about them. It might be felt that perhaps

I have read too much for such an experiment – perhaps I should have stuck with a short piece, like the passage quoted above. That would help me to be attentive to what I was doing while reading. But again, this isn't easy. I found it difficult to decide what is short or long enough for such an experiment. If too short, perhaps the result is not representative of my reading habits anyway; I feel I am doing something unnatural in reading so closely, and that is not what I usually do.

But was there nothing that struck me about this passage when I reflected on it as a real reader? There are some things. For instance, while reading the novel, I found myself nagged by a question. The first lines note that the police 'came for me last night'. It occurred to me that the narrator must then be recounting/writing this novel about experiences that have happened within 24 hours. Since this is the Prologue, it seems that the whole thing was written in that time. That's a lot of writing (361 pages in print) – perhaps it should be thought of as being spoken quite quickly, which would be a lot of speaking. As it happens, a large part of the story is spoken and recorded by the narrator, but that doesn't include the Prologue, where the starting quotation comes from. By the Epilogue at the end of the novel, it says six months have passed since the beginning. Perhaps, the 'last night' of the beginning is simply a ploy to create a sense of urgency in the reader, or perhaps the narrator should be thought of as starting to write as soon as he was able to, and finishing six months later?

My preoccupation with this point does not help a great deal in deciding which of the above accounts to go with. But it is useful to understand the process of reading anyway. It is possible to understand my interest in this point as one of the ways in which I tried to establish a link between what is real as I understand it (my notion of what a writer can or cannot do) and what is fictional (what the narrator says). This attempt to establish a link is one way of trying to distinguish between relevant and irrelevant information, which helps me make sense of the story. The point about timing seemed relevant, but didn't quite fit with my sense of what is realistically possible. Such *assessments of relevance through observations and slight hints are, arguably, the very basis of all linguistic communication, whether spoken or written – including specialised communicative activities such as a reader reading a text and feeling she has understood it.* Studies of cognition in real reading have often focused on how such determinations of relevance are made.

4. REAL-WORLD READING

The above three accounts, interesting and valid as they are in their own ways, are all too focused on the text. The first account tries to discern the reader as foreshadowed *within* the text; the second tries to outline what the reader brings *before* reading a text; and the third understands the real reader as such only *after* she has read a text. Each of these seeks to position the reader only in relation to the text. What really happens when we read a text is considerably more complex.

Like many readers I, for instance, picked up the novel *Q & A* only after watching the successful film adaptation from it, *Slumdog Millionaire* (dir. Danny Boyle, 2008). I therefore had a strong audiovisual preconception of the novel, which my reading modified substantially. The manner in which the novel in the first instance, and thereafter the film, was produced and designed and marketed anticipated who would read it, and for what reason. I have discussed such calculations in the process of producing a printed literary work in chapter 3. As it happens, I am reasonably well aware of the social and cultural circumstances in India, where this novel was written and set and published, and readers such as I were particularly targeted by the producers of the book. Readers of the earning bracket to which I belong can easily afford to buy this book, and the book had been priced accordingly. Nevertheless, that doesn't necessarily mean that the calculations of the producers had anticipated or predetermined my reading experience in every respect. They were correct only to the extent of my being a likely customer for this book. In fact, those calculations and anticipations applied to readers like me to varying degrees; and equally, readers such as I formed our varied and distinctive views through the process of our reading.

In brief, *a very complex set of interactions between author/producers of the book and market conditions, between context-specific reading habits and this text and its readers, between how the text was discussed and adapted, are all at work together.* It is possible to discern, with some research, what sort of broad patterns of print production and print reception are revealed by the career of, for example, *Q & A* through the market into readers' hands and thereafter. This is what a researcher interested in the 'reception history' of literature usually does with regard to particular texts and publishers, particular categories of readers, particular locations where reading happens, and so on.

For us, the question that follows from these accounts is: what do they have to do with our understanding of the contemporary for literature? Each of these accounts lends itself to somewhat distinctive ways of understanding literary contemporariness.

1. FROM THE IMPLIED READER PERSPECTIVE

The reader reads a text as contemporary because the idiom and strategies of the text are familiarly of our time in a general way. The reader doesn't need to draw upon her knowledge of the past and how literary expression in the past sounded. Gauging contemporariness in a work of popular fiction such as *Q & A* could simply be a matter of how easily the text reads at the level of language. When reading the beginning of *Q & A,* the somewhat non-standard colloquial constructions, attitudes to quiz shows and getting arrested, etc., are all features that the reader can effortlessly grasp. There is nothing jarringly quaint or dated in there. A more challenging experimental work would resonate with the reader's sense of language and world in a different way (perhaps not as ease of reading but the challenge of newness). At any rate, the contemporary text uses an idiom and strategies that immediately evoke the reader's world in some general way.

2. FROM AN INTERPRETIVE COMMUNITY PERSPECTIVE

As readers, we already have some collectively agreed preconceptions about what is contemporary and what a novel of our time should be like. These preconceptions may be exactly of the sort that are cited from an implied reader perspective – but, in this case, we don't think of these as idioms and strategies that the text uses, but as features that we already know and look for. The sense of familiarity and immediacy or the ease of reading mentioned above is not because the text makes it so; these are found because the reader is predisposed to finding it so.

3. FROM A REAL READER'S PERSPECTIVE

As real readers, we constantly try to match our particular experiences of the world we live in with those found in the text. In reading *Q & A*, for example, I try to match images of Delhi and Mumbai that I have in mind with those described in the novel. I also bring my understanding of real time to the time of narration/writing mentioned in the novel. If these come together effectively, with an immediacy that is plausible to me, I think of the novel as contemporary.

4. FROM THE REAL-WORLD READING PERSPECTIVE

We usually know that *Q & A* was written in 2005 before reading it. Even if we don't know that for sure, we can tell it is from roughly that time from the information on the book covers, and from the reviews and advertisements that brought the book to our attention in the first instance. We may have seen the film adaptation recently. All these ensure that we approach the novel and read it with a secure sense of its being a text of our time. The other three points above are really academic considerations; we are unlikely to be called upon to identify the contemporary qualities of a text simply by reading it, without any sense whatever of when and how it became available to us.

Despite the latter observation, it would be imprudent to dismiss the others. Our sense of the contemporary in literature, it seems to me, involves all those possibilities to some degree, and a systematic approach to contemporary literature should consider all of them together.

The four accounts of reading above have a bearing on our consideration of the reception of live/recorded performance and e-text, below. Since the reading of written or printed texts is the conventional norm for literature, reception of these other forms of literature is most easily understood as a departure from that norm.

WATCHING PERFORMANCES

Much of the above outline of *the reader's approach to a written text is analogous to a viewer's approach to a live or recorded performance*. The manner in which the written sequence of a text may anticipate the reader, or have an 'implied reader', is similar to the manner in which a sequence of images/sounds (or of scenes) may be thought to have an implied viewer. Just as a habituated reader brings certain predetermined strategies to reading, so too does a habituated viewer for understanding screen or stage performances. Real viewers naturally try to match their experience of the world to stage or screen performances, and so do real readers to written texts. I have observed earlier that the producers of literature in print target readers and market books in ways that influence how we think of literature; so do those involved in producing screen or stage performances.

To analyse the distinctive features of the viewer's relationship to the stage or screen will take more space than is available here, and in any case is not relevant here. Performances are of interest here only insofar as they are within literature, which means, as I observed in chapter 3, in terms of their relation to written/printed literary texts. Describing the characteristics of this relation is also a way of clarifying the differences between readers and viewers. Inevitably, that is also likely to put us in a position to characterise what is contemporary in performance from a literary perspective. The points in the box are a few that come to mind.

DIFFERENCES BETWEEN READERS AND VIEWERS

- *The obvious difference between a written text and an image (or clip from a movie, scene from a play) is that the latter can contain a lot more compressed and simultaneous information than the former.* Imagine, for example, a scene in a printed story where four characters are playing the Chinese game mahjong and chatting in a room. If this were a descriptive passage, there would be some attempt to render the setting vivid along with narrating what passed between the four. But, however carefully the text might dwell on this, it wouldn't be as vivid as it could in a film or on stage, which *is* visual. We will be able to hear the dialogues, observe the costumes, take in the decor of the room, take note of the light, and so on, simultaneously and almost instantaneously. What might call for several passages of reading to gradually obtain an impression can be very quickly conveyed on screen or stage. Also, where the written story is necessarily read in a linear fashion in a book, and therefore information is given in sequence, in the film or on stage several bits of information can be juxtaposed to acquire linked significance. In the film, for example, the arrangement of mahjong tiles on the table before the players may seem to signify something in relation to their exchanges with each other as those happen.

- Related to the above point: as readers, it is not as easy for us to gauge from the written text the time and space in which the mahjong scene occurs, as it is for us when viewing a performance of this scene. The text might give us only an inexact sense of the size of the room where the players are, and we often read dialogues without having a clear sense of how long the conversation might actually have lasted. In a stage or screen version, these would be as clear as they are in life. *The relation between fictional time/ space and real time/space is generally more loosely conceived by readers of written texts than by viewers of performances.*

- The written story can take the liberty of simply telling us clearly what is in a particular character's mind while she plays mahjong: thoughts and feelings that might not be apparent to the other three. This won't distract us parti-cularly from what's happening in the scene; we are used to this. In the film or on stage, this cannot be done easily, only perhaps by inserting some such laboured device as a voiceover or soliloquy (which may be distracting). A film trying to convey a character's thoughts while she is playing mahjong in this scene is likely to compensate for not being able to show them – by suggesting them through the actor's expressions and gestures, background music, and so on. *The devices for conveying and apprehending the psychology of characters are different for written text and performance.*

- *The perception of unorthodox writing is obviously quite different from what appears unorthodox in a live or recorded performance – these are different media and are received differently.* Conveying the unorthodox nature of a written text in a performance (or *vice versa*) can therefore pose particular challenges. If it so happens, for instance, that the written description of the mahjong players uses some made-up words (which are nevertheless understandable to readers); depends in some way on the sounds and rhythms of the narrative; or has fragmentary sentences and paragraphs, the effect of these on readers may be nearly impossible to convey to viewers of a stage or screen performance. That effect could perhaps be approximated by being unorthodox in terms of the viewer's expectations of what should happen in a performance.

These are merely a few indicative points; there are various other ways in which the differences between written text and performance, and therefore the possible relations between them, can be thought about.

Insofar as understanding what is contemporary in literature goes, some of the factors that are relevant to reading written texts (and discussed above) become comparatively less so where performance is involved. For instance, in examining how readers may read the opening sentences of the novel Q & A, we had observed that the reader may well have to think about the location and period, that these are key aspects of how we read contemporary literature and understand it as such. The text may seem to deliberately play with the reader's expectations in this respect: at the beginning of Q & A, the reader is left guessing and looking for clues until the fourth paragraph. In a film version, such as the adaptation Slumdog Millionaire, such strategies are of no importance to the viewer: the period and setting of the story is immediately self-evident, and the sense of this being a contemporary story (however exotic or familiar the setting might be) is immediate too. Similarly, where a past setting is evoked in a contemporary performance, there is less of a call on the viewer's knowledge of the past than is the case for the reader of a text. Going back to the example discussed in chapter 3: where the contemporary reader of Eileen Chang's story 'Lust, Caution' has to call upon some historical knowledge of Shanghai during the Japanese occupation to have a clear sense of the setting, the viewer of Ang Lee's film has less need of this. In brief, in this regard, written texts reveal sparingly, and viewed performances reveal superlatively.

In considering how the relation of literary text and performance impinges upon reception of contemporary literature, we do not need to dwell further on the minutiae of the process of viewing. We can move on to the broader contours of reception that are manoeuvred for, or that work upon, that relationship, with the above observations in mind.

To convey briefly what's involved in such broader contours of reception, let me go back to the novel *Q & A* and the film adaptation *Slumdog Millionaire*. The main protagonist of the former is a young man, orphaned in childhood, who manages to survive by his wits among the poverty-stricken and exploited rungs of Indian society. The novel is about how, despite his lack of formal education and general ignorance, he wins an enormous reward in a television quiz show by answering 12 consecutive questions correctly. By sheer coincidence, the questions happen to recall crucial moments in his life, painful experiences that fortuitously provided the answers to precisely those questions. The novel recounts these experiences after he is arrested on suspicion of having somehow cheated on the show. The device of improbable coincidence during a quiz show allows the novel to present a wide-ranging picture of what being down and out in India, mainly in cities such as Mumbai, Delhi and Agra, is like.

The device also helps to translate the specific social and cultural context of contemporary India for international audiences, because the particular format of the fictional quiz show is now familiar to audiences worldwide. It is based on the quiz show format that originated in Britain as *Who Wants to be a Millionaire* (from 1998), and has been adopted or adapted in different languages in over 80 countries (including India, as *Kaun Banega Crorepati*) – one of many instances of contemporary mass media programming depending on worldwide replication of successful formats. It provides a complex structure that many readers can therefore easily follow, and brings with it some of the sense of drama and suspense that has made the quiz format so very successful. The novel as written text already had a strong performance-based appeal.

In adapting the novel as *Slumdog Millionaire*, British director Danny Boyle thus started with a text which was already well disposed for audiovisual translation with an international audience in mind. The fact that the film (like the novel) has primarily (and somewhat implausibly) English dialogues, and its *Who Wants to be a Millionaire* format, ensured interest among UK, US and other

Anglophone audiences (especially in India, where it was also dubbed in Hindi). Given the setting, the Indian audience was no doubt of particular interest to producers of the film. The film took many obvious liberties with the novel, so that only some episodes and the main quiz show-inspired frame remained. To a great extent, these liberties were taken to render the film friendly to viewers familiar with formulaic Hindi films from the Bombay film industry (often called Bollywood). Bombay films have an enormously influential role at various levels in everyday life in India, and indeed a very considerable and widely dispersed following beyond India. The practices and expectations of such Hindi films provided another performance frame, overlapping with the quiz show format, through which to sieve the text for recorded performance. This frame happily resonated with the novel, too, since Hindi films and actors figured significantly in some parts of it. To some audiences, this aspect of the film would seem 'exotic', but in a way that coheres with the Indian setting, and that can be connected to one of the most easily identifiable of Indian cultural products – Bombay films. Others, more familiar with such films, would simply feel at home with it, despite its being in the English language.

That is not simply a technical matter. It is evident that the techniques of Bombay films are drawn upon numerously: certain dialogues and shots, the impossibilities that underpin the film plot in addition to the improbable coincidences of the novel, and the background music and dance sequence particularly recall Bombay film formulae for the cognoscenti. But beyond that, this is also a matter of appealing to the sensibilities and sensitivities of Bombay-film audiences. One of the noteworthy shifts between the novel and the film adaptation is in the representation of sexual oppression. The novel features a gay paedophile film star, a quiz-show host who is also a sadistic sexual predator, episodes of homosexual activity, and a parent molesting his daughter. None of these finds their way into the film. In the novel, the hero does not ultimately find love. He falls in love with a prostitute, who is savagely beaten by one of her clients (the quiz-show host) and made to disappear by her pimp. In the film, the hero's beloved does become a prostitute and a gangster's moll for a while, but in a typically 'feel-good' vein there is abiding love with a happy ending. At the level of sexual politics, to take one level of audience sensitivities, the film sieves out much that might have disturbed. The film was adapted to the standard audience expectations of Bombay films, and made to adhere to a familiar and safe formula.

In brief, taking account of international audience expectations of the television quiz-show format, and Bombay film audience expectations (at various levels, including in terms of sexual and social mores), determined shifts in the film relative to the novel. In such shifts, we are able to discern concessions made to the different expectations that audiences for popular contemporary literary texts and recorded performances habitually work with. In the case of adapting *Q & A* as *Slumdog Millionaire*, these shifts evidently worked for audiences. The superlative success of *Slumdog Millionaire* in the box office is a measure of audience expectations being met at both international and, particularly, Indian levels: for a while it topped the worldwide box office, and recorded one of the highest earnings for any Western release in India. The success of *Q & A* has been relatively modest (especially in India), and spurred largely by the film adaptation.

Other examples of related texts and films, dealing with other contexts, may work on audiences to completely different effect – this is no more than a particular, though suggestive, example.

ENGAGING WITH E-TEXTS

E-text literature simply feels contemporary to readers (in this section, by reading I mean a combination of reading, viewing and listening) in a way that talkies in the 1930s might have felt. Actually, e-texts appear to be more challengingly new now than talkies in the 1930s because their production, as observed in chapter 3, is not wholly controlled by publishing or media institutions. Literary e-texts therefore have an as-yet marginal air about them. Their availability to readers is often not mediated in an institutional manner, and they can be read without the usual trappings of organised publicity and opinion-forming strategies. They figure rarely in school and university literature courses at present, and are very seldom reviewed in papers and magazines. Scholarly studies of e-texts – still a modest number – invariably treat them as symptoms of a new phenomenon in literary production and reception, which are yet to fulfil the extraordinary potential of their medium.

At present, the e-texts that have been noted in systematic approaches to literature are those that resemble conventional ideas of literature in print (like Ryman's *253*, certain blogs, some fanfiction), rather than those that exploit the distinctive qualities of the e-text medium. In other words, the former have received attention because they can be easily transferred into print and produced in the conventional way by publishers. Or, at the least, they can be put in the spaces on the internet that are controlled by publishing and media corporations. But these are admittedly a minute fraction of an immense field of literary writing and reading. Literature in e-text is consequently still regarded as a cutting-edge matter, which hasn't quite made it into mainstream respectability.

That may be oft-averred, but there is little doubt that e-text literature cannot be disregarded in any systematic study of contemporary literature. On the contrary, its inventiveness and newness seem to call for particular attention. This was evident in some of the points I outlined with regard to literary production in e-text, and can be reiterated here by elaborating on the corresponding receptive dimension. In making the relevant points in chapter 3, I have in fact already taken account of reading to some extent. The following two points recall those and briefly chart their implications further.

1. ACTIVE READING

If we recapitulate some of the observations about e-texts in the previous chapter, they come down to essentially one predominant feature with regard to reading: *readers can be more active in engaging with e-texts than with print/written texts*. The e-text could enable and encourage the reader to read in a non–linear manner, to jump back and forth between different e-texts, to juxtapose writing with sound and images, to annotate variously, to manipulate the text, to leave a comment for public consumption, and so on. Any one of these possibilities effectively enables the reader to do something that readers of printed text usually don't.

From the literary reader's point of view, the additional scope for work in reading e-texts could be understood in a number of more or less coherent ways. On one hand, these may seem to liberate the reader, and conventional reading may consequently appear to be comparatively constrained and limited. On the other hand, these could be regarded as unnecessarily undermining our appreciation of literature, our grasp of the aesthetics of literature, which are tied to writing and print. Some may argue that the greater amount of work that the reader does in reading e-texts, work that may even involve manipulating the text, dilutes the distinction between author and reader. Others might feel that the reader's sense of being more autonomous, almost an author, is illusory. A great deal of the authorship of e-texts is not immediately apparent any longer, because it doesn't consist simply in putting written text on paper. It consists in processes that are less visible and that readers are less aware of, like writing programs, offering or not offering hyperlinking options, and so on. Perhaps it is the e-text reader who is tacitly manipulated more comprehensively and unwittingly than the reader of printed texts.

2. COMMUNITIES AND ACTIVISM

The possibilities of communicating and building networks across all sorts of territorial boundaries have had a substantial impact on reading e-texts.

In some cases, these processes have led to the consolidation of reading and writing communities that existed before the development and wide-scale accessibility of the internet. Fan communities particularly come to mind. Fans of certain authors, books, films, television series, and so on, used to read in a specialised way and produce writings inspired by the texts they admired by actually meeting at fan events, or producing magazines (fanzines). With technological advances for social networking, such fan communities have naturally grown, and for some popular texts (such as the *Harry Potter* series, Tolkien's *Lord of the Rings*, Japanese manga comics) these are often numerous and large international collectives. In such circuits, there is a constant production and flow of creative e-texts, inspired by the admired original, which are written and read by fans. Such production and reception has been so prodigious that 'fanfiction' is now regarded as a specific genre, which is often discussed in terms of a distinctive jargon. Equally significant is the growth of similarly extensive fiction e-communities (primarily), and communities of bloggers (often around a theme). I have mentioned some efforts by internet firms to structure these for profit generation in chapter 3.

Interestingly, *international literary e-communities can occasionally mobilise themselves or be mobilised for certain kinds of literary activism.* Such mobilisation can take place against the control of corporations over production, or for social causes. For example, when the corporation Warner Brothers sought to control the use of the Harry Potter brand in fan websites by issuing closure notices in 2000–01, one of the largest fan networks – The Daily Prophet – called for a boycott of all Warner Brothers products. In that instance, Warner Brothers capitulated by largely withdrawing the notices. The same network started a literacy campaign in 2008, claiming that exchanges around Harry Potter fanfiction may encourage youngsters to cultivate literacy where existing education systems are failing them.

Such activism can also take a more explicitly political turn. As the arguments for and against military invasion of Iraq by the US and UK governments were raging in early 2003, for instance, several compilations of anti-war poetry were produced, used in demonstrations, and figured in petitions. One of these was published as a freely accessible e-chapbook anthology entitled *100 Poets against the War*, edited by Todd Swift (27 January 2003), using responses to a call issued through the internet. Similarly, Sam Hamill posted an electronic request for anti-war poetry in late January 2003 and received responses from 11,000 poets; organised (through the website www.poetsagainstwar.org) a day of anti-war poetry readings in USA and elsewhere on 12 February; and arranged for a collection of 13,000 'peace poems' to be handed to various government representatives on 5 March. A selection of these, edited by Hamill, was later published in print under the title *Poets against the War* (April 2003). In both these cases, circulations of e-texts across a range of literary communities were crucial.

What such general observations do not convey are the considerations involved in engaging with a particular e-text. There are, of course, numerous kinds of literary e-text, and how we receive any one depends on the preconceptions we have about that particular sort of e-text (analogous to studying a specific poem in terms of our preconceptions about the genre of poetry). A considered typology of various kinds of literary e-text is bound to take considerable space, and is beyond the scope of this book (see Further reading). But a simplified, twofold division of types, clarified by one example, could be helpful.

A fairly straightforward distinction can be made along the lines mentioned in passing above: between *e-texts that resemble conventional print texts, and e-texts that use their medium in unexpected and innovative ways.* The former are less work for a reader, and readers can become habituated to their e-text characteristics relatively easily. A critic who approaches certain personal blogs as literary texts, for instance, can quickly adapt preconceptions about the conventional personal diary or journal to analyse these. All that this critic has to do is think about what reading and writing texts on the internet involves (also already a habitual business for those who surf the internet regularly), and determine how these may modify preconceptions about the conventional personal diary. However, *when faced with a literary e-text that uses its medium more inventively, so as to create something that seemingly doesn't resemble any conventional print text, the critic would probably need to go back to basics – start reconsidering the nature and scope of literature, the fundamental structures of reading and writing, and so on.* This is more work for the systematic reader. Such literary e-texts are most likely to be in hypermedia form, similar to the e-poem 'The Hugo Ball' discussed in chapter 2.

By way of an intriguing example of the latter, Nanette Wylde's 'Storyland' (first version 2002, second 2004, at www.preneo.com/nwylde) can be considered. It was included in the Electronic Literature Organization's *Electronic Literature Collection*, Volume 1 (Hayles *et al.*, 2006). As with 'The Hugo Ball', this cannot really be quoted, and is best experienced at first hand. The useful brief description given by the author to introduce it in the collection reads as follows:

> *Storyland* (version 2) is a randomly created narrative which plays with social stereotypes and elements of popular culture. Each sentence is constructed from a pool of possibilities, allowing each reader a unique story. The reader presses the 'new story' button, and a story is created for that moment in time. It is unlikely that any two stories will be identical. *Storyland* exposes its narrative formula thus mirroring aspects of contemporary cultural production: sampling, appropriation, hybrids, stock content, design templates. It risks discontinuity and the ridiculous while providing opportunities for contemplation beyond the entertainment factor.

In other words, the first screen opens with a (somewhat surreal) story which is revealed gradually sentence by sentence, and seems to feature stock characters and familiar — clichéd — phrases from popular literature, television shows, films, and so on. When the 'new story' button at the bottom is pressed, the screen goes blank for a moment, the colourful 'Storyland' title at the top flashes with a musical jingle in the background (reminiscent of advertisements or cartoon shows), and a new story starts appearing sentence by sentence. If this is repeated several times, the reader gradually perceives that though each story is different, all are composed of certain set phrases with subjects and objects and adjectives substituted.

There are several features in this e-text to challenge the literary reader. Like most e-texts, it invites interaction: in this instance, the simple physical task of clicking the 'new story' button whenever the reader wishes. The consequences of doing this are fairly radical though — the story changes entirely. There is no stable text to refer to and analyse; every time the reader presses that button, or leaves the text and returns to it, there's a different story. It thus works through a simple device to draw attention to the power of the reader over the story.

Bereft of a stable text to which the reader can return, the reader looks for something to link the constant flow of different texts. This is likely to make the reader wonder about her strategies for reading and her preconception of what a story is. It might reassure the reader that, despite the changing text, she can find certain stable elements, in repeated phrases and stock images and characters, across the different stories. That, in turn, might make the reader pause and ponder where this sense of stability is coming from, if not from a stable text itself. It might occur to her that, in fact, it derives from the shared context of popular culture — a general familiarity with popular fiction, shows, films, etc. In other words, it may seem that the context of reading confers a certain degree of coherence even to a constantly shifting text. At the same time, the reader may be struck by the idea that this e-text is a good demonstration of what a story generally is: perhaps essentially no more than variations within a limited range of expressions, forms and personae that readers are acclimatised to. The reader may feel pushed to consider whether that can apply to literature in other genres, not just fictional prose.

While such questioning of the reader's role and the structures of literature is under way, these questions also draw attention to the as-yet unusual e-text medium itself. Evidently, the technology that goes into making this particular e-text is quite different from the technology involved in print, or in live or recorded performances. Something more than simply writing in a language or performing an audiovisual scene is involved here. There are evidently well-defined formulae for mixing and combining phrases and subjects and objects and adjectives at work. To put it otherwise, the technology here involves juxtaposing writing with more or less tractable (even if not fully revealed) algorithms. That may lead the reader to consider whether this isn't in fact always the case in literary writing and reading (or indeed any linguistic communication). Literary writing and reading are always based on complex algorithms, which we are all so accustomed to and have internalised to such an extent that we don't think about them. Perhaps this hidden algorithmic level of the technology of all writing is simply being made visible here because the algorithms are simpler and therefore jar on our habitually complex expectations. Quite possibly, what we regard as literary reading and writing are no more than based on the distinctively literary nature of the algorithms for such reading and writing.

What such e-texts as Wylde's 'Storyland' push us to do is, in fact, to reconsider our deep-set understanding of what is literature and the means through which literature appears to us. These are actually fairly startling thoughts for the conventional literary reader to encounter; and many of us may feel that an e-text such as this is not really literature at all as we understand it at present. And yet, it does make us feel that there is something literary happening here: perhaps a new kind of literature is being prefigured, even if not fully realised, in such e-texts. I can think of no more concrete example of what dealing with something *contemporary* in literature could consist in. In fact, each of the e-texts chosen in the volumes of the *Electronic Literature Collection* gives rise to similar challenges and self-questioning for readers of literature, which clarify some of the limits and possibilities of contemporary literature.

REVIEWS AND CRITICISM

Reviews of particular literary texts that appear in magazines, newspapers, journals, radio or television culture shows, and so on, are usually understood as introducing and judging something new for readers. Passing judgement need not be a necessary component of a review, but it is often expected – reviewers' approbation is used by publishers and booksellers to publicise texts, and many readers look for guidance from reviews in choosing what to read. *The reviewer is in the useful position of being a reader mediating for other readers, setting the tone for how the contemporary in literature should be assessed and received. The reviewer plays this useful role by appearing to be somewhat more than a run-of-the-mill reader – assuming the role because her opinion is apt to be taken more seriously than those of other readers.* This might be because of her academic standing or credentials as a literary author and commentator, or perhaps simply because her views appear in a highly regarded publication. The reviewer therefore does her mediating by exercising a sort of readerly authority, and indeed by maintaining a tone of authority in the review. Of course, readers who are not perceived as having that sort of authority – thought of as 'ordinary' readers – are now also able to put their assessments and judgements in the public domain, primarily through the internet. Most internet book retailers encourage readers to leave review-like comments and judgemental ratings, and reviews galore are posted in blogs. But the reviewing spaces remain quite distinct: the authoritative reviewer's and the 'ordinary' reader's views appear in quite different places.

Critical interpretations of contemporary literary texts in scholarly books or journals usually appear well after the reviews, and serve a different purpose. Though they do play a part in making and breaking reputations and keeping some texts alive in the study of literature, these are seldom recruited for publicity or for mediating readers' interests in new literature. In general, these appeal either to readers who have already read certain texts and wish to obtain a deeper understanding of them, or to researchers and scholars with an (often professional) interest in some aspect of contemporary literature. *Such critical interpretations take a more considered view of the text than a reviewer might, by:*

- *reading it carefully within relevant broader contexts (other books by the same author, other texts on related themes, trends in contemporary literature, specific theoretical approaches to texts, and so on); and*
- *looking closely at the text itself and discovering nuances and implications that may not be evident in a less careful and informed reading.*

Most critics acknowledge that these two dimensions of critical interpretation are inextricably linked: knowledge of broader contexts is needed to discern textual nuances, whether obvious or not; and, equally, close attention to specific literary texts feeds into a critic's knowledge of broader contexts. However, the latter dimension is more commonly emphasised in relation to critical interpretation. The notion that there are inexhaustible hidden or unobvious depths in literary texts, which the skilled interpreter may tease out, has been the mainstay of literary criticism. Teaching and learning critical interpretation is therefore thought of as not simply a matter of gathering information on the history of literature, on a large number of literary texts and scholarly works, and so on. More importantly, it is believed to involve analytical methods for, and experience of, reading so as to delve beneath the skin of literary texts – to understand texts more deeply than an untrained reader might. The literary critic therefore usually exerts the authority of specialist knowledge.

On the face of it, reviewers and critical interpreters often seem to do very similar things, and are often the same persons. Similar kinds of background information and discernment of textual nuances may appear in a review and a scholarly paper. But the broad distinction made above is relevant. Let me try to convey the distinction in a limited way with reference to my own recent attempts at critical interpreting. Consider, for instance, two novels that appeared in the USA and UK, respectively, while discussions about the 2003 invasion of Iraq and its aftermath were occupying public attention: Nicholson Baker's *Checkpoint* (2004) and Ian McEwan's *Saturday* (2005). Baker's novel presents a discussion between two friends: one of them wishes to assassinate US President Bush for the violence unleashed in Iraq, and the other tries to dissuade him. McEwan's *Saturday* describes a day in the life of a distinguished London-based surgeon, which also happens to be the day of massive anti-war protests in the city. Reviews and critical interpretation of these – considered one after the other – involved the following distinctive sorts of approaches and observations.

1. REVIEWS

Both novels were received by reviewers in interesting ways. Reviewers of Baker's novel largely wondered whether it is permissible to write about, even fictionally, the assassination of the US President, and didn't seem particularly interested in the content of the novel. Their views were coloured by the political polarisations that the Bush administration and the invasion of Iraq had aroused. McEwan's novel was initially greeted by a spate of glowing reviews, until the novelist John Banville published an influential and damning response to it in 2005. Banville felt that the novel was badly written and ideologically suspect with regard to the invasion. These reviewers were influenced, in brief, by the overwhelming preoccupation with the situation in Iraq at the time, and tried to locate the novels as taking a position with regard to it. It was obvious that reviewers don't necessarily concur in their judgements, just as readers generally don't. And, evidently, reviewers try to assess texts in terms of what seems to be relevant when the text appears. The point is not to be preponderantly informative or analytical, but to be so to the extent that the text under review would be received as immediately relevant – at the cutting edge of contemporary literature.

2. CRITICAL INTERPRETATION

By the time I attempted a critical interpretation of the two novels (Gupta, 2011), I had a somewhat different objective. I had more space, to begin with, than a reviewer usually has. I had the advantage of being aware of the debates between those reviewers. I knew that my readers would be limited to well-informed, literary readers (usually academic). My sense of the newness and relevance of these novels was not quite as immediate: I situated these amidst other literary texts from that context, with hindsight about how that conflict progressed, and so on. Rather than thinking of them immediately as new and at the cutting edge, in other words, I had them contextualised against broader themes of war and literature. In discussing these, it seemed to me that, in one respect, they were similarly structured: both were carefully designed to make it impossible to attribute a clear pro- or anti-invasion agenda to their author. They had been structured, I argued, precisely to avoid the kinds of attributions that their reviewers made. That seemed to me to contextualise these novels *and* their reviews at the same time. My critical interpretation did something that would have been of little interest to reviewers or readers of reviews when they appeared.

As I have indicated above, *one of the grounds that is shared by reviewers and critical interpreters is that they both seem to speak with authority. For a systematic approach to contemporary literature, it is expedient to be aware of where precisely this authority derives from, and to be able to question any apparently authoritative statement.* No systematic study can take any authoritative statement or any authority as infallible. There is no reason to be overly suspicious of literary reviewers' or critics' claims of literary authority: it is understandable that those who have had the time to inform themselves of literary matters and analyse texts are more likely to offer useful insights than those who haven't. That is saying no more than, for instance, that I am justified in trusting an experienced plumber more than one who offers to cut his plumbing teeth on my leaking pipes. But claims of such literary authority are often not based merely on information, analysis and experience, and it is worth contemplating how the following play in reviews and interpretations.

1. LANGUAGE OF AUTHORITY

The voice of authority is often borne by the confidence with which judgemental statements are asserted. If a statement such as 'This is a luminous and powerful work of fiction' or 'This poem is infantile waffle' comes with an argument to back it up, then of course the reader is in a position to dispute or accept it in a considered fashion. If it is merely stated with complete conviction, it may sound authoritative, but without reason – the opposite might be said with equal conviction and will be no more or less meaningful. Such confident but unsubstantiated statements appear often in reviews, and sometimes in scholarly papers and books. Confidence, in such instances, is mainly a matter of syntax, and depends on whether statements are constructed in tentative, qualified or imperative ways. A great deal of mediation of contemporary literature for readers seems to be based on confident judgemental statements given in an authoritative manner, and they seem to be taken seriously. Publishers and booksellers know this well, and often pick out such approbatory statements from reviews (deliberately disregarding any arguments given) for publicity.

But it isn't merely in such obvious ways that the language of authority carries unjustified weight. Sometimes, particularly in academic writing, the manner in which arguments are presented may seem to weigh in authoritatively irrespective of what the argument says. So, carefully depersonalised expressions, the use of technical-sounding terms, a sprinkling of footnotes, etc. (academic discourse), seem to confer scholarly status in themselves. These are, of course, all significant insofar as they relate to what is said, but not otherwise. Thus depersonalised expressions are necessary to maintain an objective stance in presenting arguments; technical terms usually have precise connotations, which it would be tedious to repeat constantly; it is necessary to show how an argument relates to existing arguments, hence footnotes; and so on. It is not the conventions of academic discourse that make them meaningful, and no authority rests in being able to use them; it is the purpose for which they are used that is significant.

2. STANDING OF AUTHORITY

We often take a review or critical observation more seriously if we know who is saying it: for instance, if it issues from the pen of a well-known novelist or a distinguished professor. Our inclination to be taken (or taken in) by confidently pronounced judgement or poker-faced academic discourse is considerably strengthened if we feel that these come from someone who is entitled to use them. Such public or institutional standing inspires trust, in much the same way as I may feel inclined to trust an experienced and qualified plumber rather than an inexperienced novice. Depending on trust in this manner might be useful for readers who are not being systematic about their study of contemporary literature. That's similar to my trusting a plumber of standing rather than a novice – I have to fall back on trust rather than knowledge because I am ignorant of plumbing. However, for a systematic understanding of literature, especially contemporary literature, public or academic standing has little weight. As a rule, reviewers and critics of good standing are perfectly capable of making rash judgements and being desperately wrong in their arguments.

3. THE AUTHORITATIVE SOURCE

We are similarly inclined to read a review that appears in a highly regarded magazine or television programme, or a critical study in a prestigious journal, more seriously than those in less-well-known sources. This is similar to my having more respect for a plumber who can show me a certificate of membership in a venerable trade association than one who can't – I assume that he must have met certain standards to have been accepted there. Similarly, it can be assumed that a rigorous selection and assessment process must have been met before something appears in a respectable source. This is not unreasonable for the cursory and unsystematic reader, but for a systematic approach, the authoritative source has as little weight as the reputation and academic credentials of a reviewer or critic. *All* that is of moment for such an approach are the information, evidence and arguments that are offered.

It might seem that these points are fairly obvious, and in any case apply to the study of literature generally, rather than to contemporary literature particularly. And perhaps I have taken an overly didactic, finger-wagging tone in making them (as Dr Guru acidly observed on reading this). It is, of course, up to us – readers of this book – to decide whether or not these are reasonable and relevant points. But they do raise issues that are of particular moment for studying contemporary literature. Reviews, as I have noted, are designed to mediate between contemporary texts and readers. Usually relatively few interpretive texts are devoted to specific contemporary literary works; so doubtful assertions of authority may be accepted too easily in the few that are available. Where a range of interpretations have discussed a literary text over a considerable period – a text that is therefore not quite contemporary any longer – readers have more considered perspectives and alternatives to judge by. Otherwise, we have to depend on the persuasiveness of analysis and relevant information that supports such critical readings.

READING TRANSLATION

In chapter 1, I presented arguments against confining our reading to only contemporary literature in original languages, and in favour of extending our reading to translations too. I observed that most of us take recourse to translated texts because we don't know the original language in question. Translations should be read with an awareness of reading in translation – but not in the way a student of translation (someone doing Translation Studies) might. A student of translation would actually need to know the language of both the original and the translated text (source and target languages) to understand how they work in relation to each other, why the translator has made the choices she has, and so on. These considerations are not really material to those of us who are reading in translation because we don't know the original language. Nevertheless, I noted in chapter 1 that, for our systematic approach, we do need to be aware of translations as translations. Though I have blithely discussed translated texts above without further ado, what reading a translation as a translation implies when we don't know the original language could be made clearer. Since the process of reading and reception is outlined in this chapter, it is appropriate to return here to the issue of reading translated literary texts. All the more so since our sense of the contemporary world, and therefore contemporary literature, is, as argued earlier, dependent on a constant flow of translations – reading translations has a crucial place in contemporary literature.

The implications of reading translations as translations are best considered by reading a specific translated text thus. To make the most of such an exemplary exercise, it makes sense to turn to a text in which the precise use of language is unavoidably important, and where translation could be a particular challenge. Poetry exploits all aspects of language (meaning, sound, figures of speech, etc.) to the maximum, and it is well known that written Chinese and English follow distinctive linguistic systems – so an English translation from a Chinese poem should serve well here. The following is Gregory Lee's translation (2008, p. 43) of the poem 'No Mourning for Language' by Duo Duo (originally published in 2003):

> No mourning for language
> The report of a detonation is the beginning of understanding
>
> Just give thunder this order – make no sound
> no accounting for wolves, no – yet another salvo
>
> > Let history tell lies, let the deaf monopolise hearing
> > Words, convey nothing at all
>
> Thunder is not thunder, silence is thunder
> Incomprehension – therefrom emerges the most stubborn culture

> Incomprehension, so the ocean is vast beyond comparing
> Incomprehension, so the whole world is one

There are apparently no obviously context-specific references or allusions here – no names of people or places, for instance. In reading the translated text by Lee, we may have such systematic observations as the following.

1. SOUND

In English, the aural qualities of the poem (sound to the ear) read smoothly. Similar sound-patterns (assonant and consonant) – such as mourning/report, wolves/salvo, lies/monopolise, incomprehension/ocean – mark an incantation-like movement. That quality is accentuated by the occasional rhyme (thunder/culture), and repeated words (thunder, incomprehension). The use of 'therefrom' sounds a bit awkward, and is possibly an attempt to keep a feature of the original text in the translated version – it is evidently used so that 'incomprehension' can be placed at the beginning of that line. But, on the whole, it works well as poetry in English; it sounds like poetry. Readers who do not know Chinese cannot know how close these qualities are to Duo Duo's original, but perhaps there is something of this incantation-like quality in the original. Our ears, at any rate, associate such a quality with this poem, without necessarily knowing whether that should be attributed to Duo Duo or Lee (or both).

2. SENSE AND STRUCTURE

The poem plays between the apparently opposite notions of meaningful language and incomprehensible sounds/silence. These apparently opposed strands are switched. On one hand, the switching suggests that language is dead (but not to be mourned), meaningless (like the deaf listening, words conveying nothing), and misleading (so that history lies). On the other hand, sounds without words (detonations, thunder) or silence, and their obvious consequence (incomprehension), are meaningful. It is the latter that gives rise to something sustainable (stubborn culture), and apprehensions of greatness (the vast ocean) and unity (one world). There is an air of momentousness about asserting the greater significance of incomprehension over meaning, largely due to the loud, warlike associations (in English) of detonations, thunder and wolves. As readers, we would generally expect this reading of the sense and structure of Lee's translation to be close to Duo Duo's original. In a common-sense way, we usually feel that the ideas/arguments in the original text are easier to convey in translated versions than their aesthetic or poetic qualities (such as how it sounds).

3. IMAGES

This could work in various ways, depending on how culturally aware and informed we are, and what associations we bring to our reading. Speaking for myself, for instance, I was especially interested in the image of the (oft-repeated) thunder. It is brought up in a strikingly paradoxical fashion: 'Just give thunder this order – make no sound'. It is paradoxical, of course, because thunder *is* sound. But also, from my non-Chinese perspective, the idea of giving an order to thunder seems to go against the grain of mythical associations – for instance, the Greek god of thunder Zeus, or the Hindu god of thunder Indra, usually do the ordering. I might feel that is part of the paradox. But a look at a reference book on Chinese mythology suggests that the Chinese god of thunder, Lei Shen or Lei Gong, carries out instructions from Heaven to punish wrongdoers. So the image here may well ring somewhat differently to those of us who are Chinese readers. Similarly, having recently read Jiang Rong's novel *Wolf Totem* (2004; translated from the Chinese by Howard Goldblatt, 2008), the significance of the image of wolves for a Chinese reader seems of interest to me. The novel explains in considerable detail Chinese perceptions of the image of the wolf as contrasted with those of Mongolian herdsmen from the steppes.

4. CONTEXTS

In English, the disaffection with language, history and apparently meaningful comprehension, and the desire to find meaning in their opposite – with a bang – seems quite understandable in the terms of our time. It could perhaps be an expression of feeling fed up about the manner in which people are manipulated by language (in the media, in advertisements, in political rhetoric, etc.). We may associate such manipulation by language as a characteristic of globalisation (of which more in chapter 6) and the spread of consumer culture. Uniting the world by incomprehension could be a symbolic way of opposing the apparent meaningfulness of global consumerist culture. This could well apply to the powerful growth of consumer capitalism in China, which is often discussed in the news within China and elsewhere. But, given the information (which appears with Lee's translation) that Duo Duo's earlier efforts as a poet were during the Cultural Revolution in China, and that he left China after the Tiananmen Square protests and clampdown in 1989, it seems likely that the disaffection is not simply confined to global capitalism. It could well be due to scepticism about existing and past ideologically restrictive regimes generally, whether communist, capitalist, or other, and an inexpressible desire for change. Such doubts and disaffections and desires are not unfamiliar in our time, whether we happen to be in China or in some other country.

Irrespective of how to – or off – the point these observations might be, they convey to some degree what's involved in reading a translation as a translation if we do not know the original language. *Being aware of reading a translated text here consists in undertaking, so to speak, a series of translations that are not linguistic. These involve bringing our sense of the different contexts in question, insofar as we understand the differences, to bear upon the text that we read. That could work at every level of our reading – aural and aesthetic, structure and sense, associations of images, relevance to context, and inferences made from these. Such awareness could lead us to inform ourselves more of the context we are unfamiliar with, or modify our sense of the one we feel at home in.* In such reading, we conduct in our minds a kind of debate between what we know, and what we guess, and what we don't have a clue about. Such reading, in other words, places the contemporary literary text in the midst of the world we are familiar with and live in, and that which is less vivid to us. We juxtapose our sense of differences and variations in the contemporary world in practical ways in reading texts in translation. As observed in chapter 1, that is the general character of contemporary life for most of us now, and we live knowingly or unthinkingly amidst a constant whirl of translations.

REFERENCES

Baker, Nicholson (2004). *Checkpoint*. New York: Knopf.

Banville, John (2005). 'A Day in the Life'. *New York Review of Books* 52: 9, May 26, 12–14.

Boyle, Danny, dir. (2008). *Slumdog Millionaire* (film). Los Angeles, CA: 20th Century Fox.

Duo Duo (2008). 'No Mourning for Language' (2003). Trans. Gregory Lee. *Wasafiri* 23: 3, 43.

Gupta, Suman (2011). *Imagining Iraq: Literature in English and the Iraq Invasion*. Basingstoke, UK: Palgrave.

Hamill, Sam, ed. (2003). *Poets Against the War*. New York: Thunder's Mouth Press and Nation Books.

Jiang Rong (2008). *Wolf Totem* (2004). Trans. Howard Goldblatt. London: Penguin.

McEwan, Ian (2005). *Saturday*. London: Vintage.

Swarup, Vikas (2005). *Q & A*. London: Black Swan.

Swift, Todd, ed. (2003). *100 Poets against the War*, 27 January. www.nthposition. com/100poets0.pdf

Wylde, Nanette (2004). 'Storyland' (2002). www.preneo.com/nwylde. In N. Katherine Hayles, Nick Montfort, Scott Rettberg and Stephanie Strickland, eds (2006). *Electronic Literature Collection*, Volume 1. Electronic Literature Organization. http://collection.eliterature.org/1/works/wylde__storyland.html

FURTHER READING

Books for further reading in chapter 3 on book history, performance, and e-texts also cover reception and reading, and thus are relevant here. The following are in addition to those.

IN A GENERAL WAY

Chartier, Roger (1995). *Forms and Meanings: Texts, Performances, and Audiences from Codex to Computer*. Philadelphia, PA: University of Pennsylvania Press.

ON READERS AND READING WRITTEN/PRINTED LITERATURE

Crone, Rosalind, Katie Halsey and Shafquat Towheed, eds (2010). *The History of Reading: A Reader*. Abingdon, UK: Routledge. [Wide-ranging collection of essays and extracts with sections on – among other areas – theorising

readers, reading communities, and individual readers. Includes writings by
Wolfgang Iser and Stanley Fish, who are mentioned above.]

Miall, David S. (2006). *Literary Reading: Empirical and Theoretical Studies*. New
York: Peter Lang. [Particularly useful discussion of the empirical dimensions
of reader–response, covering surveys and cognition.]

Squires, Claire (2007). *Marketing Literature: The Making of Contemporary Writing
in Britain*. Basingstoke, UK: Palgrave. [Has an account of the manner in
which British book publishing and distribution is affecting reading habits.]

ON READING TEXTS AND VIEWING PERFORMANCES

Brooker, Will and Deborah Jermyn, eds (2003). *The Audience Studies Reader*.
Abingdon, UK: Routledge. [Includes sections on cultural texts, gender and
reading, and interpretive communities.]

Fortier, Mark (2002). *Theory/Theatre: An Introduction*, 2nd edn. London:
Routledge. [Has a useful chapter on reader response and reception in relation to theatre.]

Schram, Dick, ed. (2009). *Reading and Watching: What Does the Written Word
Have that Images Don't?* Amsterdam: Stichting Lezen. [Collection of essays on
reading texts in relation to engaging with films, images, games and other
kinds of visual forms.]

ON READING E-TEXTS

Looy, Jan Van and Jan Baetens, eds (2003). *Close Reading New Media:
Analyzing Electronic Literature*. Leuven, Belgium: Universitaire Pers Leuven.
[A particularly useful introduction.]

Trend, David, ed. (2000). *Reading Digital Culture*. Oxford: Blackwell.
['Reading' is used in the broad sense of assessing the contexts of digital culture here.]

ON CRITICISM, REVIEWING AND AUTHORITY

Garrett-Petts, W.F. (2000). *Writing about Literature*. Peterborough, Ontario:
Broadview. [A guidebook for students aspiring to become literary critics.
I have not listed it here for that purpose, though, but because it gives a sense
of what academic discourse in literary criticism consists of.]

Hans, James S. (1992). *Contextual Authority and Aesthetic Truth*. Albany, NY:
State University of New York Press. [Considers literary concepts of
authority and authorship, and makes a case for context-specific aesthetic
authority.]

Pool, Gail (2005). *Faint Praise: The Plight of Book Reviewing in America.* Columbia, MO: University of Missouri Press. [Gives a view of the processes underlying book reviewing in the USA, and of the influence that reviews exercise.]

5

PERSPECTIVES AND ISSUES 1

SUPERSIGNIFICATIVE TERMS

In the previous chapters, we considered some ways of approaching contemporary literature in a systematic fashion. Chapter 1 discussed academic strategies for analysing literature generally, and how the contemporary fits therein; while chapter 2 reckoned with specific strategies for describing what is contemporary in literature. Chapters 3 and 4 charted factors that determine the production and reception, respectively, of such literature. Although these observations are exemplified with references to texts deemed, broadly, of our time (say, as this is written in 2011), the emphasis has been on understanding the area of contemporary literature flexibly. In other words, I have tried to discuss what seems contemporary now with a sense of what has been regarded as contemporary in the recent past and of what may come to be contemporary in the future. I have also attempted to present observations so that they may be meaningful in different linguistic and cultural contexts (despite writing in English). To a large extent, then, the emphasis so far has been on coming to grips with the broad idea of the 'contemporary' in relation to literature, rather than with enumerating literary perspectives and issues that *are* contemporary in our time.

In this and the final chapter we turn to literary perspectives and issues that are contemporary in our time. Such an enterprise appears to be fraught with difficulties. To begin with, even as I write 'our time' here, that time has, in an immediate way, passed, and with it whatever was contemporary then has become a tiny bit less so. It seems that, on the moving boundary of time, nothing that I could describe as contemporary perspectives and issues can remain so for long. By nevertheless doing so, I might now decisively have to limit the flexibility and openness to contexts and developments that I have been courting so far.

Moreover, examining contemporary literary perspectives and issues appears to raise the prospect of engaging with a survey of these. I have argued on several occasions against using surveys, and indeed thinking in terms of surveys, to approach contemporary literature in a systematic and yet broad and open way. But it does seem impossible to say anything about perspectives and issues without enumerating them or offering a list of some sort. In doing so, however, I am apt to find myself in the uncomfortable position of contradicting arguments offered earlier. Distressing questions seem imminent: How comprehensive does a list of perspectives and issues need to be? Since I do not have too much space in hand, how can I sensibly limit my list? Is it possible to come up with any list that can meaningfully convey something as broad as contemporary literature in general? Would not any list be based on retrospection, rather than noting what's ongoing and potential? And so on.

A listing of perspectives and issues is inevitable for our purpose, however. For literature, these are obviously an uncontainable plethora; anything that happens in life, or that can be imagined, might appear in contemporary literature (love, death, war, business, madness, travel, childhood, crime, disease, gardens, forests, kinship, friendship ...). And any such literary theme could naturally be sieved through contemporary perspectives, be coloured by present-day concerns and attitudes in different locations, irrespective of how universal or timeless it might seem. Naturally, the list I offer below is not of that sort, and it is still designed to keep observations open and flexible. In brief, I thread this discussion of contemporary literary perspectives and issues by focusing on what may be called *supersignificative terms*. The advantages of doing so become clear as I explain what such terms are.

The supersignificative terms I have in mind are of three sorts: those that enable various kinds of analysis (e.g. 'everyday life', 'ideology', 'identity'); those that refer to analytical frameworks (e.g. 'postmodernism', 'postcolonialism', 'globalisation'); and those that refer to oft-debated issues (e.g. 'news', 'human rights', 'environmentalism'). What brings these quite different sorts of terms together, to my mind, is that they are supersignificative, by which I mean that they share the following features.

- Such terms appear to be immediately meaningful and relevant in a large number of different contexts, and are used in, and travel easily across, a range of national, linguistic and cultural boundaries. They appear constantly in this fashion in the mass media, academic writings and discussions, and institutional deliberations. Such terms often enable forums for exchange and for the formation of alignments across variously located groups.
- Supersignificative terms are accommodative of different contexts. In other words, while maintaining a broad integrity, they can be applied with different nuances in different contexts. Terms such as 'identity', 'environment' and 'globalisation' can be understood with different emphases, depending on where and in what language they are evoked. They acquire a clear and definite application in relation to local circumstances, while remaining loosely understandable across languages and locations.
- Supersignificative terms accrue connotations in a fluid manner. Put otherwise, such terms gather an expanding range of applications and meanings with use. The more they are used in different circumstances and contexts, the larger the range of meanings and applications that they extend to. Thus, 'globalisation' had a fairly limited economic thrust in the 1970s and early 1980s, but gradually extended to processes concerned with political organisation, cultural production, communications and networks, changes in society, and so on – and continues to gather further nuances and suggest further connections as the term is used in different contexts.
- These terms are therefore difficult to define in a succinct fashion: they always seem to mean more than a succinct definition can suggest. If, for instance, 'globalisation' is defined as 'processes of global integration', that does convey its essential meaning. But it is also immediately evident to us that this isn't particularly helpful.

'Globalisation' can be understood only by thinking of specific processes and institutions in specific contexts, and with a sense of what it means for different areas (politics, economics, education, culture, etc.) in different periods, and by considering how it is used (by whom, why and where). At times, it might even seem that when we use the term 'globalisation', we are actually not really talking about 'global integration' at all, but about local concerns. A meaningful grasp of the term 'globalisation' can therefore follow only from a complex discussion rather than a succinct definition.

- Given that supersignificative terms are accommodative and fluid, it is not surprising that they seem to inform each other and overlap. *Discussion of these seems often to be conducted by relating them to each other*: in conjunctions like 'postcolonial identity' or 'environmentalist ideology', or in juxtapositions like 'globalisation and identity' or 'postmodernism and everyday life' or 'everyday life and the environment', and so on. Between them, supersignificative terms can be brought to bear upon specific themes, such as love, death, war, business, madness, travel, childhood, crime, disease, gardens, friendship, and so on.

- Each of the above features of supersignificative terms suggests that we regard such terms as particularly resonant in our time. These are terms that we use thus because *they seem to us uniquely useful to describe contemporary lives and times and experiences*. These terms don't really name something, or refer to a specific idea or act that is out there; they gesture towards the complex dimensions of the contemporary world we live within. In brief, we use such terms to be able to articulate what is contemporary for us, and equally we confirm our contemporary awareness by using such terms.

For a systematic rendering of the perspectives and issues of contemporary literature, supersignificative terms provide a useful way in. They present the possibility of making a relatively manageable list, and they bear upon most perspectives and issues of literary interest. The relationship of literature to such terms inevitably involves an apprehension of the contemporary – such terms have, by definition, a particular contemporary resonance.

A discussion of these is, however, more easily thought of than undertaken. Identifying relevant supersignificative terms for discussion is the first step, and I feel I have done this already: those given above in an exemplary fashion are examined here. This chapter and the next discuss the following by turn: everyday life, ideology, identity (supersignificative terms that enable analysis); postmodernism, postcolonialism, globalisation (terms referring to analytical frameworks); and the news, human rights, environmentalism (examples of oft-discussed issues). 'News', which appears in the latter category, is discussed first below in relation to 'everyday life' – they seem to me to be mutually clarifying. It is impossible that the discussion of any of these can be anywhere near adequate in the space we have. Each term evokes too complex a field of meanings and applications to be conveyed here, and many volumes have been devoted to each of them. The discussion here is naturally indicative rather than adequate, and follows a consistent pattern. Each term is discussed below in relation to one specific work of literature, with a view to clarifying *some* of the salient points of debate centred on that term. In the process, I expect a reasonably systematic understanding of the perspectives and issues of contemporary literature to emerge – an understanding that can then be extended to other themes and contexts and cultures and texts, and to other supersignificative terms.

EVERYDAY LIFE AND NEWS

Gordon Burn's novel *Born Yesterday: The News as Novel* (2008) is an extended fictional treatment of news that was reported in Britain over the summer of 2007. The novel was conceived, as the dust-jacket blurb says, on the understanding that news itself has increasingly become fiction-like, and that the boundary between reality and fiction is blurred in news stories: 'The news – all news now – is essentially fiction: an accretion of rumour, surmise, spin and speculation gathered around a tiny nucleus of verifiable fact. There is increasingly little of what, back in the days pre-dating the world-wide web, the blogosphere and rolling-news channels, used to be thought of as the plain, unvarnished truth.' In exploiting the fictional aspect of news, Burn's novel appealed to readers who had a shared sense of the news in 2007. The author noted in the Acknowledgements that the novel was addressed to readers who would recognise its themes as recent news: he intended 'for yesterday's news to become a novel while the events and characters it depicted were still fresh in people's memories' (p. 215).

The various themes of the novel, which would recall the news of summer 2007 in Britain for those who followed it, include Tony Blair's stepping down as Prime Minister in favour of Gordon Brown; the disappearance of a three-year-old child, Madeleine McCann, in Portugal and the complicated investigation that followed; attempted car bombings in Glasgow airport and central London; the beginnings of a crisis in the banking sector; and a host of more fleeting newsworthy items of interest. These are interwoven in an extended narrative, at times in a first-person voice, at others from the point of view of one of the characters, and often from an omniscient narrator's perspective.

The treatment of these newsworthy characters and events in the novel is distinctly un-news-like. The language of news is a distinctive one, which we generally recognise immediately as such: it seldom deliberates in an in-depth way on characters and their feelings and motivations; usually affects a factual and to-the-point air; and comes with preconceptions of significance (arising because some celebrity or public figure is involved, because the reported event could have large-scale consequences, because an event informs us about public-interest matters, because something unusual is perceived, etc.). Burn's treatment of the familiar newsworthy figures and events from 2007 deliberately eschews these strategies and gives them a novelistic turn. *Born Yesterday* often makes links and draws on information beyond the remit of news stories; imagines what a figure in the news might have felt or thought; and describes characters and locations in an impressionistic fashion. Much of the novel seems to read what's *behind* the news stories and images – seems to be *about* the news – in a manner that is not likely to be found *in* the news. For example, in describing a photograph of Prime Minister Gordon Brown visiting a factory, we find the following observations:

> Brown's grin was fixed, as always, as a grimace; there was some gurning, a movement that suggested chewing, the clearing of a shred of tomato skin maybe from in front of his bottom teeth; a hint that if anything upset his rather delicately balanced equilibrium he could at any second and without warning revert to being Bad Gordon – the Gordon of

kicking the furniture and control-freak tendencies; meanspirited, domineering; the Gordon of the shaking hand, the clouded mien, prone to sudden and terrible rages.

(p. 90)

This definitely reads more like fiction than news. From the news photograph (and many news items of the time), a personality is inferred, a psychological portrait is drawn, as an imaginative reader – or an able novelist – might. This passage, and the novel as a whole, accentuates what can be made of the news, and what the news leaves unsaid.

Burn's interesting play on news and fiction leads towards some inferences that are to the purpose here – which brings us to the other supersignificative term in the subtitle, 'everyday life', from a tangent.

1. EVERYDAY LIFE AS THE HORIZON

The novel raises an obvious question: what is it about events and persons that render them significant enough to feature in the news? The blurb and passage quoted above give some hints. *The news extrapolates what appears to be significant from an ongoing flow of interactions and events*, which includes routine and habitual doings and exchanges, the kind of quick surmises and assessments that enable us to lead our daily lives, amid our daily movements and spaces – in shops and offices and homes and streets. Equally, *the news confers significance by selecting certain events and persons from this ongoing flow of interactions and happenings*. As against much that is trivial or commonplace in this everyday flow of our lives, the news brings up events that are significant because they have a public appeal or impact. These seem to deserve more general attention than we would give to an ordinary personal or small-scale happening. That everyday flow against which, or from which, the significant and newsworthy arises can be thought of as 'everyday life' in the first instance. *Everyday life forms a horizon of our enormously complex and lived existence against which what is significant is understood as such – by becoming newsworthy*. That can be extended further: matters of historical significance, for instance, extrapolate the significant or confer significance in a similar fashion, only with a more retrospective and wider view than the news. News is more immediate.

2. WHAT IS LEFT OUT OF THE NEWS

Burn's novel shows that *by extrapolating the significant or conferring significance, the news also leaves out many aspects of everyday life that were necessarily involved when the newsworthy events and interactions actually occurred.* In a way, Burn's account could be regarded largely as a reinsertion of everyday elements into 2007 news stories. This involves taking into account the kind of quick assessments of personality that we constantly make when we meet others (much like the characterisation of Gordon Brown above), being sensitive to locations and atmospheres and moods, making associations with our own experiences, bringing in apparently unrelated information to understand an event, etc. – all strategies that Burn's news as fiction displays.

3. MAKING NEWSWORTHY

It can be inferred from the above that *what is significant and newsworthy amidst everyday life is not necessarily obviously or self-evidently so, but is made so by the manner in which news is selected and presented.* The perception of such significance has to do with how the news is produced and received. The blurb quoted above observes that it is the conditions of news production and reception (taking in the worldwide web, rolling news channels, etc.) that render news more akin to fiction. The autonomous rationale of newsworthiness is implicit in the conditions of news production and reception. Thus the news could be thought of as imposing a self-fulfilling structure on the complex and unstructured blur of everyday life.

4. NEWS AS EVERYDAY

Finally, inevitably news now feeds into how we live from day to day. This is the take-off point for Burn's novel: that, as noted in the Acknowledgements, contemporary readers of the novel would be aware of 2007 news, and bring that awareness to their reading. This would be natural since awareness of the news is part of our everyday life: we read newspapers or watch TV news daily, we discuss news items with each other and develop our view of the world accordingly, we sometimes respond to the news by being charitable or joining protests or worrying about our savings, and so on. *The news is so intimately and immediately enmeshed in our everyday life that it becomes an aspect of its unstructured flow.*

Throughout the twentieth century, particularly in the latter half, a great deal of effort has been devoted by sociologists, philosophers and others to developing systematic approaches to this most intractable and yet essential aspect of human existence: everyday life. Attempting this with reference to some more structured area of study – such as the news or history or psychology – is one of the ways in which this has been undertaken. That's the ploy we have worked with. Others have sought to identify areas within everyday life for particular attention, such as how day-to-day disaffections are expressed by people, what sorts of collective behaviour and performance can be charted, what is involved in popular culture and the use of language. *These attempts also press thinkers to sharpen their ideas about how they think: in other words, it makes them reconsider what they understand by the news or history or psychology, for instance.* At the same time, everyday life is always there, it is lived and talked about constantly, and it is in fact what we think of most immediately as our present. By its very nature, 'everyday life' is a supersignificative term that captures the many-sidedness of contemporary life.

One influential attempt to give a sociological account of everyday life, Michel de Certeau's *The Practice of Everyday Life* (translated from the French by Steven Rendall, 1984), notes the importance of reading and telling stories as everyday practices, and observes that literature can be regarded as 'a repertory of these practices' (p. 70). In fact, we do generally think of literary texts as close to everyday life as we live it. Therein we often find close renderings of exchanges, events, persons, interactions and feelings apparently as they might actually happen or might really be perceived and felt by us. *Literary texts frequently create the illusion of being records of everyday life.* Even when familiar (newsworthy or historically salient) themes and persons come up, as we see in Burn's novel, a sense of everyday reality is inserted in their depiction. Moreover, we read literary texts amidst our everyday life, which inevitably influences our reading.

In relation to approaching systematically what is contemporary in literature, a few briefly stated points related to the above observations are relevant.

- Observations above about gauging the contemporary in terms of familiar attitudes and idioms in literary texts, or in terms of the closeness of our lived experiences to the author's lifetime, are to do with our general grasp of everyday life. This sense of familiarity and closeness derives from how in tune we feel the text is with the often unremarked aspects of our day-to-day lives: what sorts of expressions we are accustomed to, what sorts of gadgets we are habituated with, what major (newsworthy) events have occurred, etc.

- In our reading of texts that are clearly not contemporary, we still naturally bring our everyday experiences to bear on them. So in reading, for instance, a Shakespeare play about a jealous husband, we may draw upon what jealousy means to us and the personal circumstances in which we have experienced jealousy. This is what gives a contemporary turn to whatever we read. That turn is exploited to produce contemporary adaptations of texts from the past in, for instance, live or recorded performances. These are the grounds on which I have included such adaptations as within the remit of contemporary literature.

- In previous chapters, I have noted how recent news is used in contemporary literature (for example, with reference to the 'war on terror'). Evoking recent news is a time-honoured way of evoking the contemporary. Burn's strategy of inserting or fleshing out the everyday dimensions of newsworthy events is in fact constantly found in contemporary literature.

- We could let accounts of everyday life in literature affect our everyday life. We may emulate certain characters from fiction, draw inspiration from verse, respond to current events with attitudes gleaned from a play, and so on. Just as reading and writing happens amidst the everyday, literature impinges upon the everyday.

IDEOLOGY

Orhan Pamuk's novel *Snow* (2002; translated from the Turkish by Maureen Freely, 2004) describes a visit by a minor poet, Ka, to the town of Kars to write a journalistic report on women who had allegedly committed suicide in protest against a government ban on headscarves. Kars, it turns out, seethes with contending political claims and commitments, which lead to dramatic confrontations when the town becomes snowbound and temporarily cut off.

The headscarf ban was one of the measures taken by the government of the secular republic established by Mustafa Kemal Atatürk in 1923, which followed a firm policy of modernisation along broadly West European lines (secular democratic nationalism with regulated capitalism). In *Snow*, the police, army, bureaucrats and upper classes of Kars (as of Turkey at large) ensure adherence to Atatürkian principles, while various political alignments define themselves against the ruling dispensation. There are radical Islamists (led by a character called Blue), who are convinced that the country should be governed strictly in line with Islamic tenets. They are prepared to take militant action against the government and more widely against what they regard as a hostile and imperialist West. They are responsible for an assassination, which Ka witnesses, and for championing the headscarf. There are moderate Islamic factions that, less aggressively, maintain that Islamic culture should prevail in public life although other faiths and groups have their place. Revolutionary socialists appear in Kars in the form of a theatre troupe led by Sunay Zaim. In snowbound Kars, they conduct a short-lived coup to establish a Marxist state. This is expected to work in the interest of the working classes and, through strongly centralised political and economic policies, to lead the way towards an equal society. But debilitating contradictions arise even during Sunay's brief period of power, all the more starkly due to his penchant for theatrical public gestures. Other factions with strong convictions focus on ethnic factors. A number of the minority Kurdish population, for instance, regard the Turkish government as an imperialist force; some seek an independent nation of their own, and are divided between those who combine this with Islamist convictions or with socialist ideals. Anarchists appear in the brew of political convictions, expecting a new order to emerge only after the current order is destroyed. And so on. Numerous differences fracture each of these political alignments, and simultaneously they are also often able to find some common ground across the widest divergences (for example with regard to Western imperialism).

Ka finds the charged atmosphere in Kars invigorating. Though his muse had been dormant earlier, in Kars he is driven to write particularly inspired poetry. The poems are described prosaically, but aren't actually transcribed in the novel, and are eventually lost. He falls in love, and at the end loses his lover İpek; he has numerous discussions on religion and art with different people, and is unable to decide whether or not he is an atheist; he becomes the mediator between revolutionary socialist Sunay and radical Islamist Blue, witnesses two assassinations and the coup, and observes violent public performances and clandestine meetings. After Kars, he takes refuge in Frankfurt, where he is eventually assassinated. The narrator notes that it wasn't clear who was responsible, but he 'heard quite a few conspiracy theories: he'd been assassinated by the Islamists, MİT, the Armenians, German skinheads, the Kurds, Turkish nationalists' (p. 386).

In a loose way, we usually think of terms like revolutionary socialism, secularism, radical religiosity, nationalism, anarchism, etc., as matters of ideology, and of ideology as something to do with politics. Or rather, we think of the systems, convictions and actions associated with those terms as ideological. At times we seem to think of ideology as restrictive, as a rigid and stifling imposition; at others we might have a more affirmative sense of ideology, as necessary for collectively reaching towards desirable goals; and sometimes we think of ideology in a neutral way, as something that is inevitably and pervasively embedded in all aspects of our social life even if we aren't aware of the particular ideologies at work. These loose notions and attitudes regarding ideology can be sharpened here by closer contemplation of *Snow* – with a view to understanding its supersignificative applications, contemporary resonances, and bearing on literature. In the process, some of the prodigious number of formulations and discussions of ideology in philosophical, sociological, historical, political, cultural and other kinds of studies are implicated. I don't mark them out specifically here; they are easily followed up through further reading. In each of the following observations on *Snow*, the relevant generalisation about ideology is italicised; together, they convey the relationship between ideology and contemporary literature to some extent.

1. IDEOLOGY ATTACHES TO A COLLECTIVE

In Kars, when different characters talk about and act upon ideological convictions – Atatürkian secularist, socialist, Islamist, ethnic nationalist, etc. – they usually have other people in mind and not simply their own unique situations and interests. Insofar as they proclaim themselves as socialist, secular, nationalist and so on, they speak of convictions that apply beyond their individual lives, to a group or collective of some sort (such as Kurdish, Turkish, Muslim, working class, women). *Ideology, in brief, has to do with convictions and systems that are relevant to how people are placed (or place themselves) as belonging to some group or other.* Of course, people can belong to several groups at the same time, so that some Kurds are Islamists and some are socialists, and some nationalists are Islamist and some are secular, and so on.

2. GUIDING PRINCIPLES AND BEYOND

Each ideological position seems to emphasise basic guiding principles: nationalists foreground the importance of allegiance to the nation and its legitimate citizens; Islamists espouse unswerving religious adherence to Islamic tenets; socialists emphatically seek equality through joint ownership and centralised planning. However, *each ideological position has wider implications, usually beyond what seems to be immediately relevant to its guiding principles.* Thus religious ideology is not confined to religious observance and institutions, any more than socialism restricts itself to economic administration. Ideologies extend widely from their core convictions to family life, education, legal systems, leisure and entertainment, and other areas of social and political life. With certain guiding principles, each ideology seeks to establish a general and consistent social order (which may or may not be accommodative of alternative guiding principles).

3. BY WHOM AND WHERE

How ideologies are expressed and acted upon depends significantly on where they are advocated and by whom. Kars has a particular history (as a town in north-east Turkey, with powerful influences from past Russian and Ottoman governance) and a particular mix of peoples in its population (along different lines, of Turkish and Kurdish ethnicity, largely Muslim, with different levels of affluence and education). These determine what seems ideologically expedient and immediately relevant to, say, Blue or Sunay Zaim. Ka's view of

Kars and its inhabitants is coloured constantly by its particular history, environment, and social and cultural life. At the same time, though, both Blue and Sunay have larger than local horizons implicit in their Islamic and socialist convictions, which extend to other contexts and even to all humanity in their view.

4. IDEOLOGICAL STATE APPARATUSES

Kars, like Turkey (or any context with a stable government and social order), has a dominant ideological set up: the Atatürkian secular republican state. *The dominant ideology is promoted and maintained by various mechanisms: through an army and police force; through legal, educational, financial, mass media, and other institutions and provisions; through propaganda and public works; and so on (collectively thought of as 'ideological state apparatuses').* Ka and others are constantly aware of such state apparatuses for maintaining the dominant ideology as they traverse Kars and meet. Beyond the dominant ideology of the Turkish nation, people such as Blue and Sunay are able to perceive a dominant global ideology too – that of the West or of international capitalism.

5. DOMINANT IDEOLOGY

Groups and persons locate themselves and their agendas in terms of the dominant ideology. Such groups and persons may think of themselves as opposed to, willingly or unwillingly subject to, or in sympathy with the dominant ideology. The events that motivate Ka's visit to Kars in the first instance (women allegedly committing suicide because of the government ban on headscarves) are regarded as opposition to the dominant ideology. The revolutionary socialist coup is an attempt to overthrow and replace the dominant ideology and its state apparatuses in snow-bound Kars. Some episodes in the novel are devoted to Blue's attempt to get different ideological groups in Kars (Kurdish nationalists, anarchists, etc.) to produce a joint statement against the larger ideological forces of the West.

6. COMPETITION OF IDEOLOGIES

Alongside positioning themselves in relation to (opposed or sympathetic to) the dominant ideological establishment, different ideological factions compete with each other. In Kars, this is a matter of passionate debates and confrontations arising from irreconcilable differences in principles. The Islamists' conviction in the superiority of those who subscribe to Islam, for example, simply cannot be reconciled with the egalitarian aspirations of socialists or the secularists' principled indifference to religion in matters of political and public import.

7. IN EVERYDAY LIFE

The range of co-existing ideological perspectives in Kars, which are all located apropos the dominant Atatürkian state ideology and simultaneously in competition with each other, *is intricately enmeshed in everyday life.* Ka's presence in Kars is registered in the local newspaper in both friendly and hostile waves, depending on the ideological tide of the unstable period he finds himself in. In an everyday way, conversations of all sorts and interpersonal relationships (even love) circle around the tensions of ideological commitments in Kars. Everyone's daily life in Kars accommodates or resists in small ways the structures that maintain the Atatürkian state ideology, and is thrown out of kilter by Sunay's brief revolutionary coup. Fear and acts of violence arising from ideological clashes pervade the air of Kars, and finally Ka's assassination becomes subject to various ideologically loaded explanations.

8. PERFORMANCE AND INTERPRETATION

In the public advocacy of ideologies, performance and interpretation are important. That many of the most dramatic political events and announcements in Kars are framed by public performances and texts — Sunay's coup, the assassination of Sunay, Blue's statement to the West — is no accident. Numerous interpretations of the news are often cited with amusing effect in *Snow.* In fact, the various characters in the novel perform their own ideological positions for others' benefit, and try to interpret each other's positions (in, for instance, trying to work out whether or not Ka is an atheist).

9. IN LITERATURE

It could be argued that literary texts are inevitably written and circulated and read amidst ideological arrangements and debates. Consequently, a systematic approach to literature cannot but seek to discern how ideological convictions may be reflected or evaded in literary texts. Ka's poems are composed in the midst of, and in response to, the charged political environment of Kars. Ideological nuances may be seen in them according to the reader's perspective. The novel deliberately thwarts such reading by not reproducing the poems (which are lost), and simply gives a carefully ambiguous prosaic account of each. In a way, the absence of Ka's poems itself accentuates our thwarted desire to interpret them so as to throw light upon Ka's own ideological leanings. As it happens, the tendency to discern ideological nuances in literary reading and interpretation was also a key theme in the reception of *Snow* itself. Much critical engagement with the novel has pondered the many ideologies which it depicts.

The italicised generalisations above about ideology, which are exemplified with reference to *Snow*, are obviously relevant to literary texts generally in their different contexts. These generalisations have been explored in relation to literature at large, and specific literary works, in numerous volumes. Since we are, much like the fictional citizens of Kars, always in the midst of ideological debates and dispensations of some description, we read and write literary texts accordingly. Understandably, our sense of what makes our world contemporary, and what is contemporary in literature, is intimately connected to the ideologies that surround us and impinge on our lives. A systematic study of contemporary literature therefore usually demands, in greater or lesser degree, some grasp of the ideologies of the present. At the least, such study calls for consideration of those aspects of the protean and supersignificative term 'ideology' that are relevant to the production and reception of literature now.

IDENTITY

The term 'identity' is now used in academic, media and other public discussions with particular (and particularly complex) connotations that would scarcely have registered in the early twentieth century. It still carries the conventional senses of being an official way of being identified (as in 'identity papers'), or of being a philosophical term related to certain abstract debates (on, for example, what does it mean to be an individual, and how does the mind recognise persons?). However, especially since the 1960s, the term 'identity' is more likely to evoke notions of *belonging to groups and of relations between groups.*

These could be geopolitical groupings (as in 'national identity'), or groupings according to beliefs and customs (as in 'religious or ethnic identity'), or groupings based apparently on innate or physiological markers (as in racial, gender, sexual identity). Each of these kinds of groupings, obviously, overlaps with others in complicated ways. More importantly, *talking about identity in this contemporary fashion implies considering the relations between such groups: in terms of minorities and majorities, power relations, rights and prerogatives, tensions and conflicts.* This means that talking about identity (almost inevitably when it comes to discussing literature) is now often a matter of talking about the politics of, and social attitudes to, identity. Identity has become a key term in contemporary ideological debates. The supersignificative ring of the term arises from these developments, and has been prodigiously discussed. Some of the key points of discussion are best picked up by considering an example – in this instance, with reference to a work of literature that relates text to recorded performance (a film).

Iranian director Abbas Kiarostami's film *Shirin* (2010) is composed entirely of shots of an audience at a performance (a film or play) based on a classical epic. We – the viewers – are shown the audience through a series of close-ups of women, generally one at a time, registering their expressions in response to the performance they are watching. There are some men in the audience, who are occasionally seen indistinctly in the shadows behind the foregrounded women. The women are of different ages, some young and others middle-aged or elderly, and all wear the headscarves or *chadors* that are obligatory in Iran. Throughout, we aren't given a view of the performance they are watching, but we have a reasonable sense of what's before them from the dialogues and soundtrack. In fact, the responses of the audience on screen and the progress of the film are tracked in terms of the story that unravels through the dialogues we hear, and the attendant sounds and background music. That we are generally accustomed to watching such performances means that we can easily imagine what this one might look like; and those of us who have some acquaintance with Persian literature will have no difficulty whatever following the episodes of the story being performed. The story is that of Khusraw and Shirin, of which many text versions (usually verse) from the medieval period onwards are available.

Since our only access to the performance that the women watch is through the dialogues and soundtrack, we have a strong sense of it as a written or recited text. This particular version of the story is obviously based on the poet Nizami Ganjavi's late-twelfth-century epic *Khusraw u Shirin*. The film credits, however, not Nizami's poem, but the prose adaptation thereof (1998) by novelist Farrideh Golbou (or Faridah Gulbu), whose novels are noted for dealing with the social condition of Iranian women. The screenplay for Kiarostami's film was adapted from Golbou's prose version by the author and director Mohammed Rahmanian. The Shirin, first princess and later queen of Armenia, of Nizami's poem is an exceptionally strong female character in medieval literature anywhere. She combines forthright passion and sexual allure with a determination to meet her lover Khusraw, prince and later king of Iran, on an equal footing. Though they fall in love in their youth, Shirin allows their love to be consummated only when Khusraw is mature and both have fulfilled their public responsibilities. Throughout, Shirin maintains the upper hand in their relationship. In the dialogues that we hear in Kiarostami's film, the story is told emphatically from Shirin's point of view, beginning and ending with monologues addressed to her weeping companions. She registers along the way the male 'childishness' of the lustful Khusraw, the 'games that men play' in war and power struggles, and in her final tragic monologue (after Khusraw is assassinated) asks her companions whether they are perhaps weeping 'for the Shirin that hides in each one of you'. Since the women in the audience, whom we see on screen, are also weeping at this point, these words seem to be addressed to them.

Our contemporary sense of the importance of identity could be brought to bear on our viewing/reading of Kiarostami's *Shirin* in several ways, which also highlight some of the key points of literary debate concerning identity. These are outlined below largely in terms of the questions we might ask ourselves when engaging with *Shirin*.

1. IDENTITY-BASED PERSPECTIVE

The obvious question that we may ask is: why does the film focus only on the female members of the audience? This ploy effectively focuses attention on the reception of the text we hear in the background along the lines of gendered identity – both individual (since each female spectator has an independent appearance on the screen) and collective (since the images of each work together with others to convey joint patterns in their responses). Collectively, all who are featured seem to become entirely absorbed in the performance, irrespective of age and background, and clearly identify with Shirin's vicissitudes: they brighten up when things go well for the heroine, weep when tragedy strikes, flinch when men fight and kill, and so on. The selective view of the audience also accentuates the gender dimension of the text/performance that they watch, the familiar (at least to this audience) story of Shirin and Khusraw. On the one hand, we may feel that it is the characterisation of Shirin in that story itself which engages the women in the audience thus. On the other hand, we might equally feel that it is because we are given access to the story through the gaze of women in the audience that the role of Shirin is emphasised. No doubt both possibilities are interlaced, and what we have is an apprehension of literary text and reception along gendered lines. In a general way, *the relevance of identity (gendered or other kinds) in a literary text may arise from either the content of the text or the associations brought by a reader/viewer, or, most likely, from both.*

2. ESSENTIALIST AND SOCIAL-CONSTRUCTIONIST

We may naturally wonder what characterises the gaze of the women in the audience as a specifically female gaze (if indeed it is that). What distinguishes and brings together female responses, and therefore suggests a gendered identity at work in engaging with literature? We could take two directions here. On the one hand, perhaps the women view the story in a gendered fashion because they are innately or biogenetically similar as women, and thus different from men. This is thought of as an essentialist understanding of gendered identity. On the other hand, perhaps the gendered perspective appears because the women viewers have been brought up to think of themselves and their role in society as women – they are conditioned by social circumstances to assume a gendered perspective. This is regarded as a social-constructionist account of their identity. A marked common denominator for the women we see in the film is that they all wear the mandatory headscarf or *chador*, which presents an obvious reminder of the *social* positioning of women in Iran. *Countless debates have sought reconciliations between, or differed vehemently on, essentialist and social-constructionist understandings of identity.* Essentialist accounts cause unease because they could undermine claims of equality between men and women, and yet occasionally essentialist accounts have been used strategically to counter essentialist assertions of male domination (by claiming defiantly, for instance, that women may be innately superior to men in some ways).

3. NORMS AND SYSTEMS

We may also find ourselves wondering about the role of those indistinct, shadowy figures in the audience: the men. If selectively observing the women in the audience accentuates gendered identity, this must have some relationship with male identity. The male perspective is obviously not presented directly in the film, but indirectly through the empathy that women in the audience feel with Shirin's character in the story.

Despite her royal status and real power (she does rule over her subjects), her relationship with Khusraw is complicated by his expectations as a man, and expectations of him as a man. He expects to dominate her, and is expected to demonstrate martial strength and engage in contests with other men. He regards Shirin in the first instance, and despite his love for her, as someone to be sexually conquered. Shirin's determination to meet on equal grounds (not to be a conquest and a prize) despite her love for him is an uphill task, and involves an exceptional assertion of will. In brief, both are caught in a male-dominated society (a patriarchal society) in which expectations of men and women (as conquering and subjected persons) are powerfully predetermined.

Thus it is evident that *social norms and systems are the basis of an unequal relationship along the lines of gender — and such norms and systems may also explain unequal relationships along the lines of race, class, religion, and so on, where they occur.* That the contemporary women, whom we watch, identify with the medieval character of Shirin as closely as they do shows that their situation is not dissimilar. We might feel that the indistinct male figures in the shadows are not individually identified because the patriarchal norms of society are embedded in the background rather than asserted by individual men.

4. RELATIONSHIPS BETWEEN IDENTITIES

It may occur to us that *each aspect of identity focused in a literary text may be understood in relation to other aspects of identity*. In *Shirin*, for instance, national identity is clearly related to gendered identity. The women in question here are Iranian, and respond in terms of circumstances in Iran. Their headscarves gesture towards the national context, a few decades after the 1979 Islamic revolution, living in a theocracy.

Yet other kinds of identity-based groupings that must be there in this audience do not have any marked role in the film; age, class, ethnicity (such as Kurd, Turkmen, Armenian etc. in Iran) do not have a distinctive part to play. We may wonder, however, to what extent the position of other identity-based groupings may be analogous to that of women. *Are there similarities in the relations between dominant and dominated groups along the lines of, for instance, race, sexuality, ethnicity, religion, and those along the lines of gender? What sort of joint commitments or disagreements may consequently arise between different identity-based groupings? These are questions at the heart of writing and reading literature in terms of identity*. 'Identity' is a super-significative term because it extends to such a wide and diverse range of groupings.

5. THE VIEWER'S OR READER'S IDENTITY

Finally, we may ask ourselves about our own responses to *Shirin*. The unusual experience we have of watching an audience watching a performance is likely to render us sensitive to our own position as spectators. That the depicted audience is focused in terms of gender might make us ponder our own gendered perspectives: do we bring our own male or female perspectives to bear upon our understanding of the classic *Khusraw u Shirin* and to Kiarostami's *Shirin*? Do we read and interpret the text in the background and the film we watch in terms of our citizenship, perhaps as Iranian, as Middle Eastern, as European, and so on? To what extent may our sense of our identities – as black or white, heterosexual or homosexual, Muslim or Buddhist – determine how we engage with this literary work? If we consider this systematically, we are likely to find that *an identity-led engagement with the literary work is also an engagement with our own identities, and therefore of how we understand our place in the contemporary world.*

The italicised sentences above highlight some of the general notions that have occupied thinking about and within different identities, and have influenced writing and reading of contemporary literature. Such notions are obviously and inextricably entwined with ideological considerations and experiences of everyday life now.

POSTMODERNISM

The supersignificative terms that are discussed in this section ('postmodernism') and the next ('postcolonialism' and 'globalisation', examined together at the beginning of chapter 6) have surfaced mainly through scholarly debates in literature and other areas. They often feature now in popular print and broadcast media texts (news features, documentaries, commentary and opinion pieces, serious chat shows, etc.), where they are used in less rigorous and more impressionistic ways. These terms refer to particular analytical frameworks for understanding the relations between contemporary ideologies, identities and everyday lives. However, analytical definitions of, and debates on, these terms are often superseded by their popular evocations; these terms increasingly refer loosely to social conditions and cultural processes that have an immediate contemporary resonance without needing to be carefully unpacked.

Postmodernist theories and critical perspectives were elaborated and debated primarily in the 1970s and 1980s, especially in the academic area of literature and cultural studies. In other areas, such as sociology and economics, the terms 'modern' and 'postmodern' are often used interchangeably, or not particularly distinguished. For our purposes, the following three quickly sketched points cover both the academic import and the popular resonance of postmodernism.

1. MODERNISM AND POSTMODERNISM

*Post*modernism seems obviously to refer to social conditions and cultural productions that appear *after* modernism. Though we might feel that 'modernism' and 'postmodernism' should refer to subsequent chronological or historical periods, in fact neither term has a firm chronological basis. Rather, they are before or after more in terms of the ideas they evoke than the chronological periods they may be associated with. Very briefly, *modernism is associated with social conditions and cultural products wherein a coherent perspective of the world is sought – a coherent way of linking all ideologies, identities and everyday lives of our time.* This could involve looking for an overarching ideology or a universal set of values (scientific, aesthetic, political, etc.). As opposed to that, postmodern conditions and cultural productions are regarded as unconcerned with the desire to find a single coherent perspective of the world. *Postmodernism involves being reconciled to having different and contradictory ideologies, identities and experiences of everyday life contending with each other and co-existing, and not needing to resolve these within any single coherent perspective.*

2. LITERARY DEVICES

Postmodernism, as differentiated from modernism, can be recognised in certain features of contemporary cultural products. *In developing a coherent perspective of the contemporary world, the modernist literary text often uses new (or 'experimental') devices that systematically undermine traditional literary expectations* (of plot and structure, characterisation, style, etc.). This could occur, for instance, in consistently using a stream-of-consciousness technique, or methodically playing with references to myths, or using language in a studiedly inventive manner. By contrast, *postmodernist literary texts deliberately cultivate inconsistency and an unsystematic appearance. Such texts often juxtapose incommensurable narratives, and court incompletion, dissonant images, contradictions (e.g. in plot, characterisation, style), fractured forms, irresolution, and so on. The result might be as startling and new as modernist texts, but in a distinctively pluralistic or multifarious way* (as opposed to a coherent way). This applies to other kinds of cultural products, too (films, visual arts, architecture). These cultural products seem to derive from and reflect our contemporary experience of everyday life, ideologies and identities, which themselves are often multifarious and incoherent, and we may feel that it is impossible to consolidate those into overarching frameworks.

3. UNDERLYING SYSTEM

Some thinkers (see Further reading) have persuasively maintained that the postmodern social condition, and cultural expressions thereof, are, despite appearances, due to a well-coordinated economic and political system − a contemporary capitalist system. Briefly, the argument is that the currently dominant capitalist economic and political system is coordinated by encouraging and enabling an apparent multitude of contending ideologies and identities, and incoherent experiences of everyday life. Since the capitalist system is increasingly ensconced in, or bears upon, most parts of our world, postmodernism also seems relevant to numerous contexts.

These three points are stated above in a rather abstract manner. As elsewhere in this book, what postmodernism implies for literary production and reception now is best taken up with reference to a specific example.

Haruki Murakami's novel *After Dark* (2004; translated from the Japanese by Jay Rubin, 2008) weaves together several incidentally linked narrative strands or stories that unfold in Tokyo over a single night. A young trombone player, Takahashi, runs into teenager Mari in an all-night diner and starts chatting. It turns out Mari has decided to spend the night in the city away from home. They meet several times in the course of the night and talk about their lives: Takahashi mainly of his troubled childhood and his father, and Mari of her relationship with her beautiful sister, Eri. Eri was Takahashi's classmate at school, and, as Mari tells him, has been asleep for six months − not in a coma, simply sleeping. At regular intervals, the novel turns to views of the sleeping Eri as from a camera, though the camera-like narrative voice often verbosely anticipates the audience's feelings. To begin with, she is found in bed beside a television which apparently screens the room she is in; at times, a masked man appears and watches her; she wakes up once and seems to cross into the room on the television screen; and finally she falls asleep again. When Takahashi leaves Mari after their first meeting, she is approached by Kaoro, a friend of Takahashi's and a hotel manager, who asks her to help communicate with a Chinese prostitute (Mari had learned Chinese). The prostitute has been savagely beaten up in Kaoro's hotel by a client, who then escaped unobserved. Mari accompanies Kaoro to the hotel and they arrange for the gangster whom the prostitute works for, an eerily expressionless man on a motorbike, to pick her up. Kaoro later finds a photograph of the prostitute's client from surveillance cameras and gives it to the gangster. Alongside these interwoven strands, the doings of the client Shirakawa after he attacked the prostitute and absconded are traced at regular intervals. He seems to be a high-flying computing and financial executive (with aspirations to take over Microsoft), who works through much of the night in his office in an efficient and mechanical manner. He talks on the phone to his wife, and buys milk on his way home, while the gangster searches for him.

Though the different strands of the narrative are linked in different ways – mainly by the connections between characters – they don't actually come together. Each strand seems linked and separate at the same time. In itself, each strand retains a sense of unresolved mystery till the end. Apart from the connections between characters, a degree of coherence is provided by the omniscient narrative voice. This is an acutely self-conscious narrative voice, which deliberately withholds more than it reveals. By turn, it assumes the objectiveness of a camera-like gaze, observes and invades different private spaces and conversations with omniscient ease, and yet affects the uncertain feelings and thoughts of a film audience or voyeur or surveillance worker. At times, one of the characters seems to apprehend a deep level of connectedness at work in their world. When Takahashi, for instance, tells Mari of his experience of watching criminal trials (he wants to study the law), he comes up with the following suggestive image to convey his sense of deep, hidden forces being at work – a disquieting image, which seems to be significant for the novel as a whole:

> A giant octopus living way down deep at the bottom of the ocean. It has this tremendously powerful life force, a bunch of long, undulating legs, and it's heading somewhere, moving through the darkness of the

ocean. I'm sitting there listening to these trials, and all I can see in my head is this *creature*. It takes on all kinds of different shapes – sometimes it's 'the nation,' and sometimes it's 'the law,' and sometimes it takes on shapes which are more difficult and dangerous than that.

(p. 97)

But the novel doesn't allow for much more coherence between the different and unresolved strands it weaves together than the incidental connections between the characters, the contradictory narrative voice, and Takahashi's vague image. There's also, of course, the fact that all the above happens in the city of Tokyo – the narrative voice at times assumes a bird's-eye view (also camera-like) of the city.

After Dark seems to present a postmodernist perspective and be amenable to postmodernist readings. The following three sets of observations on the novel follow the order of the three points above.

1. NO OVERARCHING PERSPECTIVE

The series of incidents in the novel could be thought of as fragments of the everyday – or rather, every-night – life of the city. The focus on night rather than day shrouds these incidents in mystery, and yet they convey the patterns of night-time in a big city: they are set in diners and bars and hotels, amidst late-night eccentrics and workers and antisocial elements.

The female characters seem to crystallise the simmering violence of a patriarchal social environment: the beautiful Eri reduced to a state of passive vulnerability (rather like the fairytale 'sleeping beauty'), exposed to the gaze of an unidentified masked man, a television camera, the narrator; the immigrant and physically abused prostitute; the self-possessed and plain schoolgirl Mari struggling to find her place; and others. Youthful aspirations and idealism are conveyed through the conversations of Mari and Takahashi. The brutal regimes of power and exploitation are suggested through the dangerously relaxed Chinese gangster and the sadistic corporate high-flyer. The various identities of these night-time citizens of Tokyo, from different strata of the city and partakers in different economies, are fleetingly brought together in the narrative.

But all these elements of the novel do not quite gel into a whole. The characters seem to occupy different worlds, and to entertain irreconcilable and often inexplicable motivations, which do not really meet even if their lives and paths criss-cross in various ways within Tokyo during one night. No ideological or social perspective is offered, or seems able to contain them all.

2. NARRATIVE STRATEGIES

This overall impression of fragmentariness and irresolution in *After Dark* is, however, not accidental or unintentional – carefully deployed narrative strategies are used to construct that impression. The voice of the narrator, as observed above, plays a deliberate game with the reader. On the one hand, it claims a camera-like distance and objectivity from what it describes (the metaphor of the camera is mentioned often throughout the novel). On the other hand, it self-consciously intrudes and moulds the view by choosing what to focus on, and by imbuing its gaze with collective anticipations and feelings. The contradictions of this narrative voice are available briefly in its characterisation of itself when describing the sleeping Eri:

> Our point of view, as an imaginary camera, picks up and lingers over things like this in the room. We are invisible, anonymous intruders. We look. We listen. We note odours. But we are not physically present in the place, and we leave behind no traces.
>
> (p. 27)

Actually, the fantastical image of Eri's long sleep itself disturbs the otherwise realistic, even though fragmentary and mysterious, flow of events. It interrupts the logic of the narrative by apparently bearing an out-of-this-world symbolic resonance. Also, the manner in which the different narrative strands are connected is a deliberate ploy to exacerbate the disconnected effect of the novel. The connections between characters appear to be entirely coincidental; they cannot be used to establish any greater design for the novel as a whole. And yet these connections allow the narrator to weave the strands together.

3. A DEEP ORDER?

However, we are invited to, and feel tempted to, look for some underlying design through these connections and through the nar-rator's contradictory voice. And in looking for some coherent perspective, we may well end up bringing it to our reading of the novel. This is not because such an underlying design is offered by the novel, but because we already have certain ideas about how our contemporary world works, and those may seem to chime with our reading of the novel.

So, for instance, we are accustomed to being bombarded constantly by numerous unrelated images through the television, newspapers, magazines, the internet, film shows, billboards, and may have concluded that these are all aspects of a gigantic media industry. We may have reasonably clear ideas about an economic and political system that produces such a constant variety and plethora of images, and why they are produced. Further, we may also have made some general inferences about the manner in which our exposure to such images affects contemporary society: increases the aptitude for buying commodities, creates an illusion of choice where none really exists, etc. With these ideas in mind, we may find confirmation of them in *After Dark*. There are suggestive gestures towards image production in the novel – for example, in the narrator's camera-like affectation, in the television screen that seems to suck in Eri at one point, in the hotel surveillance system that Kaori uses – which we may regard as aspects of exactly the kind of media industry, the political and social system, which works in our world.

Alternatively, we may bring our sense of how gender identities and patriarchal power works in our world to find an underlying coherence in the novel. Postmodernist fragmentariness may thus itself seem like a manifestation of a deeper ideological order and system (such as postmodern capitalism).

It is ultimately difficult to say whether there are definitively postmodern texts (which exhibit certain characteristics) or simply postmodern readings (a way of understanding texts in terms of contemporary circumstances). Postmodernism is conceived and talked about in between literary production and reception, amidst contemporary contexts, and encompasses both.

REFERENCES

Burn, Gordon (2008). *Born Yesterday: The News as Novel*. London: Faber.

de Certeau, Michel (1984). *The Practice of Everyday Life*. Trans. Steven Rendall. Berkeley, CA: University of California Press.

Golbou, Farrideh (or Faridah Gulbu) (1998). *Khusraw u Shirin*. Tehran: Rowshangaran va Motaleate Zanan.

Kiarostami, Abbas, dir. (2010). *Shirin* (DVD). London: British Film Institute.

Murakami, Haruki (2008). *After Dark* (2004). Trans. Jay Rubin. London: Harvill Secker.

Pamuk, Orhan (2004). *Snow* (2002). Trans. Maureen Freely. London: Faber.

FURTHER READING

ON NEWS AND EVERYDAY LIFE

Allen, Stuart (2004). *News Culture*, 2nd edn. Maidenhead, UK: Open University Press. [There's a useful chapter on 'News, audience and everyday life'.]

Bird, S. Elizabeth (2003). *The Audience in Everyday Life: Living in a Media World*. New York: Routledge.

Sheringham, Michael (2006). *Everyday Life: Theories and Practices from Surrealism to the Present*. Oxford: Oxford University Press. [Covers different philosophical approaches to everyday life, and explores everyday life in relation to literary, performative and visual cultural productions.]

ON IDEOLOGY

Hawkes, David (2003). *Ideology*, 2nd edn. London: Routledge. [Covers formulations of ideology and relations to culture – mainly from a leftwing position – with a historical perspective, until post-September 11.]

Heywood, Andrew (2007). *Political Ideologies: An Introduction*, 4th edn. Basingstoke: Palgrave. [Gives succinct accounts of different political ideologies. The discussion of ideology in relation to *Snow* above is of political ideology.]

ON IDENTITY

Gupta, Suman (2007). *Social Constructionist Identity Politics and Literary Studies*. Basingstoke, UK: Palgrave. [The first half deals with concepts of social constructionist identity, and the second with their institutionalisation in literary studies.]

Jenkins, Richard (2004). *Social Identity*, 2nd edn. Abingdon: Routledge. [A general overview of concepts of and debates about identity in different disciplines.]

ON POSTMODERNISM

An area gifted with many readers, of which some are listed here. These carry extracts from works by Fredric Jameson, David Harvey, Jean Baudrillard and others who are able to perceive, as I noted above, the logic of capitalism underlying postmodernist incoherence.

Brooker, Peter, ed. (1992). *Modernism/Postmodernism*. Harlow, UK: Pearson.
Docherty, Thomas, ed. (1992). *Postmodernism: A Reader*. Hemel Hempstead, UK: Harvester Wheatsheaf.
Drolet, Michael, ed. (2004). *The Postmodernism Reader: Foundational Texts*. London: Routledge.
Nichol, Brian, ed. (2002). *Postmodernism and the Contemporary Novel: A Reader*. Edinburgh: Edinburgh University Press.
Waugh, Patricia (1992). *Postmodernism: A Reader*. London: Bloomsbury.

6

PERSPECTIVES AND ISSUES 2

POSTCOLONIALISM AND GLOBALISATION

Like 'postmodernism', the term 'postcolonialism' appeared with constantly expanding connotations and applications, primarily in literature and cultural studies circles, from the 1970s. The term 'globalisation' also became similarly supersignificative over the same period, but it occupied mainly sociologists, economists, political scientists and anthropologists. Until recently, 'globalisation' had a relatively modest purchase in literary studies. Quite possibly, literary interest in the former had worked against the latter. At any rate, the relationship and difference between these two terms apropos contemporary literature is productively explored by considering them together. 'Globalisation' has been markedly successful in reaching outside academic circles, and is now used prolifically in popular and public discussions. Comparatively, 'postcolonialism', though also evoked similarly at times, carries more of a whiff of scholarly investment.

In a valiantly summary fashion, the following could be said briefly about these terms.

A postcolonialist perspective engages with contemporary ideologies and identities by examining the history and effects of European (primarily) colonial expansion since the sixteenth century (beyond and within Europe).

The argument goes as follows. Distinctive ways of categorising groups of people, instituting power relations, regulating everyday life, and organising knowledge were developed in the process of colonial expansion. These underpin current social conditions and attitudes in a vast number of contexts – perhaps everywhere, whether among those who were colonised, those who did the colonising, or even those who weren't directly involved in the process. How that works can be discerned by analysing a range of cultural productions and receptions accordingly, especially fruitfully in literature. Since colonial relations were essentially unequal and exploitative, their persistence in contemporary circumstances also tends to be so. However, ways of opposing inequality and exploitation (of decolonisation) had also emerged from the colonial situation. For many scholars, assuming a postcolonialist perspective goes hand-in-hand with a political commitment to take such opposition to its logical conclusion in the contemporary world. *The idea is to understand the colonial structures within contemporary inequalities and exploitations – in what seem to be postcolonial societies now – and redress them. Concurrently, the idea is to oppose the persistence of colonial relations (and appearance of new kinds of colonial relations) in the contemporary world and to realise a just postcolonial order.*

Globalisation refers to processes of integration towards the development of a worldwide order, and the study of globalisation involves the analysis of such processes. In early usage, the term referred mainly to:

- economic processes (e.g. corporations operating across countries, international movement of labour and commodities, international arrangements for regulating trade and markets);
- political processes (e.g. setting up international laws and policing, transnational forums such as the United Nations, promoting global political norms such as democracy and human rights); and
- technologically enhanced communication processes (particularly associated with the World Wide Web and global information corporations).

The implications of these processes for contemporary ideologies, identities and experiences of everyday life have associated the term with a large number of other areas. The degree to which cultures and environments are erased or transformed (cultural globalisation), and the extent to which different groups gain or lose from these processes, have been hotly debated by those studying globalisation. Various levels of ideological polarisations have followed: for instance, between those who feel globalisation is desirable and those who feel it should be opposed (anti-globalisation); between those who defend local interests and those who feel all interests are best served by further global integration. There are numerous intermediate positions. *For cultural productions and receptions, including literature, globalisation has a twofold relevance: on one hand, these reflect on and take positions regarding globalisation processes; on the other hand, these are themselves subject to globalisation processes.*

Evidently, though with different arguments, both postcolonialism and globalisation:

- extend a world-embracing way of thinking;
- have to do with large-scale social changes in, or relevant to, the contemporary world;
- involve ideological convictions and political commitments of contemporary moment; and
- provide methods for analysing cultural productions and receptions of various sorts, including literature.

The enormous plethora of unresolved debates that have revolved around these terms, and what they imply for a systematic approach to contemporary literature, are naturally impossible to summarise here. By focusing on one literary text, however, some of the key moments in debates around both terms can be clarified to some extent.

Martin Crimp's play *Cruel and Tender* (2004; first performed in London) is set against the ongoing 'war on terror' which began after the terrorist attacks in the USA of 11 September 2001. This is an adaptation from Sophocles's classical Greek play *Women of Trachis* (*Trachiniae*, fifth century BC), and is best considered with the classical play in view.

Sophocles's *Women of Trachis* focuses mainly on Deianira's inadvertent poisoning of her husband, Hercules. Hercules had conquered and sacked a Greek island-state because of his desire for the ruler Eurytus's daughter Iola, whom he sends to Deianira's care before he returns home. Deianira pities the girl and takes her in, but feels nervous about losing Hercules's love and sends him a love potion. The love potion, originally given to the unwitting Deianira by vengeful centaur Nessus, actually turns out to be a deadly poison, which causes Hercules's slow, agonised death. The larger part of the play depicts Deianira's anxieties as she first discovers the motive for Hercules's absence and then realises that she has poisoned him, and she finally commits suicide. Hercules appears in the latter part of the play and makes arrangements for his own demise amidst excruciating pain. In Crimp's *Cruel and Tender*, a character called simply 'the General' corresponds to Hercules, and his wife Amelia to Deianira. The sacked city is now in Africa, and naturally the General's destruction of it to appease his lust can only be regarded as a devastating war crime (and not his first). As in the original, the General appears late in the adapted play, and is shown as disintegrating psychologically and physically – his final words are a frenzied reiteration of his being 'not the criminal / but the sacrifice' (pp. 68–69). The General has evidently been the pawn of politicians conducting the 'war on terror'. Hercules's and the General's endings in the two plays are both similar in effect and different in import. In Sophocles's play, Hercules vividly describes his own physical and psychological suffering, and dominates the scene as a larger-than-life figure. In Crimp's play, the maddened and dying General mostly speaks of the cruelties he has perpetrated in the name of the 'war on terror', but it is clear that he is but a cog in the pervasive violence and cruelty that surrounds him.

There is simmering violence at every corner of the play: both in the enormity of the General's committing genocide and the 'war on terror', and in the everyday domestic arrangements of Amelia's household. At different points, Amelia wonders whether all men are rapists, thinks of children as little terrorists, and describes having sex with one's husband as a kind of terrorism. Casual cruelty or barely restrained violence characterises all the dialogues. Unlike for Deianira, it is unclear whether Amelia is aware that it is poison that she sends to the General – and it is obtained not from a vengeful centaur, but from a weapons scientist with anti-war convictions (a curious but not improbable contradiction). The counterparts of the deferential messengers and attendants of Sophocles's play here are devious political actors who control the 'war on terror'. The loyal chorus is replaced by three women (Housekeeper, Physiotherapist,

Beautician), who are aware of their class difference and self-interest, and are unable to sympathise with their masters. The captives here (especially Laela, the counterpart of Iola) are far from silent background figures, and are shown assimilating themselves effortlessly to the manipulative nature and callousness of consumer society.

A reader with interest in postcolonialism may note the following in Crimp's *Cruel and Tender*.

1. THE SHADOW OF COLONIAL HISTORY

It is significant that the conflict in the background of Sophocles's play is a purely internecine one, between Greek communities, and that in Crimp's play it is an international one, across national boundaries. That the city where the General has committed genocide is in Africa (we are told it is Gisenyi, a city in Rwanda, a former German and then Belgian colony which became independent in 1962) inserts a history of European colonisation of Africa in the interim and postcolonial dominance since (in Rwanda, the Belgian colonists exacerbated internecine conflicts, which led to several genocidal episodes around and after independence). This colonial interim gives a distinctive flavour to the power relations at work in this play, which is emphasised by the implicit reference to, and difference from, the ancient Greek context of Sophocles's play. *The shadow of colonial history, both within and across nations, is cast on contemporary international and national events at various levels.*

2. COLONIAL AND POSTCOLONIAL SYSTEMS

The 'war on terror', for which the General is an agent, is evidently a reassertion of colonial power relations in a new guise in an apparently postcolonial context – with the apparently moral objective of vanquishing 'terror'. In fact, in the nineteenth century, colonists often felt they had a moral mission to bring 'civilisation' to 'primitive' Africa too. It was evident then, as it is often observed now, that such *colonialist moral objectives usually hide the economic and political self-interests of powerful countries*. The point to note is that these kinds of old and new colonialism are quite different from classical assertions of power. In Sophocles's play, it is the individual hero Hercules who is responsible for his actions. In Crimp's play, the General is merely a pawn in a power system, wherein politicians and the media and military technologies (representatives of each appear in the play) have their parts. *Colonial and postcolonial relations work through a system, rather than through ambitious individuals.*

3. THE ROLE OF IDENTITY

The immediate way in which colonial relations work is through differences in identity. In Crimp's play, Laela and her brother (the Boy) are African – visibly (particularly in performance) racially identified in a way that is immaterial to Sophocles's play. Though racial differences and prejudice are not foregrounded in Crimp's play, they do have disturbing undercurrents throughout, given the colonial legacy (in the colonial period, racial prejudice was programmatically hardened, often as a matter of policy). For instance, when Amelia asks Laela to stick out her tongue to confirm whether she can speak and hasn't been mutilated, the spectacle might remind us of a slave-owner checking out the fitness of a slave (a familiar image associated with colonial slave trade). The race issue works with particularly disturbing effect in contemplating the General's war crime. We might wonder whether his ability to murder large numbers of people in Gisenyi isn't as much a sign of his regarding them as disposable by dint of their racial and ethnic difference (genocide licensed by a 'war on terror') as of his uncontrollable lust.

4. EFFECTS AT DIFFERENT LEVELS

The distortions of colonial inequities and attitudes are felt not only within colonised societies, but also within colonising societies. The violence of the neocolonial 'war on terror' abroad is reflected within the domestic sphere of the General's home. And since this conflict now involves not just specific nations, but international arrangements generally, the effects are felt beyond old colonising and colonised areas. As is the case with identity-based inequities, they operate across, or seem to be analogous across, different kinds of identities. So the undercurrents of racial violence are reflected in the more up-front apprehensions of sexual violence and class and national conflicts in Amelia's household.

5. PREJUDICE AND DESIRE

While colonial domination is exercised through identity-based prejudices, the relations between coloniser and colonised (or between dominant and marginal groups under apparently postcolonial conditions) is more complex than simply being prejudiced and exploitative. However unpalatable, the fact is that the General's feelings for Laela are not of hatred or contempt, but of overwhelming and possessive desire. Despite her discomfort, Amelia largely assumes a protective attitude towards Laela and her brother. For Amelia, Laela is both a rival in love and an adoptive child.

6. DECOLONISATION AND HYBRIDITY

The effect of the colonial relationship can also lead to changes that can, paradoxically, be enabling for the colonised − and put them in a position to oppose colonisation and perhaps overcome postcolonial inequalities. As Laela and her brother live in Amelia's household, they gradually assume a sort of position of power themselves. The boy takes to war games with his toys, against Amelia's wishes. Laela's growing facility with English and awareness of the tensions between the General and Amelia allows her to manipulate both. As the play progresses, Amelia and Laela seem to establish a sort of comradeship, and at the end, the General's main concern is Laela's future welfare (he tries to get his son James to 'take' her). At the end of the play, after the General is committed in an asylum, it is Laela who is left in charge (in the last line, telling the housekeeper to clear up), and James is seen holding the boy in his arms. Something of the cultural and identity-based differences between the characters − the General, Amelia, Laela, James, the boy − seems to rub off on each other and reach towards new identities (so to speak, hybrid identities).

7. REITERATION THROUGH POSTCOLONIALISM

It is possible that the above observations from a postcolonial perspective are themselves not wholly free of the kinds of inequalities and exploitations that they denounce. Perhaps in thinking of Laela and Amelia, for instance, so fixedly in terms of their colonial heritages and identities, colonial terms of thinking are as much reiterated as questioned. Also, possibly, an overemphatic interpretation in terms of colonial history and postcolonial or neocolonial circumstances has the disadvantage of overlooking other contemporary circumstances that are not entirely rooted in that history: for example, in relation to the role of servants and the class system, or the hold of news media on public perceptions, which the play depicts.

A reader of Crimp's *Cruel and Tender* with globalisation processes in mind might have the following observations to make.

1. CONTRADICTIONS IN GLOBAL INTEGRATION

The backdrop of the 'war on terror' against which the play unfolds is essentially a move towards global political integration. The idea is to bring about a worldwide regime and instil certain universal political convictions, whereby acts of terrorism will cease to be meaningful or considered necessary. It would seem, then, that the 'war on terror' is a particular aspect of what we think of as globalisation processes. Crimp's play highlights a debilitating contradiction in this effort, in that the attempt to overcome terrorism is itself coercive and violent and assumes a brutal military form. As an agent of the 'war on terror', the General is simply an agent of terrorism and violence himself: as Amelia puts it, 'the more he fights terror / the more he creates terror' (p. 2). In this regard, the play positions itself as anti-globalisation: it draws attention to the fact that *programmatic attempts at imposing global integration and instilling global ideologies can be oppressive and self-contradictory*. Indeed, the play depicts a world that seems to be subsumed by violence from micro (the home and family) to macro (national and international) levels.

2. INEVITABILITY OF GLOBAL INTEGRATION

At the same time, *there is an air of inevitability in the manner in which integrations above and beyond local contexts — in everyday life and across different identities — now take place* and are shown in the play. That Laela manages to adapt herself so effectively in the new environment of Amelia's household is because there are common denominators in most contemporary settings. There are standardised ways of dealing with different aspects of life. English is increasingly operating as a globally dominant language, and Laela had already been learning English at the Tuseme club in Gisenyi. Arrangements for providing and consuming modern comforts are evidently not foreign to Laela. From a conversation between James and Amelia, we are told that Gisenyi is no stranger to Mexican restaurants and flat-pack furniture. The setting of the play, Amelia's home, is temporary and modern in a way that doesn't suggest a clear location. The pervasive reach of news media means that not even the General is immune from charges of war crimes and public accountability.

3. VISION OF GLOBALISED WORLD

The allusions to Sophocles's *Women of Trachis* in *Cruel and Tender* serve to put the realities of a contemporary globalising world into perspective. Hercules's adventures were a matter of serving kings and gods, and ultimately serving himself (even his crimes enhance his heroic stature). The interests that the General serves are less tractable – ultimately, they are political interests that extend violently across the world. The General's penchant for violence makes him a criminal rather than a fallen hero. Insofar as the General understands his mission, as he explains to his son James, it was 'to burn and to cut to purify the world' (p. 57). For the General, the world that he has purified is not one of gods and kings and individual heroism, but of shopping malls and school playgrounds, luxury apartments, internet chatrooms, cameras and telephones. His is *a vision of a contemporary world described by communication technologies and institutions which are part of everyday life (at least middle-class everyday life) in widely dispersed contexts.* These represent the processes of global integration.

4. ACCESS ACROSS BOUNDARIES

The commissioning and first productions of *Cruel and Tender* involved companies and organisers in Austria, Britain, Germany and France – a matter of international collaboration. It has also been performed in Italy, Canada, Ireland and elsewhere. As a live performance, it was made available in a fairly wide number of countries within a short period. If it were turned into a film, or recorded and put, for instance, on a website, it could reach an enormous and widely dispersed audience very quickly. Much would depend on how effectively the producers and agents and publicists involved in promoting versions of the play in different media worked. The backdrop of 'war on terror' is meaningful worldwide now, and it could be of interest from different perspectives in different contexts. There exist, in brief, technologies and channels of global production and circulation that determine how far a play like Crimp's penetrates and what sorts of reception it receives. *The potentially wide reach of contemporary literary production and circulation and reception is an important dimension of the relationship of literature to globalisation processes.*

The italicised sentences above identify some of the points of debate among scholars of postcolonialism and globalisation, respectively. As their relationship to the example of *Cruel and Tender* shows, there are some common grounds between them and, at the same time, different emphases.

HUMAN RIGHTS

The final sort of supersignificative terms examined here – in this and the next section – refer to issues that are regarded as particularly relevant now: in this instance, 'human rights' and 'environmentalism' (and broadly, concern about the 'environment'). These terms have been important for a while, but were not quite as weighty and pervasive, say, earlier in the twentieth century as they seem now. Certainly, these terms didn't evoke the current range of ideological and identity-based complexities until quite recently. They seem now to accumulate new associations and shades of meanings without losing older ones, and we are consequently aware that they refer to some of the big issues of our time. They come up often in the news, in relation to our professions, businesses, domestic arrangements, in serious discussions of all sorts, and even in our incidental witty or ironic exchanges. 'Human rights' and 'environmentalism' appear with somewhat different nuances, depending on where we are and what language we speak, and yet they are recognised as meaningful in broadly the same way in many places now. Naturally, various analytical frameworks – postmodernist, postcolonialist, globalisation theory – have been particularly centred on the issues in question. Neither human rights nor environmentalism is a particularly literary issue; if anything, these are apt to be regarded as political or social or cultural issues. But these issues have their literary dimensions as much as any other. Insofar as they possess particular contemporary resonance, they are germane to a systematic reckoning with contemporary literature.

When we talk of human rights, we usually have the following in mind.

- *Human rights primarily have to do with protections that everyone should enjoy simply by dint of being human.* That means such rights should apply universally, irrespective of what sort of person is in question, where, and under what circumstances. These could be matters of protection from torture or deliberate humiliation, unjust treatment due to membership of some group, and so on.
- *We generally think of human rights in relation to their infringement by a powerful organisation* (or representatives of such organisations) – such as a corporation or army or government. So, a government that allows women to be treated unequally is thought of as denying women their human rights; or a corporation that imposes inhumane working conditions on an employee could be regarded as infringing his human rights. An individual harming someone for his own interests is thought of as committing a crime rather than infringing human rights.
- *Although human rights are often thought about negatively (in terms of infringement and protection of something we already have), they could also be thought of positively (in terms of being given something we should all have).* So fundamental freedoms of physical movement or of expression, basic sustenance, etc., may be thought of as rights that every individual everywhere should have, and should be given if not.
- *Since human rights are universal, and primarily a matter of protection from and by powerful organisations, their maintenance depends on having some sort of statement of agreement which is binding on all such organisations.* Although imperfect in various ways, the Universal Declaration of Human Rights adopted by the United Nations General Assembly in 1948, which all United Nations member states are expected to follow and enforce, is now usually referred to as such a statement of agreement. Governments of various countries and some transnational organisations (such as the

European Union) may add to and refine these, and arrange for them to be policed and upheld – usually by enacting laws.

All this may sound reasonable and clear, but in fact there are various unresolved ambiguities and disputes about the above points. Often, how a statement of, or law to uphold, human rights may apply in a specific situation is unclear, and the complexity of specific situations has to be considered carefully as they appear. It is such ambiguities and disputes that give the issue of human rights ongoing and growing relevance, and the term 'human rights' its supersignificative character. The following are some examples of the kinds of ambiguities and disputes that have been prolifically pondered.

- It seems reasonable to feel that some individuals should not, or cannot, enjoy what we usually think of as a full range of human rights, perhaps for their own good or for that of others. So it might be argued that some exceptions need to be made for children, for prisoners, for persons in a persistent vegetative state, for patients with psychological disorders, and so on. But setting the boundaries for what rights are accepted and what aren't in these cases can be extremely contentious.
- We sometimes accept that there could be circumstances under which protection of some human rights can be reasonably with-drawn or curtailed by those responsible for upholding them (usually governments): such as during wars, at times of serious social discord, when large-scale natural disasters strike, and so on (in general, thought of as a 'state of emergency' or a 'state of exception'). Again, it is very difficult to agree when such cir-cumstances clearly could be said to exist, and what should or shouldn't be allowed when a state of emergency is seen to exist.
- Groups with different ideological convictions or identity-based traditions occasionally find that they have different notions of what should be regarded as human rights. For example, to a secular group, it seems unquestionable that equal standing before the law irrespective of gender is a fundamental human right, while some conservative religious dispensation may call for laws based on the inequality of men and women as an article of faith.
- Even when the tenets of human rights are widely agreed, who should police and ensure them turns out to be a particularly

troubling business. If an organisation is set up for this within a country, or with international powers, there are usually questions about who should police that organisation. There are always doubts about the motivations and composition of such a body itself.

There are numerous such doubts and debates related to human rights. Literary works appear constantly in almost every contemporary context, examining situations where human rights are flouted or appear contentious in some way. We are more or less certain to have come across these in our various contexts. Any such example could clarify further how literary texts are *used* to address the kind of ambiguities and disputes about human rights outlined above.

Underlying the points outlined above there is one basic and obvious consideration: what does it mean to be human and therefore have rights? Or rather, to pose that question in a more meaningful fashion: when thinking about rights, to what extent should we understand being human in terms of being individuals, and to what extent should we understand being human as a matter of belonging to larger structures (as individuals within groups, communities, countries, etc.)? Arguably, literature explores this very big question variously; literature explores and expresses the many dimensions – all dimensions – of being human. This means that *it is not simply the case that some literary texts are used to ponder particular debates about human rights; in fact, literary texts in general constantly explore what it means to be human and thereby clarify the very basis on which human rights are contemplated.* Contemporary literature explores the range of individual and social concerns of our time and thereby clarifies what we can understand as being human, and as human rights, now.

Current discussions of what it means to be human, and therefore to have inalienable rights, often refer back to the largest and most programmatic genocide in the twentieth century, the Holocaust – the systematic murder of Jews, Gypsies, homosexuals, disabled people, and other (particularly Eastern European and Russian) civilians, by the Nazi regime from the late 1930s to 1945. Reference to the Holocaust to understand the universality of human rights is a natural recourse (and, indeed, the Universal

Declaration of Human Rights was a result of it) since it exemplifies the consequences of a regime's *not* recognising human rights, or of deliberately designating a significant part of humanity as *not* human and therefore divesting them of their rights. Literary (and, for that matter, historical and sociological) attempts to give accounts of the Holocaust have been anxious and uncertain but persistent: there have been doubts about whether it is possible for so enormous a crime to be presented in literature; whether attempts haven't distorted the significance of the Holocaust (e.g. by localising and limiting its moral significance in various ways); and whether accounts of the Holocaust aren't being unacceptably used to serve contemporary political and economic interests. However, literary reckonings with the Holocaust are generally regarded as necessary for reconfirming the universality and clarifying the character of human rights in an ongoing way. The continuing relevance of this can be exemplified by pausing on an unusual historical–fictional engagement with the Holocaust, in Jonathan Littell's *The Kindly Ones* (2006; translated from the French by Charlotte Mandell, 2009).

The narrative is from the perspective (in the first person) of Maximilien Aue, a respected businessman (owner of a lace factory in northern France), and consists in his memoirs. Though the dates are not mentioned, it can be inferred that these are written perhaps in the mid- or late 1960s. It is a detailed record of Aue's participation, as a Nazi SS intelligence officer and later bureaucrat, in every stage of the Holocaust. Aue studied the law and political science in Germany, and was awarded a doctorate in law. Generally he preferred sexual relations with men, but was also subject throughout to a sexual fixation on his sister (intense incestuous fantasies are described). His family connections, ambition and elite education – which instilled a philosophical bent of mind – led to his recruitment in Nazi intelligence services. He was deployed in Ukraine, where he participated in village-by-village and region-by-region 'cleansing' of Jews and others, mainly organising or overseeing mass killings, and occasionally killing himself. He was then sent to Stalingrad during the siege, and witnessed the brutal street-by-street combat between German and Soviet armies, and interrogated a Soviet commissar with whom he debated the ideological nuances of Nazism and Bolshevism. After a breakdown and a brief spell in Paris (during which he visited Italy and murdered his mother and members of her household for no apparent reason), he became Heinrich Himmler's representative to coordinate the Final Solution. He participated in discussions about the most efficient way to 'process' the enormous number of Jews in concentration camps in Poland, debating to what extent they should be killed in gas chambers or used as slave labour. He conducted inspections of concentration camps. He was in Berlin when the Nazi regime fell and the Soviet army marched into the city.

In the course of this career, he courts the friendship of various intellectuals: particularly, Dr Voss, a linguist with encylopaedic knowledge of 'Indo-Germanic', 'Indo-Iranian' and 'Caucasian' languages, who is keenly aware of the manner in which languages and speakers mix and overlap; and Dr Hohenegg, a pathologist who studies the effects of malnutrition in besieged Stalingrad. Aue becomes culpable in innumerable murders and acts of brutal inhumanity, and witnesses not just the suffering of Holocaust victims, but also, among other things, the psychoses that develop among mass murderers in the ranks of German and Ukrainian soldiers, brutalised feral groups of children, and the petty bureaucratic rivalries and artifices of those who manage the concentration camps. Aue was also introduced to Hitler in his bunker in the final days of the war, and reports that he bit Hitler's nose in a fit of despair.

What this brief summary of the novel belies is the enormous detail that goes into Aue's account. In leading up to his memories, Aue shows both a well-researched retrospective understanding of the Holocaust, and awareness of some of the common perceptions that attach to it. Actually, this retrospection confronts not merely anxieties about the Holocaust as they were expressed and debated in the 1960s, but also anxieties and misperceptions that continued to appear since – and are often entrenched in looking back to the Holocaust now. The account of Aue's experiences and culpabilities is a detailed flow of the minutiae of places, conversations, happenings, feelings, thoughts (close to a thousand pages of small print in the English text) which render the enormity of the Holocaust through an individual state-sponsored mass murderer's small day-to-day, or rather memory-by-memory, apprehension of events. In this account, Aue's culpability is embedded in an immense flow of events, amidst confusions of philosophical ideas, amidst numerous travels and meetings with people, and under an ideological and power system that grips ground-level reality comprehensively. What emerges from all this is a complex picture, only possible in literature, of the mechanics and consequences of the programmatic dehumanisation of certain people by others.

Insofar as that leads us back to an understanding of what it means to be human and contemplation of universal human rights, the following observations are worth making. These observations are, I think, likely to seem of contemporary and ongoing relevance in most contexts.

1. INDIVIDUALISED EVIL

We might feel tempted to look to Aue's individual psychology for an explanation of his role in genocide. We might, in other words, try to understand his culpability as a deep-seated psychosis, a symptom of an abnormal condition of the mind or an innate evil. There is plenty of material in the novel to feed this temptation: his complicated relationship with his mother (whom he kills) and absent father; his incestuous longings for his sister; his breakdowns; his forbidden sexuality. These are, however, in no evident way an explanation for the enormity of what's happening around him and what he does. *There is no evidence that his personal psychological make-up causes the genocidal ideology and world* he participates in. In fact, he locks up his psychoses in a private sphere, which is largely separate from the public and institutional sphere where genocide is grounded. His secret homosexuality necessarily puts him entirely at odds with the ideology he subscribes to. Complex relations with parents and siblings do not necessarily lead to genocide. And it is evident that Aue is able to reason in sophisticated ways, is a highly educated and thinking person. The notion that Nazi war criminals embody some kind of deep-seated and individualised and monstrous evil – a popular notion now – is simplistic in this context.

2. CONCEPTS OF PURITY AND THE ABSOLUTE

In *The Kindly Ones, the possibility and actuality of genocide is rooted in ideas of a particular sort*, not in a vacuum of ideas or in unthinking boorishness. Aue's philosophical bent allows him to state and ponder these ideas occasionally with considerable clarity. *They have to do ultimately with the concepts of purity and of the absolute.* In this view, there is a group of pure humans (in terms of race, nation, culture), which is absolutely superior to other groups – others who are therefore less than human, or impure. There is a desire for a purified nation for this group, and a world in which the absolute superiority of the group in question would be self-evident in their ability to dominate others. There is a notion of absolute order within the pure nation (or region), with pure humans working in their joint or collective interest by exterminating impure less-than-humans, and an absolute order brought about internationally by the superior group. This coincides with an idea of absolute power, which is embodied in the figure of the Führer or dictator. For Aue and others, the Führer is more a symbolic idea of absolute power than a person. In fact, the person Hitler appears ridiculous on both occasions of his appearance in the novel, without thereby undermining the idea of absolute power. We have here, in brief, an ideology revolving around notions of absolute order and power and purity of identity.

3. THE ROLE OF BUREAUCRACY

The possibility and actuality of programmatic genocide thus derived is driven by a bureaucratic system. The bureaucratic system of genocide sets up an industrial organisation, a professional structure, and acts merely to realise an idea of purity and absolute order without questioning it. Aue and the other bureaucrats of the Final Solution are simply focused on getting the job done, after having accepted that Jews and other groups are not human and need to be murdered *en masse*. They deal, as bureaucrats generally do, with the minutiae of problems of numbers and resources, efficient processes to achieve predetermined ends. This bureaucratic apparatus is in some ways similar to those we are familiar with (corporations generating profits, states trying to maintain order), in their power rivalries, determination to manage problems, and realise predetermined results. In a way, the very focus on efficient bureaucratic processing inures against the craziness of mass killing.

4. GENOCIDAL EVERYDAY LIFE

Culpability in genocide is distributed through the dissemination of ideology and spreading of bureaucratic responsibility, rather than centred exclusively on exceptionally evil leaders. The tendency to see Hitler and his immediate henchmen as sole and exceptional perpetrators of genocide continues to be strong now; Aue's detailed picture of genocide in *The Kindly Ones* works against it. As Aue notes in leading into his memoirs, every un-noted person who participated in the genocide in small ways, by ostensibly performing their functions – the worker who turned the gas taps on in the killing chambers, the station master who changed the lines for trains bearing victims to reach Auschwitz, the nurse who tended concentration camp managers and guards, etc. – were all thinking, rational people in their own narrow ways, and all culpable. All who propped up an apparatus with any degree of awareness, however indirectly, were part of the genocidal machine. *Culpabilities become distributed among the routines and habits of everyday life.*

5. THE TRANSFERABLE CONDITIONS OF GENOCIDE

Though it is necessary to analyse why the conditions of Nazi genocide appeared specifically where and when they did, the generalised features of genocidal conditions evident in *The Kindly Ones* suggest that *such conditions are transferable with slight variations in other contexts – in any context and at any time.* If the idea of individual monsters and innately evil culprits is put aside, and the abstract and systematic dimensions – the social logic – of the Holocaust are perceived, it becomes evident that this can recur with variations elsewhere. Wherever ideas of purity and the absolute have a place (in terms of true religions, or chosen peoples, or cultural superiority based on some description of identity), and wherever centralised and controlled bureaucratic apparatuses can be installed, a genocidal possibility arises. By implication, the only way to guard against that possibility is to foreground a universal notion of being human with inalienable rights, which supersedes any idea of pure groupings and absolute order to establish purity.

6. THE UNIVERSALITY OF HUMANKIND

The need for grasping the universality of being human is not merely implied in *The Kindly Ones*; the universal idea of what it means to be human is explored in certain ways. *The fact is that, at every level, the basis and order of genocidal social forces contradict themselves in the novel.* At the level of individual psychology, no subscription to a pure type of humanity is possible, and attempts to maintain it lead to terrible distortions. As noted, Aue's homosexuality itself contradicts everything he stands for. More generally, the perpetrators and victims and bystanders of genocide suffer deep psychological effects: in the inexpressible suffering of hapless victims, in the traumas of soldiers recruited to killing, in the brutalisation of children, the pervasive fear, the sense of loss, and so on. At the level of bureaucratic organisation, the absurdity of systematised mass killing manifests itself in the psychoses and insecurities that the managers of concentration camps suffer from.

Ideas of purity and the absolute fall apart at every turn. There is the unavoidable fact, often picked up in the novel, that much that is valued culturally (in music, philosophy and literature) by the so-called 'master race' is produced by Jews and others who are deprived of their human status. The scientists who study human society and biology on the ground are led invariably to conclusions that undermine ideas of group purity. For instance, Dr Voss's linguistic research, which he outlines passionately (pp. 211–17, 299–303), leads him to a view of social mixtures and movements and adaptations which explicitly undermine the entire basis of racially or ethnically pure groups. The intrepid Dr Hohenegg's research into malnutrition makes no distinction between the biological functions of different human bodies. The symptoms of malnutrition in soldiers in Stalingrad are replicated in the inmates of concentration camps.

Out of these contradictions in the social condition that result in genocide, there emerges a sense of the universality of being human – as an obverse of that condition. *This universality consists in the limitations and mortality of all human bodies, in the anxiety about killing and dying and suffering that is concomitant with psychological stability, in the unlimited possibility for adaptation and mixture and movement amidst social coexistence, in the ability to communicate across every kind of boundary, and in the desire for pleasure and comfort.* By portraying the extreme distortion of a genocidal regime in a sustained fashion, *The Kindly Ones* effectively clarifies the opposite – the universal commonality of humans – in all its complexity.

7. STATEMENTS AND STAKES

The particular rights that should follow from a universal under-standing of what it means to be human, and that should be secured in a desirable social order, are naturally not stated here. The com-plexity of the human condition suggests that any statement of these would need to deal with that complexity. But what is at stake if that universality is denied, if no arrangements are in place to secure the rights that follow, is clear.

It is up to us to contemplate what the implications of these observations are for the ambiguities and disputes about human rights noted above. Each of the general points made in these observations drawn from *The Kindly Ones* has been the subject of numerous illuminating studies in psychology, politics, sociology, cultural studies, history, etc. Each of these involves analysing different facets of the complex whole of human life and society. The literary text, like this novel, can be, and often is, a site for presenting that complex whole in all its interconnectedness and intractability.

ENVIRONMENTALISM

The term *'environmentalism' (associated with 'ecological awareness' and being 'green') now commonly refers to an area of social activism that seeks to:*

(1) *understand the effects of human activities (particularly industrial and technological activities) on the natural environment; and*
(2) *campaign for policies that enhance the conservation and sustainability of our natural environment and improve environmental conditions where these are depleted.*

Although the term found its current significance mainly from the 1970s onwards, it seems to draw in various discussions of the natural environment from well before that. It also has a productive and fluid connection to the wider connotations of the 'environment' (other than 'natural') − psychological environment, ideological environment, social and cultural environment, built environment. Designating an increasingly successful area of campaigning, it has now become a site on which many contemporary ideologies and identities stake claims, and on which investigations from different disciplinary perspectives centre. Policies to deter environmental depletion (resulting from high-profile public debates on toxic and undegradable waste disposal, global warming and climate change, species threatened by loss of natural habitat, population growth and limitations of natural resources, etc.) are firmly in the domain of media coverage now, and affect everyday life in numerous ways. Powerful moral and social norms have come to be commonly associated with the term.

Literature doesn't appear to provide an obvious space for environmentalism. It is not an area that is directly concerned with making quantifiable or evidence-based determinations of the effect of human activity on the natural environment. Nor does literature have a particularly noteworthy input into policy-making on this front. It is perhaps a measure of the supersignificative reach of environmentalism that it has nevertheless had a significant impact on literary production and reception (through 'ecocriticism' or 'environmental criticism') from the 1990s, and now has a distinctive space in contemporary literature. The following points in this regard are noteworthy.

1. RAISING AWARENESS

In the spirit of campaigning for a sustainable and improved environment, *literary texts can be useful for raising awareness of environmental depletion and its consequences*. Although evidence-based and quantifiable accounts of the latter – scientific accounts – and their policy implications are invaluable for those already interested in environmentalism (scientists, activists, policy makers, industrialists, etc.), their reach to the relatively less informed and interested is limited. However, a novel dealing with the effects of an oil slick or industrial disaster, for instance, or a work of fantasy fiction about what could occur if the environment as we know it is destroyed, may get even the uninterested thinking about environmental issues.

2. AN INEXTRICABLE RELATIONSHIP

Attention to literature from an environmentalist perspective usually digs more deeply than simply using literary texts as campaigning tools. *There is a crucial question that underpins most strands of environmentalism: what is the environmental condition that should be ideally achieved?* Or, stated otherwise, how should we describe the balance between humans and the natural environment that is most desirable? Answers to this have varied widely: from a return to the kind of natural environment that prevailed at some pre-industrial stage of history, to cleaning up to a reasonable degree and maintaining the *status quo* thereafter, to ongoing consideration according to what is practically or technologically possible, to arguing that the current state of knowledge doesn't allow for a clear answer.

Literature provides a useful arena, among many others, for engaging with this question. Even if not quite with an environmentalist perspective, the literature of different periods has reflected and explored not only what it is to be human, but also, and necessarily, the relationship between people and the natural environment. So an environmentalist perspective can be brought to bear where, for instance, literary concepts of 'nature' (usually poised between human nature and the natural world), metaphors of forests or the wilderness, descriptions and settings of landscapes, myths of Eden or floods, animal fables, and so on, are found. The idea is not that these feature in environmentalist texts, but that by reading these with environmentalist concerns in mind, a useful (that is, useful now) and broad picture of the inextricable relationship between human existence and the natural environment can be discerned.

3. RECONSIDERING CULTURAL ATTITUDES

This kind of reading of literature with an environmentalist perspective can take a more programmatic turn for the environmentalist's purpose (without necessarily becoming overly propagandist). Environmentalists have often argued that pressing environmental concerns (such as climate change and loss of natural habitats) are often not taken seriously, or are underplayed, because we are educated and brought up to be relatively indifferent to them. We are, so to speak, socialised to think of human interests as superseding environmental concerns, and to attach superlative importance to progress (in technology and lifestyles) even at the expense of deleterious effects on the environment. With that in mind, it could be argued that even unpopular environmentalist policies with little democratic support may need to be pushed strongly.

More importantly, it might be averred that a large-scale programme for changing culturally ensconced habits should be undertaken. This could be a matter of rethinking how education should work. It could, more broadly, be a matter of encouraging less human-centred and more nature-centred thinking, that is, *thinking of progress and development not in terms of exclusively human interests, but in terms of the interests of the relationship between natural world and human society as a whole.* Somewhat implausibly, occasionally a path of letting natural processes unfold according to 'natural laws' and free from any human interference is also proposed: implausible because this is apt to turn into a sort of pantheistic mysticism, and because even this sentiment is ultimately no more than human. That aside, the point is that *a broad-based reconsideration of prevailing cultural attitudes is often considered necessary from an environmentalist perspective, and in that literature – as a venerable and wide-ranging cultural form – has a potentially crucial role.* Becoming habituated to reading literature from an environmentalist perspective could be a step in that direction.

4. RECONSIDERING LITERATURE

The previous two points naturally rebound within literature itself. The previous point suggests that dominant preconceptions about how literature should be read and thought about need to be reconsidered. The manner in which we understand identity and ideologies as embedded in literature, which I have discussed above, needs to factor in the natural environment in a continuous manner. The power relations that are reflected in literature – gender relations, colonial relations, and so on – have regard not simply to societies and individuals, but also to their place within their environments. Or, rather, their place within the environment of our planet generally, since the environments of different contexts are inextricably connected and are indifferent to socially demarcated territories.

Traditional societies, for instance, had occasionally evolved arrangements that enabled a sustainable relationship with the natural environment, by ensuring replenishing and renewal of habitats. The literary forms and themes of such societies are likely to be attuned to those arrangements. Where industrialisation or colonisation has changed those arrangements in an environmentally destructive fashion, the effects are also reflected in literary expression. Whether any nostalgia or backward-looking morality arising from the contemplation of such traditional arrangements is meaningful now is also matter for literary exploration. What we look for in literature, and how we define literature, determine what we find in it; *an environmentalist perspective can perhaps lead us to reconsider what we look for in, and understand as, literature.*

These observations could be usefully considered further with a literary text in view. Peter Adolphsen's short novel *Machine* (2006; translated from the Danish by Charlotte Barslund, 2008) presents several unusual features. One of these is the time scale it encompasses. It charts the passage of an oil drop formed from the heart of a prehistoric horse, an Eohippus, to events when it vaporised and caused cancer 55 million years later. The novel starts really with a brief description of the moment after the Big Bang, and moves to the death by drowning of the Eohippus, and the decomposition and transformation of its heart into a drop of oil, then to the discovery of oil (with that drop) in Utah, USA in 1948, its passage to the refinery in 1973, and thence to a car engine in 1975, and onwards to its being vaporised and breathed in and causing cancer in 2005.

At the moment when the story touches 1975, it pauses on one of the refinery workers, Jimmy Nash, who was actually born Djamolidine Hasanow in Azerbaijan (then in the Soviet Union). His memory of a census official telling his family of the many peoples in the Soviet is recounted – it impresses him and stokes his wanderlust. He becomes a competitive cyclist but doesn't quite make it to the top, cycles across the border from Azerbaijan into Iran, and there seeks and obtains political asylum in the US Embassy and is flown to the USA. In the USA, he learns English, and becomes a refinery worker in Salt Lake City, Utah, where he loses one of his arms in an industrial accident in 1973. Unemployed and footloose, in 1975 he happens to be picked up as a hitchhiker by a young student of genetics, Clarissa Sanders. Clarissa and Jimmy drive to Austin, Texas, and talk and take LSD along the way. As it happens, Clarissa's car (a defective model deliberately left uncorrected by the makers, Ford) has the oil with the drop from the Eohippus's heart in its tank. When it vaporises in the engine, it becomes attached to a grain of sand and is released through the exhaust, and is breathed in by Clarissa 24 hours later. At this final stage, the narrator of the story appears as Clarissa's neighbour. Thirty years later (in 2005), that grain of sand and oil gradually causes lung cancer in Clarissa. She is taken to the hospital by the neighbour/narrator and dies shortly afterwards. In the final pages, the narrator describes a Native American sweat hut ritual he participated in, during which he had a vision of a prehistoric horse telling him the story which becomes this novel.

Another unusual feature of this novel is its numerous and detailed scientific descriptions of the processes at work. For example, the effect on Jimmy and Clarissa of taking LSD is introduced thus:

> At a biological level it has been established that LSD (lysergic acid diethylamide) interacts with a series of serotonin receptor subtypes (5-HT), primarily in the limbic system, but also in the hippocampus and the hypothalamus – but precisely how and which of the influences determine the hallucinogenic effect is uncertain. The increased presence of serotonin's primary metabolite, hydroxyindoleactic acid, suggests an increase in the production of the transmitter substance. LSD is probably a potent 5-HT_2 receptor-antagonist, but in addition shows agonistic activities in 5-HT_{1A} and 5-HT_{1C} receptors, which. ...
>
> (p. 64)

Similar care and detail are devoted at various points throughout: in describing the reactions of the Eohippus and the decomposition and transformation of its heart, the passage of the oil in the car, the effect of Clarissa's breathing in the toxic grain, and so on. Similar detail is also devoted at times to social matters (such as the Azerbaijani census official's description of linguistic diversity) and philosophical issues (for example, what is death?).

With an environmentalist perspective in mind, the following points about this novel seem relevant.

1. NO OBVIOUS AGENDA

Machine is not, in any obvious way, a propagandist text with an environmentalist agenda. It does not straightforwardly depict industrial or other human activities causing environmental depletion. The character of such activities is hinted at rather than foregrounded. The energetic extraction of minerals and oil in Utah, initially by the Mormons and later by large oil companies, is described without going into the environmental effects. Such doubts about the operations of large corporations as do appear are with regard to their attitude to people rather than to environments. It is observed, for instance, that Clarissa's faulty car (which could blow up under certain circumstances) is on the road, despite the Ford Motor Company's awareness of the fault, because: 'A cost–benefit analysis was carried out which showed that it was cheaper to pay compensation for 180 fatalities and 180 injured than to fit the petrol tank with one of several possible safety precautions' (p. 53). As regards environmentalism, Clarissa, a philosophical student of genetics, is found arguing persuasively against simplistic notions of 'a (misunderstood) concept such as "nature" as an ideal for humanity [because it is] at the very least profoundly naïve and probably dangerous' (pp. 54–55). Also, not insignificantly for an environmentalist perspective, Clarissa's eventual death is caused by toxic emissions from her car – by environmental pollution.

2. LARGER THAN HUMAN PERSPECTIVE

More emphatically than most literary texts, however, *Machine* presents a picture that is not immersed substantially in individual and social human concerns. The very time scale in question (from shortly after the Big Bang to 2005) puts the human presence in the universe and on our planet into perspective. More importantly, the careful scientific descriptions of processes – natural and social – are an effective way of rendering the relationship between the environment and humans, and indeed, apparently, the environment without humans. The novel gives the impression of assuming a perspective that is not, so to speak, human-centric but broader – that places individuals and human society and, for that matter, other species within and in relation to the natural environment and natural processes. It is the emphasis on natural processes, the scientific description of them, which really gives the impression of rising above a human worldview. Such processes precede the existence of humans, are indifferent to human control and motives, and follow principles that are not determined by people.

Even in the midst of human and social activity, which appear to be in our control, these processes keep unfolding in their indifferent way, outside human control – through our biological make-up, chemical reactions around and within us, the lives of other species around and within us, climates and soils, the laws of physics, the inevitable continuum of life and death, and so on. And, in fact, social processes are also shown to have their indifferent aspects, outside human control – in the dispersal and differentiation of languages, the unpredictable consequences of our actions, our limited understanding of the factors playing in our habitual behaviours, etc.

3. SCIENCE AND MYSTICISM

However, to think of this apparently larger-than-human perspective as non-human or purely environment-centred would be a mistake. Even scientific descriptions of natural processes that are indifferent to human interests and motives are couched in language, and have literary and aesthetic qualities (evocative of precision, complexity, specialism, symmetry, etc.). The view of the Eohippus's world that is presented is a creation of human understanding and imagination. This is deliberately pointed out in the early sections of the novel, when the Eohippus's reactions to her world are given through human-like thoughts, as if she talks to herself (the Eohippus is anthropomorphised). In the final passages, the language of the Eohippus is linked to mystical environmentalist apprehensions, and the nostalgia for traditional environment-friendly lifestyles, that we sometimes entertain – as a vision during a Native Indian ritual. However, this kind of mystical apprehension reads ironically here: what the Eohippus says in the vision is obviously the scientifically couched content of the rest of the novel, which is not in the least mystical.

4. QUESTIONING LITERARY PRESUMPTIONS

In various ways, *Machine* does question the presumptions of literary readers and expectations of literature. Much of its use of language appears to be distinctly non-literary to our commonly accepted way of thinking. The manner in which it weaves contextually specific details and vast time scales, the microscopic and the individual and the social and the galactic, could seem a departure from usually accepted conventions of literary coverage and expression. *Machine* might make many of us reconsider what we regard as appropriate literary language and plausible literary themes, or what we usually presume to be the scope of literature.

FINAL NOTE

Of the supersignificative terms that refer to issues which are particularly relevant now, I have deliberately chosen for discussion above two (human rights and environmentalism) that seem to be all-embracing and timeless. What it means to be human, and what our relationship with the natural environment entails, are matters that are, arguably, of constant and ongoing relevance in all contexts. To identify them as particularly contemporary *now* – as this is written in 2011 – seems to be disingenuous; surely, we may feel, these are *always* contemporary. And yet the manner in which these terms are thought about and expressed in literature is distinctively of our times and contexts, and can be differentiated from past times and contexts. They may come to be thought about differently and expressed otherwise in future times and contexts. Contemporary literature is thought of as such, ultimately, because it draws upon both what is *always* contemporary and what is contemporary *now*.

REFERENCES

Adolphsen, Peter (2008). *Machine* (2006). Trans. Charlotte Barslund. London: Harvill Secker.

Crimp, Martin (2004). *Cruel and Tender*. London: Faber and Faber.

Littell, Jonathan (2009). *The Kindly Ones* (2006). Trans. Charlotte Mandell. London: Vintage.

Sophocles (1990). 'Women of Trachis' (fifth century BC). Trans. J. Michael Walton. In *Plays: Two*. London: Methuen.

FURTHER READING

ON POSTCOLONIALISM

A particularly prolific number of readers, textbooks and guidebooks are available for this area. The following are merely indicative; there are many that are equally useful.

Ashcroft, Bill, Gareth Griffiths and Helen Tiffin, eds (2005). *The Post-Colonial Studies Reader*, 2nd edn. London: Routledge.

Williams, Patrick and Laura Chrisman, eds (1994). *Colonial Discourse and Post-Colonial Theory: A Reader*. Harlow, UK: Pearson.

Wisker, Gina (2007). *Key Concepts in Postcolonial Literature*. Basingstoke, UK: Palgrave.

ON GLOBALISATION

Connell, Liam and Nicky Marsh, eds (2010). *Literature and Globalization*. Abingdon, UK: Routledge.

Gupta, Suman (2009). *Globalization and Literature*. Cambridge, UK: Polity.

ON HUMAN RIGHTS

Goldberg, Elizabeth and Alexandra Schultheis, eds (2011). *Theoretical Perspectives on Human Rights and Literature*. Abingdon, UK: Routledge.

Orend, Brian (2002). *Human Rights: Concept and Context*. Peterborough, Ontario: Broadview.

ON ENVIRONMENTALISM AND ECOCRITICISM

Buell, Lawrence (2005). *The Future of Environmental Criticism: Environmental Crisis and Literary Imagination*. Malden, MA: Blackwell.

Coupe, Laurence, ed. (2000). *The Green Studies Reader: From Romanticism to Ecocriticism*. London: Routledge.

Garrard, Greg (2004). *Ecocriticism*. Abingdon, UK: Routledge.

INDEX

11 September 2001 terrorist attacks:
31, 50, 51
100 Poets (Swift): 109
101 Poems (Hollis and Keegan): 8
1989 Eastern Europe revolutions:
31, 51
253 (Ryman): 83–84, 85, 86, 107

Adolphsen, Peter: *Machine* 179–83
After Dark (Murakami): 149–53
"America, America" (Youssef): 8
Andrews, V.C.: 69
Aristotle: *Poetics* 71
Arnold, Matthew: "The Study of
Poetry" 16–17
Arnold, Thomas: *Chaucer to
Wordsworth* 26
Atatürk, Mustafa Kemal: 136, 137
author: 4–5, 56–62, 64, 68–71

Baker, Nicholson: *Checkpoint* 114–15
Ball, Hugo: "gadji beri bimba"
43–48; Dada Manifesto 44
Banville, John: 115
Barthes, Roland: 57

Berne Convention: 57
Bharata (*Natya Shastra*): 71
Blair, Tony: 131
Borges, Jorge Luis: "The Library of
Babel" 33
Born Yesterday (Burn): 130–35
Boyle, Danny: *Slumdog Millionaire*
98, 103–6
Brecht, Bertolt: *Fear and Misery*
49–50
Brown, Gordon: 131–32, 133
"A Bummer" (Casey): 8
Burn, Gordon: *Born Yesterday*
130–35
Bush, George: 114, 115
Byrne, David: "I Zimbra" 45

Casey, Michael: "A Bummer" 8
Cercas, Javier: *Soldiers of Salamis*
59–61, 62
de Certeau, Michel: *The Practice of
Everyday Life* 134
Chambers, Robert: *Cyclopædia* 26
Chang, Eileen (Zhang Ailing):
"Lust, Caution" 76–80, 103

Chaucer to Wordsworth (Arnold): 26
Checkpoint (Baker): 114–15
Comparative Literature: 13–14,
 37–38
context: 7–9, 22
Crimp, Martin: *Cruel and Tender*
 158–65
Cruel and Tender (Crimp): 158–65
Cultural Revolution in China:
 31, 122
Cyclopædia (Chambers): 26

Dada Manifesto (Ball): 44
Dance (Mukundan): 80–81
Duo Duo: "No Mourning for
 Language" 119–22

Eckermann, Johann Peter: 37
Electronic Literature Directory: 46,
 84, 110, 112
electronic texts (e-texts): 80–88,
 106–12
Eliot, T.S.: 57; "Tradition and the
 Individual Talent" 21; "*Ulysses*,
 Order and Myth" 20–21; The
 Waste Land 4
environmentalism: 128, 129, 130,
 165–66, 175–83
everyday life: 51–52, 128, 129, 130,
 140, 147, 148, 149, 151, 157,
 164, 170–71, 172–73; and news
 130–35
Ez-Eldin, Mansoura: *Maryam's Maze*
 33–36

Fear and Misery (Brecht): 49–50
Fish, Stanley: 96
Franco, General Francisco: 32

"gadji beri bimba" (Ball): 43–48
genre: 28, 40–43, 48
globalization: 14, 33, 51, 122,
 128–29, 130, 156–58, 163–65
Goethe, Johann Wolfgang von: 37, 38
Golbou, Farrideh (Faridah Gulbu):
 143

Hamill, Sam: *Poets against the War*
 109
Harry Potter novels: translations of 1;
 Chamber of Secrets 61–62;
 fanfiction 86, 108–9
Heaney, Seamus: "Testimony" 5–9,
 17
Himmler, Heinrich: 170
Hitler, Adolf: 49, 170, 173
Hollis, Matthew: *101 Poems* (with
 Keegan) 8
The Holocaust: 168–75
"The Hugo Ball" (Memmott):
 46–48, 84, 110
human rights: 128, 165–75, 183

"I Zimbra" (Byrne): 45
identity: 128, 129, 130, 141–47,
 148, 149, 151–52, 153, 157–58,
 161–62, 163, 165, 176
ideology: 128, 129, 130, 135–41,
 142, 147, 148, 149, 153, 157–58,
 163–64, 165, 171–75, 176
intertextuality: 33–37, 39
Iraq invasion: 8–9, 50, 86, 109,
 114–15
Iser, Wolfgang: 95

Jiang Rong: *Wolf Totem* 121
Johnson, B.S.: *The Unfortunates*
 83, 84
Joyce, James: 57; *Ulysses* 19–22

Keegan, Paul: *101 Poems* (with
 Hollis) 8
Key Concepts (Padley): 27–28, 31
Khusraw u Shirin (Nizami): 143
Kiarostami, Abbas: *Shirin* 142–47
The Kindly Ones (Littell): 169–75

Lee, Ang: *Lust, Caution* 76–80, 103
"The Library of Babel" (Borges): 33
literary canon: 4, 15–18
literary industry: 4, 18–22, 55–56
Littell, Jonathan: *The Kindly Ones*
 169–75

The Little Review: 20
Ludlum, Robert: 69
"Lust, Caution" (Chang): 76–80,
    103
Lust, Caution (dir. Lee): 76–80, 103
Lust, Caution (Wang and Shamus):
    77–78

McCann, Madeleine: 131
McEwan, Ian: *Saturday* 114–15
Machine (Adolphsen): 179–83
Maryam's Maze (Ez-Eldin): 33–36
Mazas, Raphael Sánchez: 60
Memmott, Talan: "The Hugo Ball"
    46–48, 84, 110
Mukundan, Maniyambath: *Dance*
    80–81
Murakami, Haruki: *After Dark* 149–53

Natya Shastra (Bharata): 71
Nizami Ganjavi: *Khusraw u Shirin*
    143
"No Mourning for Language" (Duo
    Duo): 119–22

Padley, Steve: *Key Concepts* 27–28, 31
Pamuk, Orhan: *Snow* 135–41
Perfume (Süskind): 34–36
performance (live and recorded):
    71–80, 88, 100–6
periodization: 3, 27, 29–33, 55
Poetics (Aristotle): 71
Poets against the War (Hamill): 109
postcolonialism: 14, 128, 129, 130,
    156–58, 160–63, 165
postmodernism: 14, 51, 128, 129,
    130, 147–53, 165; and
    modernism 148
Pound, Ezra: 20
The Practice of Everyday Life (de
    Certeau): 134
printed texts: and e-texts 110;
    publication of 62–71

Q & A (Swarup): 93–100, 103–4,
    106

Rahmanian, Mohammed: 143
Ravenhill, Mark: *Shoot/Get
    Treasure/Repeat* 48–51
Reader's Guide (Sonnenschein): 26
reading: 92–100; close and distanced
    4, 5–9, 38; e-texts 107–8,
    110–12; ordinary reader 113;
    translations 118–22; and viewing
    100–3
reviewing: 112–13, 114–18
Rowling, J.K.: *Harry Potter* translated
    1; *Chamber of Secrets* 61–62
Ryman, Geoff: *253* 83–84, 85, 86,
    107

Saturday (McEwan): 114–15
Schamus, James (with Wang): *Lust,
    Caution* 77–78
Second World War: 6–7, 27, 31,
    169–70
The Shadow of the Wind (Zafón):
    28–29, 40, 41, 43
Shirin (Kiarostami dir.): 142–47
Shoot/Get Treasure/Repeat
    (Ravenhill): 48–51
Slumdog Millionaire (Boyle dir.): 98,
    103–6
Snow (Pamuk): 135–41
Soldiers of Salamis (Cercas): 59–61,
    62
Sonnenschein, William Swan:
    Reader's Guide 26
Sophocles: *Women of Trachis*
    158–60
Spanish Civil War: 32, 60
"Storyland" (Wylde): 110–12
"The Study of Poetry" (Arnold):
    16–17
Süskind, Patrick: *Perfume* 34–36
Swarup, Vikas: *Q & A* 93–100,
    103–4, 106
Swift, Todd: *100 Poets* 109

"Testimony" (Heaney): 5–9, 17
"Tradition and the Individual
    Talent" (Eliot): 21

translation: 1, 4, 10–15; reading
    118–22
Trueba, David: 60

Ulysses (Joyce): 19–22
"Ulysses, Order and Myth" (Eliot):
    20–21
The Unfortunates (Johnson): 83, 84
Universal Declaration of Human
    Rights: 166–67, 168–69

Wang Hui Ling (with Shamus):
    Lust, Caution 77–78
War on Terror: 50, 51, 159, 160,
    161, 163, 165

The Waste Land (Eliot): 4
Who Wants to be a Millionaire (TV
    quiz show): 104
Wolf Totem (Jiang Rong): 121
Women of Trachis (Sophocles):
    158–60
World Literature: 37–40
Wylde, Nanette: "Storyland"
    110–12

Youssef, Saadi: "America,
    America" 8

Zafón, Carlos Luis: *The Shadow of the
    Wind* 28–29, 40, 41, 43